Firsthand Research

By
Anna Denisch

To request permissions, contact Our Corner Publishing at info@ourcornerpublishing.com

First Edition

Design by Arka WR | ttakooo21@gmail.com

ISBN 979-8-9863336-7-0

www.ourcornerpublishing.com

www.annadenisch.com

This book contains mature and sexually explicit content.

If you are not of legal age to view such content in your country, please put this book down.

Viewer/reader discretion is advised.

Acknowledgements

I would like to start out by thanking my cover artist and book designer for their incredible talent, hard work, and desire to create a wonderful product. I'm so glad to have them as both a friend and a partner in these publishing endeavors.

I would also like to thank my personal writing community, both online and off. To everyone who read this story in its infancy and followed it along to its conclusion, you have been such a breath of needed fresh air and optimism. I never would have been able to finish this without your encouragement and support.

A big thanks to my parents for supporting my writing goals both emotionally and financially. Please don't read this book.

But most of all, thank you, reader. Yes you. You who maybe found this book from one of my ads online. Or perhaps heard about it from a friend (tell that friend an extra thanks from me). You who might relate to one of these characters, and you who may not, but is open to new ways of thinking and experiencing the world. I may write for myself, but I publish for you. So thank you for taking a shot on this book, and I hope you enjoy it!

Table of Contents

Chapter 1
Playboy, Meet Bat

In his defense, Tony didn't know that girl was the daughter of his grandmother's rival. After all, they had met at a bar, and no one used their real names at a bar. They got together and he took her out on the family yacht because it was closer than his apartment. And he really can't be blamed for the fact that no one told him there was supposed to be a meeting there the next morning.

"So, as you can see," he explained, "it really wasn't my fault."

His sister stared at him from the other side of her kitchen island. One bag of hastily put together clothes sat on the floor next to him. Tony squinted at how bright everything was, what with all the whiteness. It certainly wasn't helping his headache any.

"Right, because you just had to have sex with her right then and there otherwise you'd die," Sandra said. She was busying about, cleaning up after the breakfast she had cooked for him. Why she didn't just hire a chef or a maid, Tony would never know.

"Exactly!" he agreed. "See, you get it!"

"*Tony*," Sandra said in that exasperated sigh that he had come to know and hate. "You can't seriously think you're not to blame here."

"No one told me they were going to use the boat! Suddenly it's my fault they never tell me anything?" Tony's head pounded and he groaned, resting his chin in his hand.

Sandra finished cleaning up, tossing the dish towel on the island with a huff. "This isn't about the yacht, Tony."

Tony looked up at her, uncertain. "'Course it is. What else could it be about?"

"You're irresponsible," Sandra said. "Nana doesn't want you to be so...oh, what's the word…"

Ronnie's head popped up over the back of the couch in the living room. "Completely useless in every way?"

Tony jumped in his seat at the sudden appearance of her voice. He debated between asking what she was doing there and telling her off. "I am not useless!"

Ronnie's head disappeared as she rolled off the couch. She walked over to them and stood next to Tony, hands on her hips. She saw the bag by his feet and her eyebrows rose. "What did you *do*?"

"He slept with Fanny's daughter," Sandra said, nonchalantly.

Tony tensed his body, waiting. And, sure enough, there was a pair of slaps to his arm. "You idiot," Ronnie said with a laugh. "Oh my god, I can imagine the look on Nana's face. Was it bad? Did the vein come out?"

"Don't be mean," Sandra said. "He's my brother, that's my job."

Tony groaned and put his head down on the counter. He knew he'd get nothing but abuse here. But he also had nowhere else to go. Well, there were plenty of places to go, but none that would actually put up with him for an extended period of time.

"Yes, but as your wife it is my duty to aid you in your sibling torment," Ronnie said. She sat down next to Tony, patting his back.

Sandra started to respond, but instead her phone rang an annoying tone that made Tony's head throb. She dug it out of her pocket and answered, walking away to the living room with a hushed tone.

"So, why did you sleep with Fanny's daughter?" Ronnie asked. "Isn't she, like, Nana's biggest rival?"

"I didn't know," Tony groaned. "And I didn't know they needed the yacht either, so don't ask."

"Do I even want to know what happened with the yacht?"

Firsthand Research

Tony shook his head, urging the pain to calm down. It had been a hell of a morning from getting caught, to being yelled at, to being thrown out of his apartment, to being forced to walk all the way here because he suddenly had no money. He didn't need another attack from Ronnie to add on to it.

Sandra walked back into the kitchen, and he could tell it was bad news by the sound of her steps. "It was her, wasn't it?" Tony asked.

"Father," Sandra said. "On her behalf."

Tony groaned. "I'm guessing they weren't calling to apologize and let me back, were they?"

"Quite the opposite, actually," Sandra said.

Tony gathered the energy to lift his head a bit, looking at her. "Give it to me straight, doc."

"You can't stay here."

His head dropped. "Not that straight!"

"Nana says you'll never amount to anything if you don't learn how to do things on your own. If you can prove that you're responsible, she'll reconsider. But until then...no one can help you."

Tony groaned and sat back, slumping in his seat. "You could just tell her you're not!"

"Lie?" Ronnie asked. "To Nana? Wow, I knew you were an idiot, but this is some next level dumbassery."

"I'm sorry, Tony," Sandra said. "We can't help you."

"Well, where the hell does she expect me to go? I have nowhere else, I... I have no one else." The realization hit him harder than the hangover, and he dropped his head.

"You could go to the cabin," Ronnie suggested.

"Yeah," Sandra agreed. "No one ever goes there anymore. They'll never even check."

Tony scratched his cheek. "That's like...hours away. I can't walk that."

"We will give you bus money to get there," Sandra said, already walking over to her purse.

"Oh no," Tony said with a mock in his tone. "Can't be seen helping the completely useless lump!"

Ronnie placed a hand on his shoulder. "You are completely useless; that's why we have to help you."

Tony gave her a look, but it fell away as Sandra shoved some money in his hand.

"You call me when you get there, okay?" she said.

"Can't. She took my phone."

"Wow." Ronnie whistled. "You really fucked up big time, didn't you?"

Tony's look returned. Really, it wasn't his fault.

*

Alice's finger's fidgeted as she looked out the window. The sun was starting to set, and she worried her bottom lip with her teeth, hoping that she wouldn't get there too late.

"Relax," Liam told her. He glanced at the GPS on his phone. "We're almost there."

"I just don't want it to be dark," Alice said. She watched the town pass by, noting out loud how it was the perfect little setting for some kind of psycho murderer or apocalypse scenario.

One of Liam's hands left the steering wheel to grab her hand. "Really," he told her, squeezing it a little. "The only kind of authors that get stuck in those scenarios are writers that actually write horror novels. You'll be fine."

Alice shifted in her seat and looked up at him. "Does that mean I'm going to find romance in this town?"

Liam glanced at the buildings around. "Looks like a quaint little place for it," he mused. "Just as long as whoever you find doesn't mind having their head removed."

Alice chuckled and her body relaxed a bit. Having Liam as an older brother was perfect for if she needed a ride somewhere or a bodyguard to travel with. Not so much help for getting a boyfriend. Very few men could handle the intimidation.

The cabin that Alice was going to be staying at belonged to her publisher. She was running into a bit of trouble with her next book and had been offered the place as a getaway to work on it. Apparently, it hadn't been used in a few years, but she was assured it would be clean for her arrival.

It was a cute little thing settled on the edge of a lake, its own pier in the backyard. There was a span of forest around, but she could still easily see the other cabins and houses nearby, and looking back down the road they had driven up showed her the lights of the town below.

"A cute romance spot," she reminded herself as she got out of the car. She repeated it to herself again as she and Liam grabbed her bags from the trunk.

She said it a third time as she walked into the cabin. The interior, at least, made it finally sound true. It was charming, decorated in tasteful wood that didn't over bear. There were columns, a fireplace, and a large, curved kitchen with updated furnishings. And the decorations were perfect, like it had come out of a magazine.

Liam whistled as they shuffled in. "I gotta change jobs," he said.

Alice chuckled at him and dragged her bags to the door to the right. The cabin had three suites; she had been told. This one was lovely, with a large, comfortable looking bed find windows looking out on the town below. That would remind her that she wasn't alone, and that others were out there as well.

Or it would remind her how far away help would be.

Before she had time to change her mind and go pick a new room, Liam was placing her bags on the bed. "Are you sure you don't want me to stick around?" he asked. He gestured to the rest of the house. "Plenty of space."

"I'm sure." Alice unzipped one bag and sighed at the concept of unpacking. "You'll get bored out here, and then you'll bother me, and I really have to get this book finished."

"Maybe you should just write another one of your normal books," Liam suggested, a bit of an uncomfortable look on his face. Which was fair. Brothers should not have to know about their sisters writing erotica.

"No, no," Alice said. "I already signed the contract for it."

Liam shook his head and wandered back out to the main room. "I know some lawyers. Could get you out of it."

Alice smiled. "I appreciate that, but I really...I should be able to do it. I just need to clear my head is all."

"I should stay," Liam said. "What if you need something in town and it's raining?"

"I'll use an umbrella," Alice told him. She placed a reassuring hand on his arm. "Don't you worry, I'll be fine."

Liam nodded and pulled her in for a hug. "Call me if you need to come back early."

"I will."

They said their goodbyes and Liam left. Leaving Alice alone. In a cabin. In the woods. She shook and walked back to her room. "Cute romantic spot."

*

It was dark by the time Tony finally got to the cabin. There had still been a bit of sun left when he got to the town, but then he had to huff it through the town and up the hill to the lake where the cabin was. Plus, he had stopped by a place in town to pick up something to eat, Sandra having the good sense of mind to give him extra money for dinner. By the time he got there he was tired and sweaty and ready to just pass out.

Firsthand Research

He didn't even register that one of the lights was on. He just adjusted his bag on his shoulder and reached down to the fake rock in the garden to dig out the key. It wasn't there. He sighed and walked around to the side of the house, checking the secondary hiding place in the bird feeder. No such luck. They must have taken the keys with them last time they were there. Well, if he was lucky, that window by the backdoor was still busted.

And lucky he was. A dozen or so years ago, he and Sandra had been playing catch inside and she had lobbed one at him that he expertly dogged. Unfortunately, the window had no such dexterity, and the ball had jammed the lock open. They had agreed not to tell anyone, and all this time later it worked out in his favor as he shimmied the window open and climbed in.

It was dark as he stumbled around, feeling the wall for the light switch. But before he could find that little bump in the wall, something round and wooden knocked into his face. He stumbled back, the light flashing on and burning his eyes.

"Oh my god!" a familiar voice said. "Anthony?"

Tony blinked his eyes open, holding one hand to his nose that pulsed with pain. "Oh, hey Alice," he said. "Cute jammies."

Alice's eyes opened wide, and she looked down at the nightgown she was wearing. It was a beautiful light blue shade with flower designs on it. Unfortunately, it left a lot to the imagination, and Tony couldn't help but imagine.

"I'm so sorry," Alice said. She dropped the bat on the ground and reached for the throw blanket over the nearest chair. She wrapped it around her shoulders. "Are you okay?"

"I'm fine," Tony said. But as he spoke a dribble of blood landed on his lip. "Ish."

"Oh goodness, here, sit down, let me get you some ice!"

Alice shuffled over to the fridge, her short, blond curls bouncing with every step. Tony couldn't stop staring at them as he slid into the living room, flopping down on the couch. She raced back over and carefully removed his hand, wincing a bit.

"How bad is it?" Tony asked.

Alice put the bag of ice to his face, and he shivered at the cold. She sat next to him, holding the bag there. "You'll live," she said. "I'm so sorry."

"'S alright," he told her, waving one hand dismissively. "Not my first time getting hit in the head with a bat. Probably not my last, either."

Alice chuckled softly. "I really didn't mean to hurt you. I thought you might be a murderer or something."

Tony looked at her out of the corner of his eyes. "Who says I'm not?"

She playfully swatted his arm and he smiled, the movement agitating the pain in his nose. He could have anticipated a lot of people being here, if anyone was so inclined to return. But his grandmother's number one selling romance author was not one of those people. Yet Alice was probably the one person in the entire world that Tony would have been okay with being here. They had known each other so long now that she almost felt like family. (And if Nana had anything to say about it, all their authors were family). Alice was comfortable and jived really well with Tony's personality. He liked her, to say the least.

"So, what are you doing here?" Alice asked. She pulled the ice bag back a bit, looking over his wound. The pain was starting to subside a bit.

"Could ask you the same thing," Tony said. He tried to smirk, but it just irritated his nose. "I mean, I do own this property."

"Your grandmother owns this property," Alice reminded him.

"Eh, same thing." He reached up, taking the ice bag from Alice. He could hold it up himself now that he was over the dramatics of being attacked. "Why are you here?"

"I asked you first," Alice said, crossing her arms.

Tony sighed. "I've been disowned," he said.

"No."

"Yes."

"She wouldn't!"

"She did."

Alice stood up, huffing a bit, the blanket left behind on the couch. "She can't just throw you out like that. You have no skills."

"Ouch," Tony said.

"I didn't mean like that."

Tony nodded and patted the couch, urging her to sit back down. "'S alright. That is apparently the point. I can't have anything that I didn't earn myself. 'Cept the clothes I managed to smuggle out." He gestured to his bag.

"She can't do this. You can't be expected to just...just what? Find a job and instantly have some place to live?"

Tony shrugged. "Apparently I can."

Alice huffed again; her cheeks tinged with pink. "Well, I won't let her. You're her grandson for goodness sakes. She can't just kick you out with no money or food or a place to go!"

She got up again, and Tony grabbed her arm. "Where are you going?"

"I'm calling her!"

"What exactly do you expect to do?" Tony asked. He tugged gently and Alice relented, falling to the couch with an exasperated huff.

"I-I'll threaten something," Alice said. "I can...I can go somewhere else after this contract is up! That's what I'll do!"

Tony laughed, if only because the idea of anyone being able to out-pay Nana was the most ridiculous idea ever. If Alice left them, she'd be ruined.

But it was the thought that counted.

"Don't worry about it," he said. "I'm sure I'll be fine."

"Well, is there anything I could do to help?" Alice shifted, pulling one leg up and turning to look at him, elbow resting on the back of the couch. He tried not to look at where the gown slid up her leg a bit.

He instead focused all of his attention on the hazel-blue of her eyes. "You could let me stay here and not tell her."

"Lie?" Alice asked. "To Nana Jan? Goodness, I must have hit you rather harder than I thought."

"That seems to be the general consensus." Tony really couldn't blame them. Nana was an imposing figure. Even he had trouble lying to her, and he was a pro at lying. "It's alright," he said, waving his hand dismissively. "Just let me stay the night and I'll be out of your hair in the morning." His hand dropped. "Wait. What are you even doing here again?"

"I'm working on a novel," Alice explained. "It's just...it's a little different than what I normally write, so Nana Jan said I could use the cabin to get away and work on it."

"Different?" Tony peeled the bag away and gently touched at his nose. It didn't hurt so much anymore, and there didn't seem to be any more blood. Thankfully, it didn't feel broken. "What like a horror book or something? Would explain why you were so wound up."

"You were breaking in in the middle of the night!" Alice reminded him, crossing her arms. "I think I had every right to be wound up!"

Tony shrugged. "So, what are you working on?"

"It's still romance," she said. "It's just...different than normal."

Tony blinked at her once, nice and slow, and his mouth fell open in understanding. "You're writing smut!" he practically accused.

"It's *erotica*," Alice said, turning back to face forward. "And it's a tasteful art form."

Tony laughed. "Naughty, naughty," he said.

Alice frowned at him, looking positively adorable with a slight pout. "Well, perhaps I won't let you stay the night, hm?"

"Alright, alright, sorry." He was still laughing, but at least trying to make an effort to stop. "I just never expected that of you."

"No one does," Alice said. "But it's such a hot market these days, and well...I thought I ought to give it a try."

Tony finally settled down, relaxing into the couch now that his face wasn't throbbing in pain anymore. "I'm sure you'll do great. Your stuff always sells like hot cakes anyway."

Alice's fingers fidgeted around each other. "Yes. I suppose they do. It's awfully...daunting."

"What are you worried about?" As far as Tony knew, Alice's books were amazing. Not like he's read them in secret or anything, because he hasn't.

"I just want to make sure it's...accurate," she said. "And it's hard because I've not...well I haven't exactly...I've never…" Alice made a face and gestured to her lap.

Tony finally looked down at it, his moment of realization delayed as he studied the way her thighs pressed together. "Never?"

Alice shook her head and then seemed to realize she was in her nightie and grabbed the blanket from behind her, laying it over her lap. Tony glared at it.

"You have to be lying?" he said, looking back up at Alice's face, covered in a blush.

"I'm not."

"So, you're like a nun or something?"

"No, I'm not like a nun! Trust me, this is not by choice." She pouted again and Tony couldn't help but notice how plump and lovely her lips were, if not a little chapped.

"It has to be," he argued. "I mean, you've seen yourself, right?" He scoffed. "I'd think you'd be beating them off with a stick."

"I have seen myself," Alice said, voice dropping to a whisper. "Other people have too, which is the problem, I suppose."

Tony glared at her. More accurately he glared at any man dumb enough to not see the clear vision of beauty that she was. But they weren't in that room, so he could only glare at her. "Fuck all of 'em," he said.

Alice glanced over at him, a bit of mischief in her eyes. "I'm certainly trying," she mumbled.

And Tony wasn't sure if it was just the topic of conversation or that look in her eyes, but he was suddenly way too hot. He gulped. "I can't believe you've gone this long without an orgasm. That's truly torturous."

The look dropped from her eye as Alice sat up straight, a bit primly. "I do not need a man to have an orgasm, thank you very much."

Tony leaned his head against the back of the couch and looked up at her. He had to take a few seconds to push away the image of Alice accomplishing that. "Ya know, it's always better with someone else, though."

Alice got off the couch, wrapping the blanket tight around her shoulders. "I'm sure it is, but seeing as how I am alone, it will have to suffice."

Tony said, "Bet I could give you one." Then he heard himself say that, and he wished the earth would just open up and swallow him.

Alice turned and looked at him with an open mouth. "Are you drunk?"

Tony shook his head, but he wished he was. "I'm just saying. You should know what it's like. And, hey, I'm available."

Alice huffed and turned back around, walking to the kitchen even though she had nothing to do in there. "You're ridiculous. We are not having this conversation."

An idea sparked into Tony's mind and he jumped up, getting a bit of a head rush. "No, no, wait, listen." Alice turned back around; lips pursed. "I *bet* you I could give you an orgasm in... five minutes."

"What kind of a bet is that?" Alice asked.

Tony smirked. The perfect cover. "If I can, you have to lie to Nana and let me stay here."

Alice's pout fell. She stuttered for a bit, clearly considering it. "I... well what if you can't?"

Tony shrugged and shoved his hands in his pockets. "Then I'll leave first thing in the morning, and you can have a terribly amazing 'loyal to Nana' story about how you kicked me out. You can even say you hit me with a bat. I'm sure Ronnie will love that part."

Alice put her hands on her hips, the blanket falling open a bit. She looked around at the room, eyes landing on the door to the suite by the front. "Fine," she said, her face turning red. "But you only get three minutes."

"More than enough time," Tony said.

Chapter 2
Sex Lesson One - Oral

Alice took a shuddering breath and led Anthony to the suite she was staying in, taking off the blanket and leaving it on the couch. This whole situation was ridiculous. Every step she took, she thought about going back on it. After all, this was *Anthony* she was talking about. The grandson of her publisher. The very irresponsible, playboy grandson of her publisher, nonetheless.

But she supposed that was why it would work. After all, this was just Anthony. She had known him a good handful of years, so it wasn't like she was going to bed with some stranger she had just met. But it's not like she ever expected to end up in bed with Anthony. Not that the idea had never crossed her mind, of course. He was very handsome.

Granted, it would be better if this were under different pretenses; if perhaps he liked her and simply wanted to be with her rather than use it as an excuse to have a place to stay. But it was, overall, a good set up. This way she would finally do it and get it over with and maybe would have an easier time getting someone to do it with her properly in the future.

Anthony closed the door behind them and there was a thick heat in the air.

"Uhm, I'll just, uh...be right back," Alice said.

She slipped into the bathroom, closing the door tight and turning on the light. She realized then that she didn't have her phone with her, and she cursed. She had wanted to call her sister for some much-needed advice, but she couldn't do that without making it obvious by walking out to get her phone. And she couldn't even look to the internet for help.

Alice leaned against the door and deflated. She couldn't do this. She was sure she had to do some kind of prep work or something. There was certainly no time to shave. And she knew that spraying perfume down there was a terrible idea, but there had to be something she could do to make it more...

alluring. She sighed and wished she had just had the courage to be a bit more outgoing back in school.

There was a soft knock on the door, and she jumped. "You alright in there?" Anthony asked. "We don't have to do it if you don't want. 'Course, that would be a forfeit on your part, and I'd win."

Alice shook her head. "I-I'm fine. Just. Getting ready."

"Doing what?" Anthony asked. Alice could feel the door move a bit as he leaned against it.

"Uh, just...freshening up." That was what people always said in the movies. She just wished she could figure out what they were actually doing.

"You don't gotta do that," Anthony told her.

"I just...I haven't exactly done anything, you know. M-maybe we should wait until tomorrow? I could, er, clean up a bit?" She could feel the heat on her cheeks, like a sunburn.

"Ah, I don't care either way," Anthony announced in that carefree tone he seemed to have about everything.

Alice was certain that wasn't true. He was the one beating people away with a stick. Clearly he had some kind of preference. Alice fiddled with the edge of her night gown. At least it would only be three minutes. And it wasn't like she was dating Anthony, so even if he didn't like it, it wasn't going to ruin anything.

Alice sighed and opened the door, stepping out sheepishly into the room. "Sorry," she offered. "I just wanted to be, uh...you know."

"Yeah, I know." Anthony took her hand and Alice felt her skin tingle. "But I really don't care."

He led her over to the bed and Alice was glad to sit on the edge of it, her legs nearly starting to shake with the nerves. She decided to look away from his wandering gaze and reach over for her phone. "Three minutes, right?"

"Mhm." Anthony got to his knees and Alice looked down at him.

"A-aren't you going to join me up here?" she asked. The way he was looking at her lap was intense, and her legs started to shake anyway.

"I've only got three minutes," Anthony reminded her. "Gotta use my best skill." Alice only nodded, wondering what that skill was. "Whenever you're ready."

Alice hit the start button and Anthony's hands immediately were on her knees. They slid up her thighs, fingers dragging against her skin, slipping their way up under her nightgown. She decided that she could not look at him, so she laid back, choosing to stare up at the ceiling instead and just let him do what he was going to do.

He found his way to her underwear. She wasn't wearing anything particularly interesting, just a tall pair of plain gray panties. She shivered at the light contact as Anthony's fingers tickled against her sides. They hooked under the edge of her underwear, and she bit her lip, lifting her hips off the bed so he could slide them off. He made a soft noise of appreciation but thankfully did not make an attempt to talk. For surely if he had, Alice would have not been able to respond properly.

For how could she even think anything other than 'oh my god, this is happening, oh my god,' on repeat as Anthony bent his head down, hands on Alice's knees, gently spreading her legs open? Her nightgown rose up a bit but she didn't dare make a move to take it off or pull it up more. Her hands were shaking too much for any of that sort. And apparently Anthony had no such indication to do something about it either. He just leaned forward, his head between her legs, slipping under the edge of the gown.

Alice felt a hot, wet breath against her skin, and she sighed out a little, "Oh," as she finally put two and two together and realized what Anthony was going to do. She turned her head to the side and glanced at her phone. Only two minutes to do it in. She very briefly thought that maybe she should have let him have the full five minutes.

But that thought was quickly chased away as Anthony's tongue gingerly pressed against her. Her body stilled, but only from the intensity of it all. There was no going back now. Anthony's mouth was down there, and this was going to happen. Her stomach did a flip, and she grabbed the sheets tightly in her hand as she waited for what would come next.

Anthony's tongue slid between her outer labia, rocking back and forth between the folds of fat, like he was trying to stretch it a bit. And it sent a tingle up Alice's spine, causing a pool of heat to warm her lower gut. And the heat only grew as Anthony angled his head a bit, his tongue slipping up. It nudged under her hood and pressed softly against Alice's clit. It was nothing compared to when she played with herself. She just chalked it up to the fact that she never had anything like a tongue to use. Nothing quite as wet, hot, or textured. But the way that Anthony was moving his tongue was certainly like nothing she had ever experienced before either.

He started in slow circles, teasing around the clit instead of actually touching it. Alice nearly clamped her legs closed, squishing Anthony's head. But his hands were on her thighs, squeezing them and holding them open as he worked. Alice could feel something, like her nerves were on fire. It was much, much more intense than being alone and she whimpered as she realized only twenty seconds had passed.

That was when Anthony's tongue started to play with her clit properly. It licked up and over it, flicking across it in long thrusts that had her legs shaking again. She could feel the pleasure building with every touch, and she was very aware of the fact that she just may lose this bet. Which meant she would have to see him every day after that. She might just have to go home early.

She could feel how wet she was getting too, which felt nice but also embarrassing because Anthony's face was *there*, and she was certain it was just going to be covered with it. She moved her hands to her face, unable to even risk being seen in such a state.

And then Anthony hummed, his lips vibrating against Alice's own, his tongue pressing down and moving from side to side.

Alice squeaked as she came. Anthony had been right; it was so much better than anything she had done alone. And where she would stop, Anthony kept going. His tongue pressed and moved against her as she crested with pleasure and then came down. Even then he kept going. Thankfully, the alarm went off before he had the time to truly overstimulate her.

Anthony's head slipped out of Alice's night gown, and he sat back on his feet. Alice didn't dare move her hands off her face.

"You alright?" Anthony asked. He had that same casual tone, as if his face hadn't just been buried between her legs.

Alice let out a shaky breath and managed to say, "Y-yeah."

Anthony patted her knee. "Told ya it's better with someone else."

Alice could only nod.

"So... I'm good to stay, yeah?"

Alice finally let her hands fall away, still only able to stare at the ceiling. She was sure she could never look Anthony in the eyes ever again. "Yes. I'll do my best to cover for you."

Anthony stood up and Alice couldn't not look at him. He had a genuine smile on his face, and she pulled herself to a sitting position, wrapping her arms around herself to try to maintain some form of dignity.

"Thanks," Anthony said. "I really do appreciate it."

Alice's mouth twitched into a little smile. "Well, you certainly earned it, I suppose."

Anthony gave her a bit of a cryptic look. "Yeah," he said, drawing the word out. "I suppose I did, huh?"

"Well." Alice crossed her ankles together, looking for her discarded underpants. "Good night."

Anthony nodded and walked to the door. "Night," he said. Then he winked at her and left.

As soon as the door was closed Alice fell back on the bed. She did that. She had actually done that. She had finally had sex. Well. She had had whatever that was, which was basically sex. It was close enough, as far as she was concerned. And now she had to deal with seeing the man she had done that with every day.

It was strangely exciting.

Chapter 3
Routine Set-Up

Alice woke up like normal. Her alarm alerted her to the time, and she rolled over, reaching for her medicine and groggily taking it. She rolled back over, cuddling her spare pillow, and prepared to go back to sleep. Then her brain decided to remind her that sleeping somewhere down the hall was an unexpected guest. One that had had his head between her legs not but a few hours ago. Her eyes snapped open, and the concept of sleep was lost to her.

How she had even managed to fall asleep last night she didn't know. She had lied there, thinking about it over and over and over until she figured she just passed out. But now she was awake again, and she was back to thinking about it. Thinking about it because it had been good. But also now it was going to be super awkward and she wasn't even sure what to say to him. If anything. Should she just pretend he wasn't there? Ignore him? After all, he had only asked for a place to stay. It's not like she had to interact with him or anything.

But he was also poor and jobless. He would probably starve to death. And it wasn't like he was going to be able to get a job in the town. At least, not easily. No no. She had to help him. She decided she would just pretend that the whole thing never happened. She would just act like he had never done anything, and she had just let him stay without the strings attached. That was a good plan.

But strings had been attached. And how could she ignore that?

With a groan, Alice reached for her phone and noted the time. It was a little early, but not crazy early. She called her sister.

Katie was the eldest of the family. She and Liam were only a few years apart. Alice had been a bit of a surprise about a decade later. Having an older sister just meant getting all kinds of (sometimes unwanted) good life advice, especially when it came to boys.

"Hey, Alice," Katie said. "How's the cabin in the woods?"

"Please don't call it that," Alice exasperated. In the background she could hear people talking. "Where are you so early? Or is it still late for you?" She laughed.

"Liam and I are helping Mom and Dad Feng Shui the house. Dad read an online article about it. You don't want to know."

"So... everyone is there huh?" Alice asked, her face already turning beat-red at the concept of talking to just Katie about it.

"Yeah. One sec, I'll put you on speaker."

"No, no, no, no, no!"

"No?"

Alice covered her face with one hand, as if her whole family was in the room staring at her. "Just...could you go somewhere private? Like someplace where everyone I'm related to isn't just standing around talking?"

"Sure," Katie said, dragging out the word as she shuffled the phone about. Alice heard a door shut, and then the noises quieted down. "So, what's up?"

"Well...uh..." Alice sighed. Better to just get it over with. Like ripping off a Band-Aid. "I think I had sex last night."

Katie was quiet for a few seconds, and Alice wondered if maybe the call had dropped or she hadn't heard what Alice said. "You...you think?" Katie asked.

Alice nodded, eyes closing under her hand. "Yeah."

"Hun, how do you not know?"

"Well... we did stuff, but not like...a lot of stuff." Alice dropped her hand, arm flopping to the mattress. "He...uh...he sort of kind of...well he…"

"He what?" Katie urged.

"Well, he sort of ate me out," Alice said, her voice rushed and filled with deep embarrassment. "Only not really. It was just...licking mostly. It was only three minutes."

"Oh, Alice," Katie said, voice dripping with disappointment.

"I know." Alice closed her eyes. Anthony wasn't exactly a stranger, but he certainly wasn't someone she knew all that well or saw often. She had practically jumped into bed with some guy like the floozie she was. The virgin floozie, but the floozie, nonetheless.

"I'm so sorry," Katie said. "I promise I'll teach you how to tell if a guy has endurance before you get to that point."

"What? N-no! It wasn't like that! I set the time limit."

"You set a time limit for sex? Oh, hun."

"No it's-It wasn't…" Alice groaned. "Just what do I do now? I have to see him every day and I don't know how to like...talk to him?"

"Why do you have to see him every day?" Katie asked. "Just stay in the cabin. If he bothers you, I'm sure Liam would have no problem coming to beat him up for you."

"Uh...well...it's complicated, but I-I do. I have to see him every day and I need to know how to handle that." Alice was beginning to regret calling her sister. But she didn't really have many friends, and certainly none she could talk to about things like this.

Katie hummed a bit, her finger tapping on something. "Well, who is he?"

"Uh. A guy," Alice said.

"Yes, you mentioned that. But *who*? Is it, like, the mailman or something?"

"D-does that matter?" Alice briefly considered just hanging up and pretending that this conversation never happened at all.

"Well, who he is is going to have a lot of bearing on how you should handle the situation. I mean...the obvious answer is inviting him in again and maybe this time see just how long he can go."

Alice could practically hear the wink. She sat up, shuffling to sit against the headboard. "That is not happening. It was a one-time deal and I mean it."

"So, who was it then?"

Alice groaned. "Just...promise not to tell anyone? And I mean it. Not a soul."

"Oh, you have to tell me now."

"Promise!"

"I promise. Not a soul. Now dish."

Alice took a deep breath. "It was Anthony. Dawson," she added as an afterthought.

"Isn't Dawson the name of your publisher?" Katie asked. Alice only nodded, which did nothing to help the conversation. "Wait. Don't tell me you slept with that, tall thing. With the red hair?"

"I won't say it, then," Alice told her.

"I don't know if I should be impressed or worried for your mental health."

"Just tell me what I should do!" Alice nearly cried. This conversation was much too long already, and she had revealed way more than she wanted to. She just needed Katie to tell her how to deal with this and let her die in her embarrassment alone.

"Well...there are a few things you could do," Katie started. Alice held the phone with her shoulder and grabbed her notepad on the bedside table. "There's always the first option I mentioned."

"One time thing," Alice said, practically growling.

"Alright, alright, just throwing it out there. Did you talk about it at all after it happened?"

"No. I kicked him out. I mean...what am I even supposed to say? Thank you?"

"Well, was it good?"

"That's not the point!"

"You should probably talk about it," Katie told her. And Alice was afraid she would say that. Because talking about things was not one of her strong suites.

"But what do I say? Like, the exact words."

"I can't tell you that," Katie said. "Besides. You're the writer; you're good with words."

"Yeah, writing them, not speaking them!"

"So, write him a letter."

"A letter?"

"Yes, a letter. Compose all your thoughts on the matter and write him a letter."

Alice could do that. She was a writer after all. The problem with talking to people was the quick time responses. Alice couldn't think that fast. She needed time to sit and process things before saying them. Speaking in real time meant too many mistakes and not saying things that needed to be said. But a letter she could write easily. She could do that in her sleep.

"So, what *are* your thoughts on the matter?" Katie asked. "I mean, why was it a one-time thing? What is he even doing there?"

"Uh, I gotta go write," Alice said. It was her number one excuse to get out of awkward conversations and this one had taken that turn about three miles back.

Katie sighed. "Alright. But I want you to know something."

"What's that?"

Katie sounded a little choked up, but clearly fake. "I'm just so proud of you."

Alice rolled her eyes. "Yes, yes, fine. Thank you."

"My baby sister is finally growing up."

"Good-bye!"

Alice listened to Katie laugh for a moment and then hung up, shaking her head. That had been painful. But it was useful. She turned her attention to the notebook and started composing her letter.

*

Of course Alice had picked Tony's old room to sleep in. He had been happy that she led him there because sex in any of the other rooms was gonna be a problem. But now he had the other problem of where he was going to sleep.

His room was off the table, obviously. He wasn't going to go and ask Alice to move all her stuff. That would be rude. But he wasn't about to go sleeping in his parent's room. And certainly not his Nana's. But they were the only other suites in the cabin. There was one more room and it was Sandra's old one. Which Tony figured was the safest. It didn't matter that he had to leave his room to go to the bathroom or anything. The only thing wrong with that was his clothing situation.

He had slept naked, because in his rush to leave yesterday he hadn't thought about pajamas. He rarely thought about pajamas. And in his early morning fog he hadn't even given it a second thought. He just shuffled down the hall to the bathroom where he would wake up more. And as he woke up, he heard noises from the kitchen. Cooking noises.

He remembered that Alice was here. And he certainly should not be walking around without any clothes on. Sure, he could probably slip back into his room without any trouble. But what if there was trouble? Alice had already done him a great deal of favors by letting him stay here, he certainly couldn't just seem like some rude person who didn't even wear clothes.

He opened the closet in the bathroom and celebrated at the stack of towels and robes in there. He grabbed a robe and slipped in. It was a lovely, satin texture, and it felt so nice he figured he didn't even need to go back to his room and get dressed. This would do just fine.

Alice was cooking breakfast when Tony wandered in. And it smelled heavenly. And she looked heavenly. She wore a frayed-out shirt that flirted around her hips and jeans that hugged her curves in just the right way. He only choked a little bit.

But it was enough to get her attention. She looked over at him, smiling. "Good morning. I hope you like eggs." She gestured to the stove she was working on.

"Oh. Uh. You don't have to cook for me," Tony said. He sat up on one of the stools by the island. There was an envelope with his name on it sitting there. He stared at it. "Is this my eviction notice?" he asked with a laugh. He wasn't really going to hold Alice to their deal if she didn't want to. He did have a few ideas on convincing her, however.

"No, no," Alice said, turning back to the stove rather abruptly. "Nothing like that. Just some thoughts."

Tony nodded and decided it was too early in the morning for thoughts. He folded the envelope and slipped it in the pocket of his robe. Alice looked over her shoulder, glancing at the action, but she didn't say anything.

"Listen," Tony said, figuring he ought to just go right out and say it. "I've been thinking about something."

"Is that so?" Alice turned off the stove and moved the pan to a cool burner. She shuffled over to the cabinets to get two plates down.

"Yeah. A job idea," he continued, tapping his finger against the counter. All of his future plans relied on this one conversation. And how Alice would react to it.

Alice scooped the eggs out onto the plates and then uncovered a second cooking pan, pouring cooked potato pieces on as well. "That was quick," she said. "Is it something online?"

Tony shook his head. He leaned up as Alice placed the plate before him, handing him a fork. "Thank you. And no. It's actually something right here."

"A job in town?" Alice asked. She stood opposite of him, he noted with a frown, remaining fully in the kitchen as she ate.

"Sort of. I was thinking I could work for you." Tony shoveled a forkful of eggs in his mouth to let her respond to that before he kept blathering on like an idiot.

"Work for me?" Alice asked. "Doing what?"

"Well," Tony swallowed hard. "Writers have assistants and stuff, right? I could...I don't know. Hold your pens? Uh. Bring you cocoa or whatever? Plus," he smirked and slid down seductively in his chair. He should have led with his strongest argument, honestly. "I have all my knowledge." He winked at her.

Alice spit some of her eggs out, specks landing on the counter between them. She coughed for a moment and grabbed for a glass of juice before she responded. "What kind of knowledge?" she asked.

"*You know*." Tony winked again. Alice blushed. Adorable. Tony leaned forward, studying the pink of her cheeks. "*Sexual* knowledge."

"Oh dear." Alice's eyes opened wide, and she turned away. "Uh, well. I'm not sure that's going to be strictly necessary."

"Ah, come on," he argued, leaning back a bit. "You're writing a sex book, and I'm sort of like, the king of sex."

Alice looked back at him, disbelief on her face.

"You need me to prove it to you again?" he asked. *Oh, please ask me to prove it again.*

"Ah, no." Alice twitched a smile. "That's alright. Thank you."

Tony shrugged. "I am pretty good," he said. "Now, I'm not trying to say you can't write or anything." The books he certainly did not read proved that she could. "But I am saying that knowing more things could help. And I know many things."

Alice tapped her fork against her plate, looking past Tony, thinking. He busied himself with eating his own food so he wouldn't vibrate to death.

"Well," she said slowly. "I suppose having an assistant wouldn't be terrible. I mean." She shrugged. "Uh, what's the usual salary range for that?"

Tony didn't think that far. "I was just thinking about like...food and secrecy?"

Alice's eyebrows furrowed. "Well surely I should be paying you."

"That's payment enough, trust me."

"Wouldn't you want money though?"

Tony shrugged. He wasn't one for thinking about the future. He just needed to focus on getting through the next few days. "I'll figure out a money job in the future. For now, I help you and you help me. Sounds good, right?"

Alice licked her lips and Tony stared at the shine that left behind. "Well. I suppose. J-just for now. You should really look into getting a real job."

Tony nodded, proud of himself. "Of course. When I'm not busy helping you, I'll be busy with that. No worries."

*

Alice liked her typewriter. She knew it was a bit obnoxious, but there was something so satisfying about the hard click of those letters that you just couldn't get out of a laptop. Plus, Anthony needed something he could look for a real job on, so he had her laptop anyway. Which was fine by Alice. Now she got to write on her typewriter that Liam laughed at her for packing.

Naomi reached out, fingers wavering slightly as they prepared to wrap around the ~~memb- coc-~~ dick.

Alice sighed and sat back. This shouldn't be that hard. She's read tons of this kind of stuff in the past. Writing it should be easy...it should be Malcolm's dick not the dick.

Thankfully her typewriter was new, a gift from her parents for her birthday, and had an actual backspace that would white out the words to retype them.

Naomi reached out, fingers wavering slightly as they prepared to wrap around Malcolm's dick. She hesitated, looking up into his ~~blue~~ copper-toned eyes, waiting. Almost as if for permission.

"Go ahead," Malcolm whispered, a soft urging for a heated desire.

Naomi pulled her hand away. "I can't. I'm sorry. I don't know how." She had never done this before. He knew that. She didn't want to hurt him, and she knew how sensitive that particular body part could be.

A heat fell between them. Malcolm placed one hand under her chin, long fingers tickling her skin. He reached down with the other. Naomi sucked on her bottom lip and Malcolm's face changed, his own fingers deftly making quick work of himself.

He looked...He felt...It was...

Alice pouted and looked down at the pile of white out forming on the page. She should really figure out what it was like first.

Anthony had her laptop, so she dug out her phone, turned off the sound, and opened an incognito tab on her browser. Face red, she went to her porn site of choice and searched for male masturbation videos. And she actually typed in 'male masturbation'. She scrolled through the video stills. Any man or woman with a camera could make a video like this. And it certainly looked it.

But none of the people or penises looked like how Alice pictured Malcolm to look. She exited out of the browser and bit her lip. Originally, Malcolm had been kind of short, with straight, black hair and piercing blue eyes. But now... now he was taller. His eyes were almost golden. And if she thought about it, he might have red hair, a little bit wavy if grown out properly.

Alice groaned and spun around in her chair. The little office room was perfect, with a large window looking out over the lake. But she was too busy staring at the closed door to notice. Anthony was just outside in the living room. And he had said he would help her with her book. He was her assistant after all.

But was it weird to go and ask your sort-of-friend-but-more-acquaintance-now-roommate if you could...what would she even ask? If she could watch him jerk off? How crass? No, no, she simply couldn't.

She wouldn't.

She had to.

Chapter 4
Sex Lesson Two – Hand Job

Tony had lied, of course. He had no intention of looking for a *job*. After all, working for Alice was a job. And if things kept going like they had last night, it would turn into a very good job indeed. But he didn't want to be bored while he waited for Alice to finish writing for the day, so he took the offer of her laptop and fiddled about online. When he heard the door to the office open (a creak he and Sandra had purposely added), he quickly tabbed over to the job-hunting sight and pretended to be considering one of the postings.

Alice took her time walking over. He listened to her take a few steps, stop, shuffle her feet like she would turn back, then approach again. He smiled.

"How's the writing going?" he asked, eyes still focused on the screen.

Alice let out a little surprised noise. "Oh! Just, uh, taking a little break. It's important to stretch your legs and rest your eyes, after all." She finally made her way to the living room. She stood next to the couch Tony was on but didn't sit down. "How's the job hunt?"

Tony glanced over at her. She was picking at her fingernails and smiling with only her mouth. She was nervous about something. "Oh, it's going," he said. "Helps that I have no experience or skills, of course."

Alice gingerly sat on the opposite side of the couch, looking at him and moving in jerky motions as if waiting for him to deny her sitting there. As if he ever would. "Perhaps you could take some course work," she suggested. "They have all kinds of skill classes online these days."

"Maybe."

Tony closed the laptop and looked over at her. He waited. She picked at her fingers and looked around at the room. It was a kind of quiet that would be awkward if he wasn't totally absorbed in how her eyes were on the greener side of hazel that afternoon; a soft, diluted color that matched her shirt.

"Actually," Alice eventually said, as if the conversation hadn't just had a lull in it. "I could use your help with something. I-if you're not busy, that is."

"Free as a bird," Tony told her. "What ya need?"

Alice gulped and folded her hands together, knuckles white. She stared down at her shoes. "Well, I could use your expertise. Your knowledge."

Tony smirked and put the laptop on the coffee table, getting comfortable on the couch. "Ah, yes. The one skill I do have. Problem in the book, then?"

Alice nodded. She turned her head so she was looking directly away from him. "I was wondering if maybe I could...if you would be so inclined...if I could watch."

"Watch what?"

"You. Uh. Do...you know."

Tony did know, but he wanted to hear Alice say it. He brought one leg over the other. "There's a lot of things you could watch, Alice."

Alice sighed, and when she looked at him, she was very nearly scowling. "You know," she accused.

"Do I?" Tony asked.

Alice covered her face with one hand. Her voice was muffled when she spoke. "I need to watch you masturbate," she said. "For the book."

Now, Tony had never exactly had an audience before. And he figured, this might be a little strange. But it was his job after all. And the blush on Alice's face was simply too cute to deny. "Anything for the book," he said.

He reached a hand down, keeping the other on the back of the couch. Alice's hand fell away in time with the sound of his zipper going down. Her face was completely flushed, and she focused so intently on his lap he could actually feel a hole burning in his skin.

Firsthand Research

Alice sucked in a breath as Tony reached into his pants. She let it out in a huff as he *presented* himself. He wasn't the most endowed man in the world, but he was pretty proud of himself. Alice bit on her bottom lip as he rubbed himself hard. Which didn't take long. Watching the way that the skin of Alice's lip pushed and pulled against her teeth was captivating. Oh to be the one biting on her plumpness like that…

"Just this huh?" Tony asked.

His voice made Alice jump a bit, and she glanced at his face before quickly staring back down at his work. "Uh, yes. That-that's very nice." She cleared her throat. "P-perhaps you could, er, narrate?"

Tony wished that Alice would look him in the eyes again. But she had to study the act itself, he figured. "It feels good," he told her. "Better when it's wet." A few droplets of precum made themselves known, as if on command of his need. He rubbed it down on himself and hummed in the sensation. "It's warm."

"Warm," she repeated, her voice dreamy. She cleared her throat again and Tony was pretty sure all of the blood in her body was in her face right now. "Could I...uh," she vaguely gestured to his dick.

Tony forgot how to breath for a moment. "Sure," he said, not certain how his voice sounded so steady. "If you want."

Oh please, please want, he thought as he focused on Alice's hands. They were smooth, and looked like they would be soft, and his mouth went dry at the prospect of those hands on his body.

"I don't know if I could," Alice said, her voice rushed. "I-I won't do it right."

"Only one way to learn," Tony said. He didn't want to seem like he was pushing, but by god if she didn't touch him soon, he might actually explode.

"Y-you'll tell me if I'm doing it wrong?" Alice asked.

"Of course."

*

Firsthand Research

Alice took a deep breath and cracked her knuckles. It was a terrifying concept: touching Anthony. After all, she had only come to watch. And what a show it had been. Antony's hand seemed to know exactly what to do, and she watched it with interest as it rubbed and twisted and squeezed. She wanted to try.

But only because Naomi was going to. It was all for the book, of course.

Having Anthony continuously stare at her was not helping. She wanted to ask him to look somewhere else, but she wasn't sure where he would start looking at. At least if he was looking at her face, he wasn't watching her mess up with his...with *that*.

She looked down at her lap, and the one hand that still laid on it, and reached over with her other hand. She searched around, much too embarrassed to actually look. Her fingers reached Anthony's dick. His fingers were still there. They brushed against each other as Anthony drew his hand back, and Alice bit her lip so hard she worried she'd draw blood. It was much too hot for the season.

It wasn't like Alice was expecting. It was hard, of course, but not like she thought. It had a bit of give to it, and the weight felt nice against her fingers. Then it twitched a bit, and her hand reflexively grabbed it.

"Ah! Sorry." Alice released it almost immediately and started to pull her arm back. She had touched it. That was all she needed.

But Anthony's hand shot out, grabbing her wrist. Thankfully it was the hand that had been on the couch, she noted, and not the one covered with his own pre-cum. Neither of them said anything, but Alice didn't pull away as he led her hand back over.

She grabbed the dick again, this time softly. Then she just held it as Anthony moved her, palm and fingers sliding over his, rather long, length. She wasn't being nearly as good at it as he had been, but he was sighing, sometimes moaning a bit. And he hadn't been doing that before. And she let that make her feel good.

"Is this okay?" she asked. She knew she should be doing more, but she was already so overwhelmed from just *this*.

"Perfect," Anthony breathed out. His voice was rough, haggard...wrecked.

Alice risked a glance at him. He had his head leaned back, eyes closed as it rested on the couch. "So, it...it really just all feels good?" she asked. Something about the way he looked so relaxed relaxed her. This was just research, and it didn't need to be so...dramatic, she guessed.

"It feels amazing," Anthony said.

Alice found that the silence was much more intimidating than speaking, so she kept talking as Anthony's hand guided her own. "It's just interesting. Because, you know, well. The vagina is sensitive, but it has like...you know pressure points? Whereas this is just...everything." This was why she hated talking in real time.

"Yeah," Anthony agreed. "It's like one, thick, long clitoris."

Alice snorted out a laugh, and Anthony chuckled. Alice swallowed the lump in her throat and figured she had enough material to work. She pulled her hand back and Anthony released it after a second of restraint.

"Thank you for the help," Alice said. She couldn't bring herself to look at him, especially since he had brought his head back up. "This was very informative." She held her hand up and out a bit, not wanting to touch anything until she could wash it.

"Don't want to see the grand finale?" Tony asked. There was a hint of something in his voice that Alice didn't pick up on as she was too preoccupied with how gross her hand felt.

"Ah, no thank you. I think I can figure out that on my own." She stood up and very nearly reached out to shake his hand. But she remembered where both those hands had been, and also that doing that would be awkward. "Thank you again," she said instead.

Alice gave Anthony a weird little smile and then raced back to the comfort of her office. She would never talk to another soul for as long as she lived.

Chapter 5
Out and About in Town

Alice bothered her lower lip with her teeth, the silence in her ear more deafening than the silence in the rest of the house. She huffed, adjusting her hold on the phone. "Oh, just say it already!"

Katie's voice was laden with disappointment. "Wow."

Alice let out a cry and buried her face in the crook of her arm. "I know," her muffled voice exclaimed. "I'm terrible. I'm awful. I'm going to die alone and when I do, I'm going to Hell."

"Well, I wouldn't say *all* of that," Katie said. "But you certainly did... that."

"What do I do?"

Alice needed Katie's help now more than ever. Being with Anthony yesterday had been helpful. Useful in fact, as she could use her own experiences in her book. But that night, as they had dinner and watched a movie on her laptop (both sitting on the couch with Alice's mind completely absorbed with how close Anthony was), she noticed he had been acting rather strange. More distant and less...exotic?

And when she woke up the next morning, the realization of exactly how everything had gone down dawned on her with a burning intensity. She had asked Anthony for help. He had, very willingly, given it to her. And she had essentially taken what she wanted and left him hanging.

"Well," Katie said, and Alice could practically hear the smirk on her face. "First, you apologize for being a big fat liar and saying it was a-what did you say- one time deal and that's it?"

"Katie, *please*," Alice begged.

"Alright, alright. You just have to find some way to make it up to him."

"Like what?" Alice rolled over in bed, lying on her back. "Make him a fancy dinner or something?"

"I'm thinking something of a more sexual nature."

Alice's eyes widened, and her heart beat faster in her chest. She told herself the idea was certainly not enjoyable. "Like what? I'm certainly not going to...to…" she wanted to say, 'give him a blowjob', but she was talking to her sister, and really, she would never say that to anyone. Her face burned with embarrassment just thinking of the idea.

"He seems like the kind of guy who would enjoy a nice night of lingerie," Katie suggested.

"Absolutely not!" Alice sat up in bed, the fire of embarrassment heating her body. She tossed the covers aside. "I am not going to buy lingerie for some guy I am not dating."

"...Are you *sure* you're not dating?" Katie asked.

Alice let out an exasperated huff. "Yes, I'm sure! How could I not be sure?"

"Well, you weren't sure if you had sex with him or not."

Alice closed her eyes and groaned. Yes, she needed advice, but she needed actual, practical advice. "Look." She took a deep, calming breath. "Anthony is not going to appreciate any sort of sexual favor I may do for him, okay? This is a business interaction. He is helping me with my book. He does not actually like me."

Katie didn't say anything.

"What?" Alice asked, checking to make sure the call hadn't been dropped.

"Oh, my dearest, darlingest, little sister," Katie said. And she said it in that way that preceded a lecture of sorts. Alice readied herself. But nothing more came.

"Your dearest, darlingest, little sister what?" she asked.

Katie sighed with a soft chuckle. "It's nothing," she said. "I'm sure a nice dinner would be acceptable. Or perhaps take him into town to get some new clothes or something, since he only has the one bag, right?"

Now that was an actual, useful, helpful, practical idea. "New clothes! Katie, you're a genius! Why didn't I think of that?"

"We rarely think clearly of the things we're so close to."

"...Right. Well. Thank you, again."

"Anytime, dear."

Alice hung up the phone and scrambled out of bed, excited with the new idea and the opportunity she had to make up to Anthony for being so inattentive yesterday.

*

"Bikes?" Tony asked, staring at the offending devices Alice was pulling out of the garage. He had been more than willing to accept Alice's offer to buy him clothes, but riding bikes down to town, and more importantly back up, was not appealing.

"Yes, bikes," Alice said. She kicked the stands out and went back inside to grab two helmets. "They're fun and healthy."

"More like terrible and a nuisance," Tony mumbled. He missed his car now more than ever. "Do we really have to ride these?"

Alice forced a helmet into his arms. "Well, I suppose you could walk if you wanted to. But you might be a bit slow getting down."

Tony turned and looked down the hill that led into town. Getting up was the part he was more worried about. Meanwhile, Alice slipped her helmet on, a lovely green shade that matched her eyes that day and the bike. The strap clung tight to her chin, squishing her face a little. Tony sighed and put his own helmet on. The things he does for basic necessities.

"You do know how to ride one don't you?" Alice asked. She swung a leg up and over, settling down on the seat of the bike.

"Been a while," Tony admitted. He had ridden bikes a lot as a kid. But the moment he got his license, he never even so much as looked at one. He gingerly straddled the seat.

"Well, don't worry. You know what they say." Alice gave him a smile and a soft laugh as she kicked up her stand. "It's just like riding a bike."

Tony gave her an unamused look, but she just laughed again, pushing away and riding down the driveway. Tony took a steadying breath, kicked his own stand up, and followed after her.

Alice rode with the practiced ease of someone who did this every day. She expertly maneuvered around rocks or branches on the road, keeping her line straight and her pedals in motion. Tony, meanwhile, shook and wavered, somehow managing to keep himself upright as his bike swerved across the sides of the road. Heaven help him if a car showed up.

Then, of course, came the steep drop that would deposit them right into town. Tony rode it carefully, keeping his hand clenched around the brake, more scooting himself down then actually rolling down it. He kept his eyes focused on the wheels and the road ahead of him, only looking up when he heard a laugh.

Alice was rolling down the hill at full speed, a sight that widened Tony's eyes and agitated his heart. She was laughing, and her legs were spread out to the sides, pedals spinning wildly as gravity took her. Surely she was going too fast. She would get to the bottom and crash. And then Tony would have to explain how he had been responsible for the death or impairment of Nana's biggest author.

But as soon as Alice got close, she regained her footing, legs spinning in time with her wheels. She hit the bottom and turned, riding around in a large circle as her speed decreased. She paused at the base, one foot holding her up as she waited for Tony.

With a grimace, Tony realized he couldn't be shown up like that. He gritted his teeth together and released the break. His bike lost its wobble as the speed evened out his motions. The rush of air on his face exhilarated him, and he allowed himself to enjoy the brief moment of flight right up until the moment he realized he *was* going too fast and would likely crash.

He tried his best to veer off to the side of the road, to crash among the soft foliage of the fall forest, but he had never been very good at steering, and he rammed right into Alice and her waiting bike.

The two toppled over from his speed, the softness of Alice's body cushioning his fall as they tangled together with the metal of their bikes.

"Fuck," Tony said as Alice groaned beneath him. "Sorry!" He kicked himself free of his bike and rushed to his feet, adrenaline keeping the pain of the fall at bay. "Are you okay?"

Alice nodded and grabbed the hand he offered. He pulled her to her feet, holding her steady and looking her over for any cuts or bruises.

"You were doing rather well right up until that end bit," she said.

He winced. "Yeah. Sorry. This is why we shouldn't have ridden bikes."

Alice chuckled and leaned down, picking her bike up and checking that it still worked. Tony mirrored her actions.

"No harm," she assured him. "No foul. Now, let's go shopping."

Tony nodded, glad that his little escapade hadn't gotten either of them hurt. Back on the bike with wiggly legs, Tony followed Alice deeper into town. It was a Thursday morning, so there wasn't much traffic, foot or car, but Tony could still feel a sting of embarrassment every time they passed someone. He was sure he looked like a toddler learning to walk.

"Here we are," Alice announced. They parked their bikes at a rack on a street full of shops. Alice reached into her bag and produced a wallet. She handed Tony a card. "There's a clothing store just across the street. Get whatever you'd like."

Tony took the card with awe. "Whatever I'd like?" Alice nodded. "Wow.

That's a lot of trust there."

"Well, within reason, of course. Just a few outfits you can wear while you're here."

"As part of my payment for working for you, right?" Tony asked. "Just to be sure."

"Mhm." Alice nodded and pointed behind her. "There's this cute consignment store down the street I spied while coming in. Meet me there when you're done?"

Tony could only nod, watching as she bounced away.

*

The bell rang out a lovely little ding as Alice entered the shop. It was as cute as she had expected. Art and clothes and various other types of crafts were spread about, each display showcasing a picture and some information about the local artist that was involved. Alice smiled at it all, wondering where she should start, and trying to figure out how much she could fit in her basket.

"Good morning," a woman with long, dark hair and glasses greeted. She wore a little name tag that suggested her name was Cyra. It was such a lovely, unique name, and Alice made a note of it for later use.

"Hello," she greeted back. "Your store is just lovely."

Cyra smiled, tucking her hair behind one ear. "Thank you. We have a real passion for promoting local work. Are you from around-I'm sorry you just look really familiar."

Alice bit her lip. That was the problem with being a successful writer. Granted it was easier than being a famous actor. But still, true fans could recognize her.

"You're not-" Cyra started. Then she shook her head. "No, I'm sure not. Sorry."

Alice twitched a smile. She hated not saying anything, but she hated more the idea of being revealed. Even if she wanted to trust the kind face of the woman running the shop, she didn't want to risk her location getting out, inviting all kinds of distractions. So, she nodded at Cyra and simply went about looking in the shop.

"Hey, I got some more of those paper flow-"

The man who had emerged from a side door stopped when Alice turned towards his voice. He was tall, and also sporting glasses. Only his made him look a bit more bookish and nerdy than the way the glasses accentuated Cyra.

"My god," he said, dropping said paper flowers on the counter. "Alice Follick as I live and breathe." He grinned a wide, tilted smile. "In our very own little shop!"

Cyra gasped. "So, you are…"

Alice blushed, caught in her less-of-a-lie-more-an-omission-of-truth. She shrugged apologetically. "I'm afraid I am."

The man seemed incapable of moving, staring at her with a slightly open mouth. Cyra chuckled and patted his hand. "Issac here is a big fan of yours."

"Oh?"

Cyra nodded. "He's got all your books. Read them each at least three times. And that's just since I've known him."

Alice smiled, a warmth spreading through her body. She did so love compliments, and nothing was as complimentary as multiple reads of her books. "Well, I'm very glad you enjoy them."

Issac just nodded.

The bell rang again, and Anthony stepped into the store, carrying a bag in his hand.

"Oh," Alice said. "That was quick."

Anthony shrugged. "Only needed a few things." He looked over at Cyra and Issac. "What's with the cod fish over there?"

Firsthand Research

Alice swatted him on the arm for being rude. To her fans no less. "This is Cyra and Issac, they run the shop. Issac, uh, enjoys the products of my labor."

Anthony gave her a look. "You can just say your books. It doesn't have to be all fanciful."

"This is Anthony," she said, ignoring his comment and introducing him to the others.

"Anthony Follick," he added, reaching out to shake Cyra's hand. Alice's eyes grew wide as she heard that name escape his lips.

"Oh?" Cyra said, looking between the two of them. "Any relation?"

"Only by marriage," Anthony said with a wink.

Alice grabbed his arm, rather roughly, and dragged him out of the store, offering a rushed apology to Cyra and Issac. She would have liked to stick around and talk with them more, but she was certain that leaving Anthony in there would only accentuate the embarrassment she felt.

"What was that?" she hissed, pulling him back towards the bikes.

"What was what?" Anthony asked. But he had a stupid little smirk on his face that indicated he knew exactly what was what.

"Why did you say that?" Alice explained.

Anthony shrugged. "I figured if I used my real name I might get found out. So, I needed a fake one."

"But mine?"

"Why not?"

"Because people are going to think we're married!"

Anthony leaned away a bit, a playful look in his eyes. "Well now, whatever would give them that idea?"

"Related by marriage?" Alice suggested. She was doing a very good job at convincing herself that the heat in her body was the outrage at Anthony's act, not the excitement the idea of being married to him created. "How else would we be related by marriage?"

Anthony shrugged. "I could have married your sister. She seems the strong type that would be down for a guy taking her name. Or, I dunno. Your brother may be a bit insufferable but, hey, I wouldn't exactly kick him out of bed in the morning, if you know what I mean."

Alice did know what he meant. And she huffed at him as she pulled her bike free. "Yes. I'm sure the very first thing people will think is that you married my brother."

Anthony put his bag in his basket and Alice noted her own empty one with disappointment. She had wanted to do some shopping herself, but keeping Anthony and his lies away from the public was her number one priority now.

"You're not really mad, are you?" he asked.

Alice sighed. "Not completely. But if you're going to use a fake name, then please just make another one up. I wouldn't want any rumors getting out. Especially not now when I need to be working on finishing this book."

Anthony nodded and he looked at his feet in shame. "Yeah. Shit. Sorry, I hadn't really thought about that."

Alice frowned slightly. That was the problem with trying to make new friends or dates. There were some things she had to think and worry about that they simply didn't. And she often forgot that her problems were not universal.

"All is forgiven," she said. "Now, let's get back to work, hm?"

Chapter 6
Sex Lesson Three – Nipple Play

Anthony had been very quiet all afternoon and it made Alice worry. He had seemed to accept her acceptance of his apology, but she wished there was a way she could prove to him that it really was okay. She figured that giving him more work to do would probably help. So, with a red face, she handed him a scene she had typed on the typewriter. After all, he had experience where she did not. He could look it over. Could find errors or room for improvements.

It had been a good idea at the start. Anthony had actually smiled when she suggested it, and he took the scene eagerly. But now her next scene sat untouched as Alice fidgeted, wondering what Anthony would think of what she had given him.

About an hour of worrying had passed. And Alice figured that if she wasn't going to get any writing done, she could at least take a look at the edits.

She slipped out of the office and crept down the hall. Anthony turned to greet her, always aware of when she was approaching. The scene lay on his lap, with a few pages scattered about the couch.

"Just thought I'd check in," she said, laughing softly to calm her nerves. "See if you needed anything?"

"I do believe that's my job," he argued. Alice looked at her feet. "Don't worry, it's good."

Alice looked back up. "Oh, is it? You like it?"

Anthony nodded and gestured her over. "I truly felt like I was a woman being ravaged."

Alice blushed and hid her face in her hands as she sat down next to him. "And all the, jargon, was okay? The, er, technical aspects."

"Yeah," Anthony said. "This is some hot stuff."

Alice felt like her face had been sunburned. She still couldn't manage to un-bury it. "Any suggestions?"

Anthony hummed. "Well, I mean, it could use some nipple play, if I'm being honest."

That got Alice to pull her hands away, purely so she could furrow her eyebrows at him. "Nipple play?"

"Yeah." Anthony nodded. "I mean, this Malcolm guy has this perfect pair of knockers right before him, yeah?" Alice rolled her eyes at the crude language. "And I mean, massaging them is great, absolutely. But, c'mon. No guy in his right mind could resist at least a little pinching."

Alice frowned and played with the edge of her shirt, watching her fingers pick at the fabric. "Well, I-I mean I know that...It's a rather popular thing in..." She gestured about. "But it's not really all that common, is it? Sexual arousal from nipple stimulation?"

Anthony looked at her, blinked, then looked down at the scene on his lap. "How do you write this, but speak that?"

"Just answer the question. Is it common?"

Anthony looked back up at her and tilted his head. His eyes roamed down to her chest and the burn on her face spread to her entire body. "I mean, it's not uncommon. Have you ever tried it before?"

Alice had to admit that she didn't. She wasn't sold on the idea that it was really a thing. Nipples were there to give milk to babies. What's arousing about that?

Anthony licked his lips, his eyes still glued to her chest. Then they bounced back up, intensity burning behind them. "I could show you."

Alice leaned away from the heat of his gaze, certain that any more fire to her body would kill her. "Show me?"

"Yeah." Anthony blinked, his eyes returning to normal. "For the book, you know. It is my job."

Alice nodded, feeling a little silly that she had let herself think it was anything else. It was just that look in Anthony's eyes, the way he stared at her. She thought maybe he had actually just...thought she was pretty. But it was for the book, of course. She was a fool to think otherwise.

She swallowed, even though her mouth had gone dry. "Well, I suppose you could give it a shot. For the book."

"For the book," Anthony agreed. And then he shifted, turning on his side and crowding forward until Alice was pressed up against the arm of the couch, practically laying down.

Anthony sat on his knees, hands reaching up and laying over Alice's shirt.

"Shouldn't I be not wearing-"

"Shh," Anthony said. "Just let me work. You'll see."

Alice bit her lip. Because the silence was the worst part. It had been different when Anthony was eating her out. He couldn't talk then. And they hadn't been so close, so face-to-face. "It's just that narration will help. With writing it all later."

Anthony nodded. "Well, great nipple play, just like great sex, begins with a little foreplay."

Anthony squeezed his hands around Alice's breasts, creating a lovely friction of pressure as the fat molded around to his touch. And it did feel nice, the squish of it as Tony's fingers pulsated, like he was drumming them on a table only the table was Alice. There was rhythm to it, and already the words of the scene were altering in Alice's mind.

Anthony's hands slid up, pulling the collar of Alice's shirt down a bit, revealing the top of her rather plain, thin, tan bra. She briefly wished she had gotten some lingerie after all. But she reminded herself this was purely academic, and she didn't need to fancy up for it.

Anthony kept pulling at the fabric, until the collar was stretched down under her bosom. "Should I take it off?" she asked.

Anthony studied the shirt then grabbed the sleeves, pulling on them as well until they were down by her elbows. Her breasts rested against the top of her shirt, her stomach thankfully still covered by the fabric, but her chest rather well presented.

"Is that comfortable?" Anthony asked.

There was a little, tight pressure on her arms, but it didn't bother her, so Alice nodded.

Anthony traced a finger over the top of Alice's bra, dipping below it a few times, dragging against the skin. Alice looked down at his handiwork, noticing with a little embarrassment how her nipples were already hard, pushing against the fabric of her bra. She noted, also, that she was getting a little wet between her legs. But surely it was just the closeness that caused that.

Anthony smiled and sighed. "You have some really great boobs, Alice," he said. And it sent a shiver down Alice's spine. "I mean," he shook his head, "seriously, who's out there not wanting a piece of this?"

'Apparently everyone' Alice thought. But she just shook her head and shrugged.

"Well, don't you worry," Anthony continued. "I'll treat them right."

Then he leaned down, placing his open mouth over one of her breasts. Alice gasped, mainly because now she would have to wash that bra sooner than she thought. But also because it felt *good*. Anthony's saliva moistened the fabric, and it eventually reached to her skin, a sticky, hot sensation that was actually enjoyable.

And his tongue! That very same tongue that had lapped an orgasm out of her (only two days ago, she realized) was pressing, wide and hot, against her nipple, warming the ripples of her skin. She let out a shaky sigh.

Anthony surfaced. "Good, yeah?"

Alice nodded. "It's surprising. But I suppose the heat and the slick make an appetizing combination."

Anthony gave her a suspicious look. "Are you sure you're not plagiarizing these books?"

"My speaking me and writing me are two very different people," Alice explained.

"Clearly." Anthony bent his head back down, giving the similar treatment to her other breast.

Alice allowed her eyes to close, giving into the warm sensations of Anthony's work. He would squeeze and massage one breast while working his mouth over the bra on the other. It was comfortable and relaxing. She felt at ease, despite the awkwardness of the situation. And surprising still was how much more aroused she was getting, to the point where she was sure she'd have to change pants after this. She always figured that being aroused was an intense, work-out kind of high. But she felt a bit like she could fall asleep right then and there.

But then the warmth and comfort of Anthony's hands and mouth were leaving her chest. She shivered in the cold, opening her eyes, feeling more awake than ever before. Because looking at Anthony looking at her reminded Alice of the situation.

"Is it okay if I keep going?" Anthony asked, gesturing to the bra.

Alice blinked at him, not fully understanding what he meant. "I mean, do you still have more to do?"

Anthony's smile was crooked, but soft. Like he was amused with her reaction but found it charming. "Plenty," he said. "Can I take off your bra?" he then explained.

"Oh!" Alice said, feeling a little sheepish and dumb for not getting it. "Y-yes. If it'll help the process along."

Anthony nodded and smiled at her fully. Then he leaned ever closer, face mere inches from hers as he reached around and grabbed at the hooks of her bra. She turned her head to the side, unable to meet his gaze.

Anthony got the bra unhooked on the first try, which really didn't surprise Alice in the least. There was a bit of an awkward shuffle as Alice sat up, pulling her arms fully out of her shirt so Anthony could slip the bra all the way off. She settled back down against the arm of the couch, shirt comfortably wrapped around her stomach, chest on full display.

And then her eyes widened and she could see her skin tinging pink with embarrassment. She hadn't shaved or plucked in a while, and her breasts sported several fine lines of hair. Thankfully they were a light color that matched the rest of her hair, but they were still noticeable.

"I'm sorry," she said, as Anthony carefully draped her bra over the back of the couch. "If I had known we would be doing this I would have…" she just gestured down, moving to cross her arms over the offending parts of her body.

"Would have what?" Anthony asked.

And Alice was hopeful. Maybe he hadn't seen. For surely if he did, he would think any number of awful thoughts about her, chief among them that she was dirty or unhygienic. And she prided herself on always being clean and put together.

"Well, uh…cleaned up?" she said, unsure how to phrase it properly.

Anthony chuckled softly. "I told you; I really don't care. And I mean that."

Alice licked her lips and then pulled the bottom one between her teeth. She wanted to trust Anthony. But she didn't know how he couldn't care. Everyone cared. Surely he did, too. But maybe part of why he always had a guy or girl on his arm was simply *because* he didn't care. Alice nodded softly, allowing that to be the story she told herself as she unfolded her arms and moved them back down.

And the look in Anthony's eyes as he looked over her certainly indicated he wasn't turned off in the least. He took one breast in each hand and just held them, moving a bit as if trying to weigh them to see which was heaviest. And the building anticipation just created more urgency and need between Alice's legs.

Anthony took a deep breath and bent his head down. He opened his mouth wide and slid his lips around one of Alice's breasts, the heat of his breath comforting, but the slick of his saliva a bit unsettling. He pulled back, his tongue sliding along the bottom until the whole area was covered in wet. And then he pursed his lips and blew on it.

Alice jumped at the shock of cold to the area. Goosebumps prickled up on her chest and down her arms, a sensation that was new, but not entirely unenjoyable.

"Bad?" Anthony asked.

Alice shook her head. "Just a little surprising, is all."

Anthony nodded and repeated the motion on the other breast. This time Alice didn't jump at the cold, and the goosebumps traveled to her back, creating a tingling sensation in her spine that travel down to her hips. They pushed off the couch a bit, trying to create a harder pressure against her groin on the cushion.

"I'm gonna do my stuff," Anthony said. "Just let me know if anything hurts, okay?"

"W-will it hurt?" Alice asked, now a little worried. She knew breasts were sensitive, of course. But she figured being made to be glorified milk bottles probably gave them a bit of tenacity.

"Some things can." He reached up and grabbed one nipple between his thumb on forefinger, giving it a little squeeze. "How's that?"

It didn't feel entirely as good as the other things he had been doing, but it certainly didn't hurt. "That's fine," she told him.

"Good." And then Anthony couldn't speak again because his mouth was back on Alice's chest.

Only this time instead of a wide, open area, Anthony seemed fixated on just the tip. He kept his mouth open around it and flicked over Alice's nipple in a similar fashion as he had with her clitoris. And there was something about the heat, and the texture, and the light teasing that just excited her even more.

Alice's hips rocked again, an urgency growing down there that she really didn't need. She wanted to focus her attention and energy on what Anthony was doing with her chest, so she could use it for the book. She had to distract herself down there so she could do just that.

Alice shifted slightly, leaning to the side so she could slide her hand down between her legs. Only Anthony had a similar idea. Only their hands touched, right there above Alice's groin.

"Ah," Anthony said, pulling his mouth away. "Sorry."

But Alice didn't want him to be sorry. She wanted him to be *there*. She grabbed his wrist, rather impulsively, as he tried to pull away. He looked at her, but she couldn't meet his gaze.

"Yeah?" Anthony asked. "You want me to?"

Alice couldn't just admit that. But she did want him to. So she nodded slightly, still avoiding looking at him. Her voice was very soft when she did manage to speak. "For the book."

"Ah," Anthony said. "Right. The book."

Alice let go of his wrist, and his hand pressed up against her, cupping her through her jeans. She took a shuddering breath at both the closeness and intimate notion of this act. And at how good it felt to have a real pressure where she needed it most.

Anthony's hand rocked against her as he resumed his work up top. With one hand down, he settled for bothering a nipple with his mouth, while his other hand worked the opposite nipple. Alice found that she enjoyed the work of his mouth much more than the work of his hand, even when his lips closed around her nipple and pulled at it gently. She figured it was the heat and wet of it all that made the sensations that much more exhilarating.

And as she felt herself getting closer and closer to orgasm, she found it was harder and harder to concentrate on it all. She wanted to take notes, to detail how it felt when Anthony pulled on the nipple and then pressed against it with his tongue; how his fingers rolled them around like an expert marble player examining his favorite ball; how he lingered between each switch, placing kisses to the skin separating her breasts. But she was cresting, cresting, gone.

Alice clamped her legs around Anthony's hand, holding it in place as her hips rocked into it, chasing that friction as she came. And Anthony didn't let up on his work on her chest, continuing to lick and suck and kiss as Alice shook through her pleasure.

And after it was all over, Alice really did feel she would fall asleep.

"So that's...that," she said, blinking at the ceiling as Anthony sat back on his feet.

"That's that," he agreed.

Alice looked down at him and he was smiling. She took a moment to gather her strength, and then slid to sit up, hiding herself as best she could as she put her shirt back in place. "I really didn't know it could be that stimulating."

"That's why you gotta do your research." He winked at her. "There are even some people that can come from just that alone."

"Really?" Alice asked. "Not anything else?"

Anthony nodded. "Oh yeah. It's not entirely common. Usually it is sort of a stepping stone to the main event."

Alice stilled, the phrasing that Anthony used reminding her of the 'grand finale' she had missed yesterday. She wondered to herself how she would have felt had Anthony not kept his hand between her legs. If he had pulled back and said 'welp I've shown you all I know, bye.'

She truly was terrible.

"Uhm, I was thinking of going to town alone tomorrow," she said.

"Don't want me to come?" Anthony asked.

"No thank you, *Mr. Follick.*"

Anthony chuckled. "Okay. Fair enough. What ya need down there?"

"I want to get some food, maybe cook something fun for dinner?"

"Yeah?" Anthony looked over at the kitchen. "We got plenty of stuff here."

Alice shook her head. "No, I, uh, want to do something special. Cook something fancy, you know?" He nodded, so she took a deep breath and went for it. "Is there anything specific you'd like?"

"Me?"

"Yes. I'd like to make something you'd enjoy."

Anthony looked up, thinking about it. "Oh! You know like, chicken parmesan?" Alice nodded. She had even made that before. "Well I was at this restaurant a few months ago and they had this thing that was like that but it wasn't chicken?"

"Eggplant?" Alice suggested.

"Yeah, that was it!" Anthony smiled wide. "It was really good, and I have been meaning to try it again."

Alice smiled back, happy that she not only was going to do something nice for Anthony, but that he was welcoming the gesture so openly. "Eggplant parmesan sounds lovely." She stood up, grimacing a bit at the mess in her pants. "I'm going to go clean up," she announced, and then wondered why she had felt the need to do that. "Thank you, again. This was very helpful."

"Anything for the book," Anthony said.

Alice nodded and turned away. For the book, of course. That's all this was.

"Oh, Alice, wait!" Anthony said.

Alice spun around, a bit too eagerly. But Anthony was just holding out her bra to her. She blushed and took it with a nod of thanks.

Always for the book.

Chapter 7
Future on the Horizon

Truth be told, it was pretty boring without Alice around. She had spent practically all the rest of yesterday writing, working on revising the scene Tony had read to include more of what he had shown her. Ate in the office and everything. Not that Tony minded. She was there to get work done, of course. But watching a movie on the laptop alone on the couch had bothered him more than he thought.

He had bought some pajamas at the shop, and the next morning he was eager to show them off to her. They were patterned, with colorful dots of sushi against a black background. But when Tony shuffled out to the kitchen, Alice was gone.

All she left was a note on the fridge saying she had made fruit salad for breakfast and to please eat some. Apparently, it's good for him. Tony ate it. But not because he was keen on being healthy or following the rules. He just didn't know how to cook and nothing else was prepared.

Tony sat down on the couch and pulled the laptop over. He sighed, thinking maybe he *should* try to get to work on some job hunting. But then he remembered he was the most unemployable person in the world and decided to distract himself with some videos.

Luckily, his salvation came in the form of a knock on the door. Now, theoretically, Tony shouldn't have gone around answering doors at a cabin he wasn't supposed to be living in. For all he knew it could have been Nana coming to check on Alice. Or Alice's brother coming to check on her. He wasn't sure which would be worse. Thankfully, he had some kind of positive karma left over from his childhood, because it was just Sandra and Ronnie.

"Glad to see you made it one piece," Sandra said, filing in.

"Nice jammies," Ronnie noted.

"Thanks," Tony said. "What are you two doing here?"

"Just thought we'd stop by to check up on you. Make sure you hadn't been eaten by wolves." Sandra stood in the center of the room, looking over all the space.

"Or eating the wolves yourself to survive," Ronnie added.

"No wolves here," Tony proudly explained. "I've been doing just fine, thank you very much. Guess I'm not such a talentless lump after all, huh?"

"Where'd you get the laptop?" Sandra asked, picking the offending piece of technology up. "Tony, did you rob a bank?"

"No, I didn't rob a bank," Tony said, rolling his eyes. "I, uh, borrowed it. From a friend."

"You have friends?" Ronnie asked.

Sandra chuckled and swatted her lightly on the arm. "Who's hanging around up here we still know?"

"I could know people you don't," Tony said.

"So, then who'd you borrow it from?" Sandra asked.

"More like who's stupid enough to lend you anything?" Ronnie added with a laugh.

Tony put his hands on his hips and scowled at her. "I'll have you know I'm a very respectable person worthy of trust."

"Are we talking about the same person?" Ronnie asked.

"Stop avoiding things and tell us who gave this to you," Sandra said.

Tony snatched the laptop back from her. "I don't have to tell you anything."

Sandra and Ronnie exchanged a glance and oooo'd.

"I bet it's a girl," Ronnie said.

"Tony, who have you coerced into helping you this time?" Sandra asked.

Ronnie crossed her arms. "Yeah, what poor innocent soul have you corrupted now?"

Tony was beginning to wish that Nana or Liam *had* been the ones to show up. At least his death that way would have gone by a lot quicker. "It's not some innocent soul, trust me."

"You know, we'll stop badgering you if you just tell us who it is," Sandra said.

Tony knew they were lying. Them knowing who it was would just make things worse. He'd never live it down. Besides, what if they found out the real truth? No, he couldn't let that happen.

"Alright," he admitted. "The truth is, I didn't actually borrow it from someone. It's mine. I have a job now."

"There's no way you got a job that fast," Ronnie said.

"Thanks for the vote of confidence," Tony mumbled.

Sandra moved to sit down at one of the stools in the kitchen. "So, where are you working?"

"Uh, it's remote," Tony said. He held the laptop up. "Why I got one of these."

"What do you do?" Ronnie asked.

"I'm an assistant," Tony said. That, at least, wasn't a lie. "A virtual assistant. It's a real thing!"

"I can't believe someone trusts you to organize their life like that. You can't even organize your own." Ronnie laughed.

"I can't believe you're so committed to this lie," Sandra added.

Tony opened his mouth, then shut it again. "You already know Alice is here, don't you?"

Sandra smiled. "Yeah, Nana told us yesterday."

"Why are you so cruel?" Tony slumped over and settled down in the stool next to her. "Well, I really am an assistant."

"So that's why she hasn't sold you out yet," Sandra said. "I was wondering."

"And you're actually a good assistant?" Ronnie asked. She was wandering around the room, looking at things.

"I'm the best," Tony said. "You can ask her yourself. I've been *very* helpful." He winked at them.

"Oh, Tony, no," Sandra said. "Please tell me you aren't sleeping with her?"

Tony shrugged. "Okay. I won't tell you."

"I thought she was smarter than that," Ronnie said.

"It's actually part of my job," Tony told them. And, if he was being honest, having a job that involved getting to have sex with Alice certainly made looking for another job much less appealing. "It's research."

Sandra stared blankly at him.

"What? It is! She's writing smut and needs help with it."

"Alice is writing smut?" Sandra asked. "Really, Tony, there's no need to lie."

"I'm not lying! Ask Nana, she'll confirm it."

"I really don't think talking to my grandmother about smut is a good idea."

Tony slumped forward and rested his head against the counter. To be fair, he wouldn't trust himself either. But this time he was telling the truth.

"You planning on staying here long?" he grumbled into the counter top.

"Just wanted to stop by and check on you," Sandra said. She patted his back. "Glad to know you're doing okay."

Firsthand Research

"Yeah. I hope you have fun with your 'important research'," Ronnie said.

Tony groaned, the only thing keeping him sane was his knowledge that he was telling the truth. It was important research, and he was doing a damn fine job of it.

*

Alice double checked the list on her phone. She had all that she needed for dinner that night. And it would fit in her basket. But there was still something she had to get. Or, at least, consider getting.

Alice held the box of condoms in her hand. She didn't plan to let anything with Anthony get that far. But she might need it. If things did get that far ahead. Which it certainly *wouldn't*. But just in case. Yes, just in case.

Alice placed the box in her basket and hurried her way to the check out, eager to get it over with so she could hide back at home. Unfortunately, there weren't any self-checkouts at this store, and only one cashier open. Alice covered the box up with the other things in her basket and waited in line with a shaking leg.

"Alice?" someone behind her asked.

She winced, worried she was discovered once again. But when she turned, it was just Nate. Her old friend from school.

"Nate!" she greeted. He smiled and she pulled him into a hug. They hadn't seen each other much since graduation, but he had been one of the only ones at school that could keep her sane during finals. "How have you been?"

"Not bad," Nate said, nodding. "Finally opened that publishing company I was always dreaming about."

"You're kidding?" Alice said, her heart swelling with happiness for him. "Nate, that's amazing! Congratulations!"

"Thanks. It's pretty exciting. Just over a year now."

The line moved forward, and Alice looked over to make sure she didn't trip as she shuffled along. "Is it around here?"

"Yeah, actually," Nate said. "Right in town. Are you living up here now?"

"Oh, no," Alice told him, chuckling a bit. "I'm still down in the city. Just came up here for a little writing vacation, as it were."

"Wow, so those are real things, and not just something they do in movies, huh?"

"Oh, yes," Alice said. "Although I do have a distracting house guest." Alice could feel the light bulb actually go off in her head. "Oh! Nate, I don't suppose you're hiring right now, are you? Any position at all."

They shuffled forward again, and Alice started placing her goods on the belt, careful to keep her unmentionable goods hidden. Especially now that someone she knew was here.

"Thinking of making a career change there, Alice?" Nate asked. "I have to say, it'd be a big step down."

"No, no, not me! My friend. He's looking for a job right now, and he has lots of experience in the publishing industry?"

"Really?"

"Mhm! Why, he's worked for one of the leading companies for years! He'd be perfect for you."

Alice smiled at the cashier as she started to check her out.

"Well, we are holding interviews for a new marketing director," Nate said.

"He'd be perfect for that!"

"Of course, I can't just give him the job. But he can certainly come in next week for an interview."

"I would really appreciate that." Alice blushed slightly as she watched the cashier scan the condoms over the sensor. But she didn't say anything about it. At least, not out loud.

"No problem," Nate said. "I'll send you all the info." He pulled his phone out. "What's the guy's name?"

"Uh." Alice bought herself some time while she paid for her goods and gathered her bag. "It's Anthony," she said.

Nate waited for a beat. "Is he like, Cher, or does this guy have a last name too?"

Alice bit her lip. She lowered her head and whispered, "Dawson."

"Daw-Dawson?" Nate asked. He laughed and put his phone away. "Good one, Alice. You almost had me there."

"It's true." Alice held her bag close and stood to the side as Nate checked out. She leaned in, her voice soft. "You didn't hear this from me, in fact, you didn't hear this at all. But he's been cut off."

"Really, Alice, it's a good joke, but there's no need to take it that far."

"I'm serious. Look, just give him a shot. I promise, he'll surprise you." He's certainly been surprising her all week.

"Alright. I'll save a slot for him." Nate gathered his bags and they walked outside. "But you better have a convincing double when you show up."

Alice shook her head, eyes rolling slightly. "He'll be there. And listen, you have to come over one night for dinner. It's been too long and I'm sure we have a lot to catch up on."

Nate nodded. "I'd love to."

"Good." Alice placed her bags in her bike and put her helmet on.

"Still scared of driving, huh?" Nate chuckled softly.

Alice gave him an unamused look and got on her bike. "Still scared of swimming?" she countered.

"Hey, mine's a pretty common fear."

They laughed together and said good-bye. It had been nice, talking to him.

Firsthand Research

It gave Alice a good break from her anxiety over how things would develop with Anthony. But as she worked her way back up to the house, it settled neatly in her stomach again.

*

Tony sat at the island and watched the world's best show. Alice cooking. It was wonderful. He'd seen her cook before a bit, sure, but nothing quite like the current task she was on.

Ingredients had been pulled out and spread out, pots and pans had been cleaned and prepped, and all the while Tony watched Alice move with growing interest. He had, at first, been a little hurt when she told him he wasn't *allowed* to help. He knew he wasn't a great cook, but she didn't know that. But now, he was glad. Because there was nothing he could do *but* stare as Alice worked.

It was stunning.

"Alright," Alice announced, looking over her spread of food. "Step one?"

Tony had finagled his way into helping a little bit by being the official recipe reader. He gulped, and somehow managed to pull his eyes down to the screen before him. "Preheat oven," he announced, wincing at how his own voice sounded. He cleared his throat.

"Check!" Alice said, leaning over to turn the oven on.

"Whisk egg and milk together in a wide bowl," Tony said, his voice much more normal now. He decided he'd keep his eyes on the screen.

"Whisk." Alice hummed and dug around in the drawers until she found what she was looking for, holding it up triumphantly. Tony really couldn't keep his eyes off her. He watched as she swayed softly while she stirred the ingredients together. "Check."

Tony blinked and took a moment to collect himself. He talked Alice through the rest of the list, cutting up the eggplant into slices, dipping it in the sauce and then the breadcrumbs. Aligning them just perfectly in the pan to bake. Even without baking at all it smelled heavenly.

"Now," Alice said, turning to the ingredients still on the counter. "Let's make the dough so it can chill before we bake them."

She was making cookies, as she had announced, walking through the door with her grocery bag earlier that day. And had gotten all different kinds of nuts and fillings so she could make them in any fashion that Tony wanted.

"Oh," Alice said as Tony switched tabs over to the cookie recipe.

"What's wrong?" he asked. She was frowning at her pile, and he worried that maybe she had forgotten something at the store. Not that he minded. He was a little concerned as to why she was doing all this cooking and baking in the first place.

"Nothing. I just, I forgot to take out the butter." She opened the fridge and pulled out a stick, frowning at it. "It's supposed to be room temperature, isn't it?"

Tony checked and nodded. "Can't we just melt it or something?" he asked.

"No, that will ruin the texture." Alice pursed her lips and hummed. "Well, just read me everything else off, we'll add it at the end." Then she reached down, placing the wrapped stick of butter between her legs, holding it tight between her thighs.

And Tony was pretty sure he blacked out for a moment. All he could focus on was that act. And the resulting look of Alice's thighs, squished tight around the stick. Even with jeans on, Tony could see the way they moved against it.

"I know it's a little weird," Alice admitted, catching his stare. "But it really warms it up quickly."

Tony snapped to attention, his mouth going dry as he studied the blush on Alice's face. "Not weird at all," he said, his voice as dry as it felt. He tried to swallow, but he had nothing to work with. It was like all of the moisture in his body had gone south for the winter.

"Are you okay?" Alice asked, moving along with the process and cracking some eggs into a bowl.

"Yeah," Tony wheezed out. "Just a little thirsty, I guess."

He would have gotten up to get his own glass of water, but he was certain that standing up would be bad for a whole host of reasons.

"Here." Alice reached up to a cabinet, the stretch of her clenched legs doing absolutely nothing to help Tony's situation, and pulled down a cup. She filled it with water and handed it over.

Tony screwed his eyes shut and gulped it down in one breath. Better, but he was going to have to specifically not look at Alice until the butter was gone.

"Are you sure you're okay?" Alice asked, turning the laptop around so she could see the recipe that Tony was not reading out to her.

Tony nodded, keeping his eyes shut. "Yep, I just uh…" He blinked his eyes open. Oh yes. What an amazing idea. "I just thought of something, you know. Something you could put in your book."

"Oh?" Alice turned, leaning against the counter as she mixed ingredients together. "Do tell."

Tony fought very hard to keep his attention on Alice's face. "Well, you know how you were saying that Naomi's never done it before?" Alice nodded. Tony licked his lips, his mouth already in need of a second cup of water. "And you were worried about how they would work their way up to it?" Alice nodded again. Tony's brain was starting to short circuit. He was losing grasp of his idea.

"I assume you've thought of a good intermediate step?" Alice asked, prompting him to go on. She placed the bowl back on the counter and finally removed the butter. She gently squeezed on it, and, satisfied with the give, unwrapped it and placed it in.

No longer a slave to that image, Tony shook his head and knocked his idea loose again. "Yeah! They could utilize some good thigh-fucking," he suggested.

Alice furrowed her eyebrows at him. "Thigh-fucking?" she asked.

He nodded. "Thigh-fucking."

Alice hummed and turned to stir the dough together. "I don't know. I mean...it's not really a pleasurable thing, right?"

"How so?" Tony thought it was *very* pleasurable.

"Well, for Naomi I mean." Alice laid out a sheet of wrap on the counter and dumped the dough out onto it, forming it up into a ball. "I'm sure for men it's great but, what does she get out of it?"

"Okay, good point," Tony regrettably admitted. "But maybe it's not all about the pleasure. It's about the closeness." He brought his hands together, linking his fingers. "And, you know, it's kind of like, the same motions. Gets ya sort of ready or used to how it'll feel or be."

He was sort of grasping at straws now. Not only was he certain that Alice would just throw the idea away, but using closeness as a reason was not going to get her to ask him for help with it. She didn't need or want to get close to him. He needed a new angle.

"I suppose…" Alice hummed again as she wrapped up her ball of dough and placed it in the fridge to cool. "Well, maybe if Naomi was trying to be... no…"

Tony really wished he knew more about the actual story. All he got so far was that one scene, that really didn't reveal much of the greater plot. He tried to figure out what Alice was thinking, watching to see if he could locate the gears turning in her head.

"I don't suppose you would mind writing it down for me?" Alice asked, smiling a bit. "How it feels for you. Maybe this is the perfect opportunity to get a chapter from Malcolm's point of view!"

She looked so interested in the concept that Tony only let the disappointment settle in a little bit. He had to remind himself that he was here to help her write the book, not just have sex with her. Although that had, so far, been the lovely cherry on top. But he didn't need the cherry to enjoy the full sundae before him.

Firsthand Research

"I'd love to," Tony said with a tight smile. "And hey," he added, because he just couldn't stop himself, "You know I'm willing to provide more than just a written account at your request."

Alice blushed and turned to start the pasta to go with their dinner. Tony, meanwhile, started drafting up his diary entry on thigh-fucking for her.

Chapter 8
Sex Lesson Four – Thighs

It had been a pretty restless night. Tony spent most of it awake, staring at his door, listening intently. He had finished his notes on the joys of thigh-fucking and had handed it over to Alice after their usual nightly movie. She had seemed overjoyed, and had rushed to the office to write, insisting that Tony didn't wait up for her.

It was a little lame, he figured. But he had kind of hoped that she would get the urge to do a little practical research. All he could imagine was her knocking softly on his door, peeking in to see if he was awake. And he would be, of course. And she would stand by the door, shuffling her feet in the shy manner she did. She would stutter out her request and Tony would toss the covers aside and she would rush in, filling up the cold space next to him with her warmth. And then they'd kiss. And then they'd get naked. And then…

Tony blinked awake in the harsh light of day. He had been having the best dream in all the worlds and that stupid woodpecker outside just had to go and ruin it. He glared out his window at the offending creature. Then he noticed how high in the sky the sun was.

Checking his watch, Tony found it was a little past nine. Alice had the unusual habit of waking up around seven. And as much as Tony dreaded getting up so early, sitting with her while she made breakfast was the highlight of his day.

Tony got up and stretched. He still hadn't shown off his pajamas to Alice, and he figured her reaction to seeing them would make up for not getting to keep her company earlier. But when Tony wandered out to the main room, Alice wasn't there.

Yet the mess from dinner was. Tony had forgotten to clean it up last night before heading to bed. He sighed and rolled his shoulders. That was probably why she didn't cook. Here Tony was, supposed to be the best assistant ever, and he couldn't even keep the dishes clean.

After getting dressed (he didn't want to risk ruining his new jammies), Tony did his task from the night before. Then he made up a mug of hot chocolate to make up for his crimes.

"Alice?" he asked, holding the mug in one hand and knocking on the door with the other. "You thirsty?"

There was no response, and Tony didn't hear the familiar click of her typewriter. He nudged the door open with his foot and nearly had a heart attack.

Alice was asleep. She was laying back in the chair, her head tilted, resting on the curved top. She had slumped down a bit, her legs spread open, her arms draped over the sides. Her face would have been peaceful and calm, were it not for the piece of paper stuck to it with drool.

"Uh, Alice?" Tony set the mug down on the desk and reached out, gently shaking her shoulder. "Rise and shine."

Alice's eyes blinked open, puffy from the lack of sleep. She focused on him. "Anthony?" she asked with a slur. "Anthony! What are you doing in my-" she moved to sit up straight, cringing and crying out as her body popped back into place. She reached up and grabbed at her neck, immediately hanging her head down.

"Easy now," Tony said, moving to stand behind her. He pushed her hands out of the way and started nudging his fingers into her muscles. She let out a satisfied moan.

"I must have," she shook her head and pulled the paper off her cheek, "fallen asleep while writing again."

"Again?" Tony asked with a chuckle. "How often does this happen to you? Should we invest in a better, comfier chair?"

Alice shook her head slightly. "No, thank you. It really only happens when I'm stuck on something and am too stubborn to walk away for the night."

"Oh?" Tony asked. He leaned over, increasing his pressure on her neck while trying to get a look at the pages spread about. "What ya stuck on?"

"Well, to be honest, I was trying to figure out how to make that whole, suggestion, from last night work. But…" Alice sighed and shook her head. "I don't know. I just can't seem to get it to work right for Naomi."

"I'd be more than happy to help you figure it out," Tony offered, all too eagerly.

"I just don't see any way I can make it pleasurable for her," Alice explained. "I'd like to, because I do think the other aspects of it work. But I just need that one last missing component."

Tony shrugged, moving his fingers lower to work over Alice's shoulder blades. She leaned forward in the seat to let him. "He could play with her breasts."

"I thought of that, actually. But see, the mouth is the part that's really the best, and it just wouldn't work."

Tony nodded, and made a note of Alice's preference; not that he anticipated being able to actually use that information anywhere. "Well, he could play with her clit."

Alice was quiet for a second. Tony wondered if maybe he was too good at his massage and had put her to sleep.

"You think that would be a comfortable position?" Alice asked. "He could…do all that and still…move?"

Tony's mouth went dry, eager with the possibility of it all. "Oh yeah. Easily."

Alice huffed softly. "I knew I should have brought those art mannequins with me. They're perfect to test positions out with."

"Ya know, you've got two life-sized ones right here." Tony gave her shoulders a little squeeze. He was definitely coming on way too strong. Not that he cared. But Alice might. This was the best deal he had going for him.

Firsthand Research

He couldn't ruin it.

"Really?" Alice asked. "You wouldn't mind?"

"Not a bit."

Alice sat up, and Tony reluctantly let go. She rolled her neck around a bit, not wincing in pain this time. "Thank you." She twisted in her seat, smiling up at him. "After breakfast?"

Tony could only nod.

*

Alice enjoyed making breakfast. It was, after all, the most important meal of the day. But she was eager to get through it, so they simply ate the rest of her fruit salad from yesterday. She could cook tomorrow. Today she had research to attend to.

It was odd how it wasn't odd, leading Anthony into her bedroom. Closing the door gave the atmosphere a hot, heavy feeling. But it was more positively charged, not at all intimidating or fearful as it had been before. Maybe it was the fact that this was less about actually doing anything sexual and more about just...seeing how bodies fit together.

"On the bed, yeah?" Anthony asked, already climbing up on it.

"Yes. I briefly considered the couch, but," Alice followed him, settling down on the other side of the bed, "I figured this would be more comfortable. For them and for us."

Anthony smiled at her, and she was so glad she had someone who was so willing to help her. Perhaps, if it wasn't too weird, she'd dedicate this book to him. At the very least he was definitely going in the acknowledgments. She just had to find out a way to thank him without letting the whole world know what they'd done.

"So, I was thinking they would be like, spooning," Alice said. Anthony nodded and turned on his side. Alice gave him one last look and then followed his motions.

Firsthand Research

Anthony slid forward, one arm snaking under Alice's body as the other draped over it. Then he pulled her back a bit, until they were flush up against one another, his arms crossed over her.

"That has to hurt your arm," Alice noted.

"It's worth it," Anthony mumbled. And his breath was hot against the back of her neck.

"I appreciate your dedication to helping me," she said. "But I need it to be realistic." She shivered a bit as Anthony's breath tickled her, sending waves of *deliciousness* down her spine.

"Trust me," Anthony said. "Any person who loves another person will put up with hours of body discomfort for them."

Alice wanted to argue, but she couldn't think of an instance where that hadn't been true. She had once fallen asleep on Liam's shoulder for two hours on a long car ride. He hadn't been able to lift his arm higher than his neck the whole next week. But he never seemed to be bothered by it. And once, not even all that long ago, Katie had been over to spend the weekend and had laid herself over Alice's lap. Even after her legs went numb, Alice had let her stay there.

"Very well," Alice said. "You may be right."

"May be?" Anthony laughed, and Alice shivered again. Anthony managed to snuggle up closer. "Cold?" he asked.

Alice shook her head. "No, I'm okay. Uh, so, how would they...you know."

Anthony pressed forward with his hips, holding onto Alice's own with the non-trapped hand. "He'd move like this," he explained. And Alice blushed, feeling Anthony already hard, pressing against her legs like that. It made her a little dizzy. "And then just reach on down like this."

Anthony's fingers edged closer to Alice's groin, but they stopped just short of pressing up against it. She looked down, excited that she might have been right about how far one could reach. But she saw that there was plenty of room, and Anthony was just being careful not to touch her, of course.

"I see," Alice said. She tried to wrap her head around it, the way the gentle rocking of Anthony against her body felt. But it was hard because it wasn't exactly how she needed it. She needed to know how it felt to have his dick between her legs, his fingers on her clit. "Do...well, do you think there's a way we could...try? Only I wouldn't want to ruin my pants." And she didn't want to not let him finish like last time.

"Could take them off," Anthony suggested, his hips slowing to a halt.

"Wouldn't want to ruin my skin either," Alice said with a breathy laugh.

Anthony made a noise, a bit like a grunt. "I could run to town and grab some condoms."

Alice picked at her fingernails, glad they weren't facing each other. "What if I already had some?"

"Do you?"

Alice nodded. "But please, don't ask why."

Anthony leaned up, his arm slipping out from under her. "Where, then?"

Alice could not bring herself to look over her shoulder. That electrifying feeling of fear was starting to form again. Once more she was about to be partially naked with Anthony, doing things of unspeakable nature. "Bottom drawer." She reached back, pointing in the vague direction of her dresser.

Anthony crawled off the bed. While he was looking through the drawer, Alice shifted around, pulling the blanket up and over her before she worked her pants off. No need to be exposed, after all.

She stayed facing the wall, listening to the jingle of Anthony's own belt as he also took off his pants. She heard the rip of the packaging.

"I hope they're the right size," she said, surprised by how little of a waver there was to her voice.

"Perfect," Anthony said.

Alice wanted to turn and look, to watch as Anthony put the condom on.

But she was already feeling pretty flushed, and she was certain that if she did that she would just burst right into flames.

The blanket behind her lifted up, and Alice bothered her lip with her teeth as Anthony slid in behind her. He resumed his position, only this time the soft fuzz of his legs pressed warm against her, and he reached down behind her first.

"Do I need-" Alice started.

"Nope. Just stay like that. That's perfect."

Alice gulped, her mouth actually flooding a bit with saliva. Must have been a symptom from sleeping in the office last night.

Anthony slid one hand under her but kept it on her waist as he worked. He shifted down a bit, and then she felt the head of his cock press against her thighs. She really thought she ought to help a bit, lift one leg to let him get between there easier, but Anthony let out a soft moan as he pushed forward. She figured the tight pressure of it must feel good to him.

To her it just felt a little strange. She had been right. There didn't seem to be anything really here for her. This was about Anthony's pleasure. Well, Malcolm's anyway.

But then Anthony seemed to be in. His pelvis pressed into the curve of her legs, and there was something rather exhilarating about it. Must be the closeness he was mentioning. Fully settled, Anthony slid his arm all the way forward, and grabbed Alice's hip with the other.

"It would probably be better with some lubricant," Alice said, cursing herself that she didn't think of it before.

"Would be messy," Anthony told her. He made that grunt again, then slowly moved his hips forward and back, rubbing against her skin. "This is perfect."

It was a little rough at first, the rubber skidding over her without any help. She almost thought to mention it, but then Anthony's hand was leaving her hip, and she heard something wet.

"Sorry," Anthony apologized. He slipped his hand between her thighs, spreading something slick around them. "I'll clean you up after."

Alice shook her head, because the presence of his saliva down there actually made the slide feel good. Like the nerves of her legs were on fire with desire. She clenched them, squeezing them tighter around Anthony as she tried to keep herself together in her own area of need.

"Fuck," Anthony hissed.

"Oh!" Alice immediately relaxed her legs, no longer thinking about the wet spot growing in her underpants. "I'm so sorry."

Tony mumbled something and shook his head, his hair tickled at her neck. "That felt good," he explained.

The arm under Alice moved forward, and Anthony's face pressed against her shoulder. His fingers reached down, and this time they didn't stop. They wiggled under the hem of her panties and pushed their way to her outer labia.

Alice sucked in a breath, letting it out in a shake as Anthony's middle finger wiggled its way between the folds of fat, pressing up against her clit. She reflexively clenched her legs again, pulling a moan out from Anthony.

"Sorry," she said again, feeling rather foolish that she couldn't keep herself still and steady.

"Stop apologizing," Anthony whispered with the hint of a growl. "I told you; it feels good. Here. It's like this." Anthony kept his hips moving, thrusting through the tightness of her legs. As he did so, he slid another finger into her and pressed both of them against her clit, dragging up ever so softly.

A burst of white-hot pleasure shot through Alice's body and she cried out, unable to contain all of that feeling in her body. If it felt like that for him, she was never going to un-clench her legs for as long as she lived.

And it didn't seem like it was going to be a long life at all. Not with the way Anthony's fingers expertly pressed against her clit. Not with the way the slide of him between her legs sent shivers down them. Not with the way he was so close, his body pressed so tight to hers, skin to skin, breath hot on her neck…

"Anthony," she breathed out. "I…Uh!"

"I know," Anthony said. "I can feel it."

Alice forced her last working brain cells to focus on that, her body starting to move on its own, pushing back to meet every one of Tony's thrusts. "You can tell?" she asked.

Tony nodded and she could hear the proud smile in his voice. "You learn to pick up on the little things."

Alice was so busy trying to decipher what her little things were, that she was almost surprised by her orgasm when it rocked through her. If it was possible, her legs clenched even tighter, and Anthony, true to his title, kept his fingers moving, pulling her though the orgasm and down from it, moaning in time with her.

As Alice came down from her high, she noticed that Anthony had stopped moving, his hips resting against hers, his dick a simple presence between her legs.

"You don't have to stop," Alice assured him. She didn't want a repeat of the other day.

"No, I do," Anthony told her with a soft laugh. It was then that Alice noticed the new weight to the condom. The sort of squishy weight.

"Oh!"

Alice lifted one leg up a bit, with great difficulty, and Anthony rolled away. He landed against the mattress, breathing rather hard. Alice figured it was okay, since they were covered by the blanket, so she rolled onto her back too and looked over at him.

Anthony had his hands under the covers, and when he pulled them out, they were holding the condom, tied at the top. It was kind of gross, and he just held it.

"Well, that was very informative," Alice said. She could feel the slick in her panties starting to dry, and her legs were cold and sticky. She needed a shower.

"Glad to be of service," Anthony said with his patented crooked grin. "Seriously. Anytime you need help with anything just let me know. Middle of the night even. I'm here for you."

Alice smiled at him and nodded. He was really rather sweet, when he wanted to be. "I appreciate it. But I think I'll be taking a shower now. And I don't suppose I need help with that."

"Ya sure?" Anthony asked, giving her a suggestive look.

Was that...flirting?

"I'm sure," Alice said. Either way, she was not ready to be fully naked with him yet.

"Alright. I should probably get one too."

Anthony crawled out of the bed and Alice shut her eyes, waiting until she heard the door open and close. She lay there for just a moment longer, staring at the ceiling, processing what had just happened.

She could already imagine what Katie would say.

Chapter 9
Reckless Idiot and Guardian Angel

Tony sat on the couch, mulling the whole event over and over in his head. He couldn't even believe it had been real. He pinched himself, again, to make sure it hadn't been a dream. But no. It was real. He really did do that with Alice.

And it had been fucking amazing.

After his shower, Tony had gone to check on Alice, make sure she was okay. But she had locked herself in the office, refusing to open the door, citing that she was filled with inspiration and had to get some writing done.

So, Tony sat on the couch, not even trying to pretend to look for work, and stared out the window, positively giddy at his own turn of luck.

His joy turned to suspicious caution as a mail truck lumbered its way up the hill, stopping at their house. Tony slid over to the window, peeking out at the man as he whistled and pulled a rather large box from his truck.

Tony didn't want to interrupt Alice's work, but what if his Nana had sent Alice a care package or something? What if it needed to be signed for? Tony could probably forge Alice's signature, but did delivery people report back on who had accepted packages? Did this delivery guy even know who Alice was or what she looked like?

Luckily, Tony didn't have to make the decision, as Alice came rushing out of the room as soon as the first knock hit the door.

Tony stood to the side and watched Alice as she smiled and accepted the package. She seemed to struggle a bit under its weight, but she shooed Tony away when he offered to help.

"You get your fan mail delivered up here or something?" Tony asked, following her back to the office to make sure she didn't drop the box or herself.

"No. No. Nothing like that." Alice blushed, which made Tony even more curious. "It's just, uh, some research. For the book. Is all."

Oh the thoughts that crossed Tony's mind as he tilted his head and studied that box. Alice caught a glimpse of his face, and her blush deepened. "It's nothing like that!" she declared before she shoved the box and herself back into the office and locked the door.

Tony chuckled, because she was cute. And since he didn't know what was in the box, he returned to the couch, eager to let his imagination do the thinking for him.

Not but a few minutes later, he heard Alice shout. He was on his feet and rushing down to break the door open in an instant. Alice was also rushing, and they bumped into each other, grabbing the other for both support and safety.

"Ah," Alice said. "Sorry." But she didn't let go of him.

"Is everything okay?" Tony asked. He looked her over for any marks of physical harm.

"Oh, yes, yes. I'm fine." Alice looked up at him, her eyes sparkling with a hint of joy that put him at ease. "I just forgot to tell you who I ran into yesterday!"

Tony sighed, his body relaxing knowing that there was no danger. "Oh yeah? Who's that?"

"My friend, Nate, from school!" Alice had a wide smile on her face, her eyes lit up by joy. Tony had no idea who this Nate person was, but he rolled with it.

"That's cool."

Alice laughed a bit, finally letting go of her hold on him. He frowned and released her as well, already missing the warm pressure of her arms. "He runs a publishing company in town," she explained. "I got you an interview!"

"Oh." Tony's frown deepened. As far as he was concerned, he had the best job on the planet. But he couldn't let Alice know the real reason this news brought his insides to a crashing halt. "Thinking of firing me, are you?"

"Of course not!" Alice said, encouragement behind every word. "You're the best assistant I could ask for. But you can't be my assistant forever."

Tony feigned insult. "Why not?"

"Well, I won't be working on this book forever, you know. And eventually I won't need a...well...a you." Alice's smile had faded, her eyes now riddled with worry as her fingers mingled together.

Tony did not want to go on this interview. But he didn't want to dampen the joy she had. And she had done him a favor in working old contacts to get it. He shouldn't be rude. "What's the job?"

Alice perked back up again, and Tony focused on that, smiling back at her.

"It's the head of their marketing department," she declared. "I think you'd be excellent at it!"

Tony just nodded. He probably could be excellent at it. If he tried. Which he wouldn't. "I look forward to proving my excellence, as always."

Alice chuckled. "I know you will. I've sent you an email with the details. He's asking everyone to put together a little presentation about what sort of plan they'd have, you know? I figure, you probably know all kinds of good techniques, working at your Nana's all that time."

Tony scratched the back of his head. His time 'working' at Nana's hadn't actually been spent working. But he did know things. He was very good at knowing things, just not so good at actually using that knowledge. Oh well, it wasn't like he was going to try with this presentation or anything.

"It's not too little of notice, is it?" Alice asked. "The interview is next week."

Tony gave her a confident smile, one he had perfected over the years to appear sincere. "Hey, if anyone can put together a presentation in a week, it's me."

She smiled back, once more full of joy. "Oh good! And if you need any help or anything, just let me know."

"Hey now, I'm the one who's supposed to be assisting you, not the other way around." Tony's smile turned to a real, genuine one as he looked at her. It was hard not to smile when she was around. "Now go on, get back to writing. We both have work to do."

Alice nodded, hesitated for a moment, then patted Tony on the shoulder before escaping back to the office. Tony stood in that spot for a brief moment, thinking on that. Then he turned and went off to avoid doing any work at all.

*

Anthony had been a little weird when Alice told him the good news. It was as if he didn't find the news good at all. She mulled it over as she avoided work. Because if she wanted to write again, she'd have to open that box and face the truth of what she had done.

She did like having Anthony as her assistant. But she was right, after all. She would be finished with this book and, she was quite confident, would never write another like it again for as long as she lived. She didn't need a... sex expert. Maybe Anthony had hoped that he could be her assistant after that. And while the idea didn't totally disagree with her, Alice was quite certain that she would be alright on her own.

She really hoped that the interview went well for him. Alice cared about Anthony, probably more than she should. They were, at the very least, friends now. And she only ever wanted good things for her friends.

And Anthony was so unique. He had this care-free, reckless lifestyle that was all an act. And Alice had always known that. Ever since the first time they met, when she was just a new author trying to get into the business, and he was working as an assistant at Nana Jan's company. He had been the one who picked her book out of the pile. The one who had sent it on to the editor that brought her on board. And even though it didn't have his name on it, she had learned that he was the one who had written the acceptance letter. And the things he said about her characters...well, no one who didn't care about life could feel those things.

Firsthand Research

Alice frowned and looked at the box, now sitting in the corner of the room. She had to get to work, otherwise she'd sit around and think about Anthony until she started thinking about things she shouldn't be thinking because they'd never happen. She had to keep a grip on reality.

But she wasn't ready for what was in the box.

So, Alice turned back to her typewriter and decided she could let that scene sit for a while; she still had others to work on, after all. She cracked her knuckles, but the sound of their pops was overcome by the sound of banging coming from outside.

Alice furrowed her eyebrows and peeked out the window. The backyard had a path leading down to a dock that jetted out to the empty lake. It was much too cold in both air and water for anyone to be out there. But there was Anthony, hammer in hand, pulling up one of the loose boards of the dock. A pile of new ones waited beside him.

Alice shook her head. She had half a mind to go out there and chide him. After all, he had work to do! And he could catch a cold! And then he wouldn't be any help to anyone.

Anthony disappeared in the blink of an eye, the only proof of his existence being the boards broken where his feet once were and the splash of water leaping into the air.

Alice gasped, then raced to the back door. She threw it open and studied the water. She couldn't see Anthony's body. Her mind raced over the endless number of tragedies that could have befallen him.

Adrenaline coursing through her nerves, Alice ran down the path. Leaves of late fall rustled under her steps. Rocks didn't dare try to trip her. She reached the water's edge and searched again. There! Anthony was just under the dock, struggling to swim, but thankfully conscious.

Alice wadded into the water. The fire of the intense situation kept the cold from her bones. Anthony spotted her and reached out. She grabbed his arm and pulled him back. He wasn't all that far away from where he could stand. Panting with effort and fear, Alice got Anthony's head above water. She continued to support him with a hand around his waist as they climbed their way back to dry land.

"Fuck!" Anthony said, his body shivering violently. He tried to drop, exhausted, to the floor.

Alice doubled her hold on him. "No," she said. "You need to get inside, now!"

Anthony was not very helpful, his feet dragging through the ground as Alice practically carried him back to the house. It probably wasn't his fault. The cold must have shocked his system something fierce. He probably couldn't control his legs even if he wanted to.

Alice could feel the cold getting to her too, although she had thankfully not been fully emerged or under for as long. She kept a hold of the situation, dragging Anthony in the house. "Come here," she ordered, in as soothing a tone as she could. "Can you move?"

Anthony stood next to her, arms wrapped around himself, shivering. He nodded.

"Good, take off your clothes," she said.

"All of them?" Anthony asked, his teeth clicking together between each word.

"Yes, all of them!" Alice hurried to the nearest room. This was really no time for modesty. She grabbed the heavy blanket off the bed and dragged it into the living room. Anthony was standing next to his shirt, pants, and socks, still donned in his undergarments.

"All of it!" Alice ordered. "Unless you want to get hypothermia and die!"

Anthony shook his head and quickly dispersed the rest of his clothes.

"Sit," Alice said, and Anthony dropped onto the nearest couch, wide eyes staring at her. "Hold this around yourself." She wrapped the blanket over his shoulders, and he wiggled a bit, holding it closed over him. She ran and grabbed a towel from the linen closet and then draped it over his head.

Firsthand Research

"Y-you're cold...c-cold t-too," Anthony sputtered out.

"Shush," Alice told him. She hurried over to the kitchen. But he was right. If she kept her own clothes on, she could be in just as bad a spot as him soon. So, while she waited for the kettle to heat up, Alice escaped to her room and discarded her own clothes in exchange for her large and warm robe.

Anthony wasn't shivering as much when she emerged. Which was either a good sign or a bad one. And judging by the slight tinge of pink returning to his cheeks, she declared it good.

"Isn't like, body heat helpful?" Anthony asked, no longer chattering his jaw. He had a sly look to his face, ruined by the lack of muscular control he had over it.

Alice tutted at him and ignored the comment, making up two cups of tea. "Just drink this."

She sat on the couch next to him and handed him a mug. Anthony snuck one hand out of the blanket, keeping it closed with the other. He shook for a second, then sipped at the tea, sighing.

"Uh…thanks," he said, glancing at her just briefly.

"You hardly have to thank me for saving you," Alice told him. "But you're welcome."

"Ya know, the more I think about it," Anthony took another sip of the tea, "the more I'm beginning to suspect you're my guardian angel."

Alice scoffed. "Is that so? I don't think I can reach that status just by pulling you out of a lake."

"Well, I can think of a few other things you've done for me," Anthony said. His shivering had decreased greatly, and his face was much more expressive. Alice was happy to know the damage had not been extensive.

"Well, still. I'm just a very good friend."

"The best," Anthony agreed.

"And as a very good friend I must ask, what were you even doing out there?" The lecture that Alice had been building up before Anthony fell in just seemed to double in size.

Anthony shrugged. He tried to play it off as being aloof, citing that, "The dock needed fixing, so I was going to fix it. Never know when you might want to use it or something." But there was a look to his face he couldn't quite hide, though he did an excellent job of trying. A look a bit like a kid that had just been caught watching T.V. when they should have been doing their homework.

"I told you I'd help with your presentation," Alice reminded him, the lecture dying in the back of her throat. "If you're worried about it."

"I'm not worried," Anthony insisted.

Alice didn't believe him, but she wasn't in the business of calling out lies. "Alright. Well, how are you feeling? Warming up?"

Anthony nodded and finished up the last of his tea. "Yeah. Thank you, again. I, uh, you know. If you weren't there…"

Alice reached over and placed a hand on his knee, protected by the blanket surrounding him. "Don't think about that," she told him. "I was here and that's what matters. Now, no more doing stupid things, okay?"

Anthony hesitated for a second then laughed. "You have met me, right? I think 'doing stupid things' might actually be my middle name."

"Well then, no more doing any stupid reckless things."

"Well now, see, that's my other middle name."

Alice shook her head at him but couldn't help but smile. Anthony's humor and lack of care may just be an act, but he was very good at it. And he was genuinely funny. Maybe if this position with Nate didn't work out, he could go into comedy.

"I think I'm alright now," Anthony said after a few seconds of silence. "But uh, I hope you know…" he bent his head and looked up at her out of the corner of his eye. "You're stuck with me now."

"Whatever do you mean by that?"

"You saved my life." He pulled his head back up, grinning. "I owe you a life debt. So, either you gotta do something dumb and reckless so I can save your life, or I'll be serving you for the rest of time."

Alice frowned at him. "If this was all some convoluted scheme to get me to keep you as my assistant, I'll-"

Anthony raised his hands in defense, the blanket slipping off his shoulders a bit. "It wasn't! I swear! I was just being funny."

Alice squinted at him because she really couldn't be sure. But she decided to believe him because he really wasn't *that* stupid. "Very well." She stood up and took the empty cup from him. "I'm going to get back to work. Try not to fall into any wells while I'm gone."

Anthony laughed and settled back into the cushions. "No promises."

Chapter 10
Sex Lesson Five – Lingerie

Tony hadn't meant to fall into the lake. It really had been an accident. He just wanted to not work. But not working when he was supposed to filled him with guilt. So, he figured if he worked on something else, he'd be fine.

But then he had fallen into the lake, and Alice had rescued him. And in those first, delirious seconds of her pulling him through the water, she really had looked like an angel.

And now Tony had to make it up to her, repay her somehow. Especially since he couldn't go on being her assistant forever.

Tony had never been a particularly good cook. He hadn't had much practice. But Alice had made him such a wonderful dinner, maybe he could do the same.

Tony opened the fridge and studied the ingredients before him, as if he actually knew any recipes. A bang came from the office, like someone knocking into something.

Tony crept down the hallway, wondering if Alice was frustrated with something in her story and taking it out on the typewriter. He raised his hand to knock. Then he heard a thud, followed by a soft "ow."

He jiggled the handle, but it was locked. "Alice?" he called out. "You okay?"

"Oh, uh, yes! Yes, I'm fine." There was another thud and then a soft whimper, that almost sounded like tears were behind it.

"Are you sure?" Tony debated breaking the door down.

"I'm fine! Just...knocked my knee against the desk is all."

Tony pressed his ear to the door and listened as he heard shuffling and grunting. "What are you doing that's got ya bumping knees against the desk?"

"N-nothing!"

Tony would find it cute if he wasn't so worried for her safety.

"You know," he said, "I'm more than happy to help. If you need it."

The noises stilled, the silence deafening. "I just...it's embarrassing," Alice finally said.

"Ah, c'mon," Tony said. "Can't be all that bad."

"I'm...stuck," Alice explained. And the muffle in her voice told him she had buried her face in her hands.

"I'm a really good un-stucker," Tony said, smiling at himself. Alice made a soft noise, maybe a sob. Tony placed his hand on the door. "Look, let me in. I can help. And I won't laugh, whatever it is."

He heard footsteps, and then Alice's voice was louder, right on the other side. "You promise not to laugh?" she asked. "Or say anything? Ever?"

Tony smirked. "My lips are sealed."

Alice sighed, and then the lock clicked open. Tony pushed the door back slowly, revealing the mess Alice had gotten herself in. The blinds were drawn, a soft yellow glow from the desk lamp the only light in the space. The box from before was sitting in the center of the room, and a myriad of lingerie had been spread about. But the lingerie that Tony was most interested in was the one Alice was wearing. Well, half-wearing. Stuck indeed.

Light pink straps had one arm stuck to her side, crossing over her back. She held a towel to her body with the hand that was still free, hiding whatever else was under there. And Tony couldn't help but stare and wonder. This was nothing like he ever imagined being allowed to see.

"Oh, Alice," Tony said. He could feel his face contorting not of laughter or jest, but of fondness and maybe love.

"That's saying something," Alice told him, looking away.

"Sorry." He moved closer, his hands reaching out. "Can I?"

Alice's already red face darkened even more, and she nodded, turning slightly, presenting her arm. Tony noticed that the towel didn't wrap all the way around her, but he bit his lip and kept his attention from wandering. There was a certain level of trust he had going on with Alice. He didn't want to break it.

Alice kept her head facing away as Tony gingerly moved the straps around, loosening them a bit until they finally released their hold on her arm. Every time their skin touched, Tony swore he could feel sparks.

"Thank you," Alice sighed out, relief radiating off her body as she stretched her arm then tightened the towel around her properly. But Tony could not unsee what he had just seen. And he wouldn't want to.

"What uh, what's with all the…" Tony gestured to the mess spread about the room.

"You said you wouldn't ask," Alice said. She was still flushed, but her body had relaxed a little.

"No," Tony reminded her. "I said I wouldn't laugh."

Alice sighed and studied the room. "I… Well, see, I figured that, you know, now that Naomi is more comfortable around Malcolm, she'd want to try to… impress him, as it were. And I wanted to make sure I wrote it right. Because I've never…well, you know. I just wanted it to be accurate."

Tony smiled at her. She really did her research. "Maybe I could help," he offered, fearful of the response.

Alice finally looked at him, shock in her eyes. "W-what?"

Tony felt a blush of his own coming on, so he turned to the side, focusing his attention on the clothes spread about. "I do know my way around lingerie," he explained. Which just made him sound awful. "I could show you how it works."

"You'd wear lingerie?" Alice asked.

Tony smiled. On purpose or not, Alice always had a way of calming his nerves. "Well, yes, but I meant that I could help you put it on."

"Oh! Oh no! No no! That would be! No!"

Tony looked back over at her. She was staring at the ground, shaking her head.

"Just offering," Tony said. He bit his lip and picked up a light blue baby-doll top. It had a bow in the front, one you could untie for easier access to the breasts. "You know, Naomi wouldn't wear something convoluted like that." He gestured to the strap thing Alice had been stuck in, now lying discarded on the floor. "She'd go simple."

Alice risked a look at him, studying the top he held.

"But she'd want to accentuate certain features." Tony circled the room, investigating the clothes Alice had bought. He found a white pair of stockings with matching thigh straps. He picked them up. "Like her legs."

Alice's body straightened up as she watched him move. There was just one missing component. Tony found it and smiled.

"And her ass," he explained, holding up the dark blue bottom that, instead of a proper backing, had supports to elevate and accentuate the cheeks.

He couldn't read the expression on Alice's face and he hoped he hadn't overstepped his bounds. It was hard not to do that when he wanted no bounds around at all.

"You just put together a whole outfit in all of fifteen seconds," Alice said. Wonder. That was the expression.

Tony felt a hint of pride, and he shrugged it off with a smile. "I told you I know my way around this stuff. Might even snag some it for myself." He chuckled and winked, hoping it would ease the tension.

It seemed to, as Alice turned away with a soft smile. "Do you think…" she hummed and bothered her bottom lip between her teeth.

"Maybe," Tony started, watching her for signs of distaste, "Malcolm helps

Naomi get dressed."

Alice looked back at him, still biting her lip. "It-it is her first time," she agreed.

Tony didn't dare let himself hope. "I know he'd enjoy it."

Alice chuckled nervously. "I think he'd enjoy taking it all off better."

"Oh no," Tony said. He found himself stepping closer against his will, drawn to the heat of Alice's body. "Trust me, the only thing better than taking this stuff off, is helping someone put it on."

"Really?"

Tony nodded. "It's like fixing someone's tie or-or cuff links! It's…"

"Intimate?"

Tony hadn't wanted to be the one to say it. "Yeah. Intimate."

Alice took a deep breath. Her attention bounced around the room. "Perhaps…if you'd still like…I could keep the towel on?" Her eyes landed on Tony, and all the air was sucked out of his body.

"Whatever you want," he croaked. "I'm here to help."

Alice looked back down, arms crossing over her chest. She nodded. "St-start with the socks," she said. "Just to see."

Tony wasn't even sure how he was moving with all the heat and energy surrounding him. He felt like he was in the back of a crowded car in the middle of winter with all the windows fogged up. But he moved all the same, kneeling down before Alice, picking the stockings out and leaving the rest on the floor.

Then he remembered how clothes worked. "Oh, er, bottoms need to go on first," he explained. He held up the clasps on the end of the thigh straps.

"Here." Alice held one hand out and Tony passed up the bottoms. "Eyes closed. Please."

Firsthand Research

Tony screwed them shut and tried to breath loud enough that he wouldn't hear the rusting of the towel as Alice stepped into the panties. He filled his ears with the rushing beat of his heart instead as he thought about the sight that was just inches before him. The sight he couldn't see.

"It's...strange," Alice said. "I don't think I've done it right."

"Want me to take a look?" Tony asked, begging her to say yes.

Alice paused for a moment. "Could you...could you do it without looking?"

Tony nodded, but he knew he was a weak man. He reached out for another piece of clothing, any clothing, and grabbed another pair of stockings. He tied one around his eyes like a blindfold, thankful they were not see-through.

"You don't have t-"

"Oh, I do. Trust me."

"No, no." Alice backed away a step. "It's really, I-I can figure it...out..."

Tony had placed a hand on her thigh. "It's just to help me concentrate," he explained.

Alice made a soft noise. "I'm being awfully difficult, aren't I?"

Tony tilted his head back, smiling up at her. "Not at all. I'm here to help you, Alice. Not make you uncomfortable. Whatever you need."

Alice was quiet for a moment. Then she stepped back up to him, thigh pressing against his fingers, making them twitch. "Thank you."

Tony nodded and leaned closer. He placed his other hand on Alice's other thigh and then slid them up, feeling for the panties. Alice let out a shuddering breath as Tony's fingers found them. The front was intact, which wasn't hard to do, so he slid his hands around her waist, feeling along the back strap.

Problem one. The first strap was much too low. It was supposed to curve along the top, not sit on it. Tony pulled it up a little, feeling Alice's body tense. He licked his lips and bit hard on his bottom one as his fingers delicately slid down, searching for the other straps. They were up much too high. He took them one at a time, holding the strap out a bit with one hand as the other gathered the fat of Alice's ass and pulled it up into shape. He let out an involuntary moan as he felt the tense muscle beneath his touch. Out of all the places Tony was most interested in seeing, Alice's ass was the top of the list. And so far, it was the only one he really hadn't seen. But oh, how he could imagine it now.

"There," he said, pulling his hands back, resting them on his own legs. "How's that feel."

Alice's breath came out in another shudder. Had she been holding it in that whole time? Tony certainly had. "B-better," she said. "I feel...taller?"

Tony chuckled at that. Always finding a way to calm him. Always. "Means it's working. Stockings next?"

"Yes, please."

"Foot."

Tony bunched up and held open one stocking and waited. Alice placed a foot against it, and he pulled it on just a bit, just to the calf. Then he did the same with the other. Now came the fun part.

Tony held in another breath. Because having actually seen Alice's thighs, he knew exactly what, and where, he was touching. He could have pulled the stockings up quickly, but where would be the fun in that? Besides, this was for the book. He was supposed to be Malcolm. And Malcolm would certainly take his sweet time.

Alice let out a soft, "oh," as Tony grabbed the edge of one stocking, skin grazing against skin as he pulled it up. He stopped instantly.

"Everything okay?" he asked. He wished he could see her face to judge her emotions.

"Oh! Oh yes! Sorry. It just…" he heard her gulp. "It feels good."

Tony smiled and nodded his head softly. "Getting all kinds of ideas for your book, hm?" He continued pulling the stocking up, feeling around the top to make sure it wasn't too tight over her skin.

"Oh yes," Alice told him. Something about talking seemed to break the heat bubble around them, like rolling down a window. "You make an excellent Malcolm."

Tony's smile widened as he slid the second stocking up into place. "Helps to have such a lovely Naomi."

He could actually feel the blush on Alice's skin as it heated under his touch. "I-I am not Naomi!" she argued.

Tony kept his focus on the conversation, tilting his head back a bit. His hands worked on autopilot as he pulled each strap up, reaching under the towel to find the hook associated with it. "Aren't all characters some version of the writer?" He started with the outer hooks on each.

"Not always! Sometimes it's people we know."

Tony took a deep breath and slid his hands up the inside of Alice's thigh, arms shaking a bit as he felt for the inner hook. One finger twitched away, grazing against the thin fabric keeping him from Alice's vagina. He cursed himself as Alice's breath hitched, her muscles going rigid. "Who, then, is she?"

Alice calmed her breath as Tony found the right hook and connected it. There was still another to go. "A-A friend."

"Uh, huh," Tony said. He laughed softly at her and stilled his shake before going back in. He couldn't slip up again.

"She is! Someone from school!"

Tony smiled, both at Alice's comment and the hook he had found. He pulled back, relaxing a bit now that half of her was dressed. "I believe you. How does that feel? Anything too tight? Too loose?"

Alice hummed a no. "It's perfect."

"Good. Halfway there." Tony stood up, could feel the hot breath of Alice against his face. Were they really that close? "Top's all that's left." He held it out to her, waiting.

Alice shuffled, then Tony felt her hand on his face. Fingers picked at the stocking. He tried not to vibrate as she pulled it off, rustling his hair in the process. He blinked in the low light, and marveled at how it danced off her skin.

"I figure, you've already seen it," she explained.

Tony glanced down. Alice had wrapped the towel tight around her waist, her chest exposed.

"Besides," she argued. "I don't think I'd want you fumbling around up here. Might scratch something."

"I'll be gentle," Tony promised. The window was back up and someone had turned on the heater.

Alice nodded and raised her hands above her head. Tony focused very hard on her face. They were too close. If he breathed as hard as his rapidly beating heart demanded, he would be panting right on her. Which was both gross and kind of rude.

Taking very deep, controlled breaths through his nose, Tony reached up and slid the material over Alice's arms. He tugged on the bottom as it settled, slipping the straps down to Alice's shoulders. All that was left was to tie the bow.

"Uh, should I…?" He gestured to the part in question.

Alice looked down at it. "Please. I was never very good at knots."

Tony gulped and reached back out, not that it was that far of a reach. Intimate indeed. And despite the fact that he had not only touched Alice's breasts, but licked and sucked on them, he still felt a general fear and anxiety. He almost wished Alice had left the blindfold on.

His fingers fumbled for a bit, but he managed to get a decent looking bow to form, holding Alice's breasts together in a very lovely fashion. "Too tight?"

Alice just shook her head. "Perfect."

"Well, uh." Tony cleared his throat. "You're all done." He thought about taking a step back but didn't.

"Thank you." Alice went to grab the towel, then stilled.

"Ah." Tony smiled at her and placed a hand over his eyes.

"All modest," Alice announced a few seconds later.

"I hope that was, informative," Tony said. The car was off, and all he had to do was step out into the cold air.

"Very. I can't thank you enough for helping. And for being so...amendable."

Tony smirked and took that step. "Don't worry about it. Like I said, whatever you're comfortable with. I'm here to help."

"And I appreciate that," Alice said, leaning against the edge of the desk. "I just...I've never been this...*exposed* around someone before," she explained. "Except maybe my family when I was a baby."

Tony let out a soft huff of a laugh and leaned on the other side of the desk. "I get it. I'm glad you let me help, though." He looked at her, lost in the deep green-blue of her eyes. "I like helping you," he said. "It makes me feel good. Accomplished, you know."

Alice smiled and nodded, glancing down at her feet for a brief moment. "You know, it's a little strange."

"What is?"

"I've done all of these...well these *things* with you, and I've never even...I haven't..." Alice sighed and hung her head, now staring at her feet.

"Never had sex with anyone," Tony finished for her. "I know. It's why I'm here to help." He smiled, trying to ease the tension returning to her shoulders.

"Never dated anyone," Alice whispered.

"You've never even gone on a date before?" Tony asked. "Like, not even a terribly awkward one when you're thirteen and your parents sit behind you in the movie theater?"

Alice bit her lip and shook her head. "It gets worse," she said, a nervous chuckle for added effect.

Tony could do the math. "You've never kissed anyone before, have you?"

Alice's smile melted into a frown, and she shook her head, her eyes starting to water a bit. "I know," she said. She sniffed. "It's pathetic."

"Hey, hey," Tony put a hand on her back, rubbing it gently. "It's not pathetic."

"Sure," Alice said. She hugged herself tighter.

"Listen, guys are dumb," Tony told her. "Trust me, I know. I both am one and have dated them. Awful, horrible people." Alice let out a soft laugh. "I think the problem is you're just so way out of everyone's league that they never even think they have a shot. I mean, really, who even comes close?"

Alice gave him a weak smile, one that has heard this sort of pep talk before. "I'm sure that's it," she said.

Tony deflated; the fun of the last moment replaced with an ache he hasn't felt since he was a child. An ache he's been running from his whole life.

"Listen. You really are an amazing person Alice, inside and out. And there's not a singular doubt in my mind that you're going to find someone perfect for you. Someone who's going to get you, who's gonna love you, who's gonna worship the ground you walk on because that's what you deserve. And good people always get what they deserve."

Alice nodded, her eyes unfocused as she stared at the ground. "Anthony?" she asked, her voice slow, uncertain.

"Yeah?"

Her head turned slowly until their eyes met. "Would you be my first kiss?"

Chapter 11
Sisterly Advice

Alice regretted the words as soon as they were out of her mouth. And with each second that passed, she regretted them more and more. She thought she had thought it through. Really, it made sense. She and Anthony had already done so much; what difference was a kiss?

But with the way Anthony stared at her, his eyes wide, mouth slightly open, she knew there was a difference. And it was a rather large one.

"Never mind," Alice said. She laughed, or tried to anyway, to help ease the situation along. She stood up and shook her head. "Forget about it." It was just a silly idea anyway.

"No!" Anthony shot up, body on high alert. "I mean, yes! I mean," he sighed and grabbed her hands, looking into her eyes, "if that's what you want."

Alice's mouth went dry, and she was sure kissing anyone right now was probably out of the question. But the truth was, she did want that. She very much wanted to kiss Anthony. She had, really, ever since they first met. Ever since she had been so nervous the first time she walked into the publishing house and had dropped her notebook on his foot. Ever since he had picked it up and smiled at her while handing it back.

It wasn't often that Alice ever really wanted to kiss anyone. Kissing, as she saw it, was a little bit gross. But she figured that was just because she hadn't done it ever. Maybe it was an acquired taste. And she had certainly had thoughts about acquiring that with Anthony.

But she couldn't say any of that. She couldn't admit she liked him, even before all of this started. Couldn't tell him that, over the course of the last few years, he had slowly crept his way into her characters, one way or another. What would he think, to know she was in this for more than just book research?

He would think she was weird is what he would think. And he would leave. Because didn't they always?

Alice cleared her throat. "I just want to get it over with, is all," she explained.

"That's not a very good reason to kiss someone," Anthony told her. But there was something in his expression Alice couldn't quite pick out. Like maybe...like maybe he *did* want her to confess her feelings. But that had to just be her imagination, right?

Alice blushed and looked down at the ground. "It's a very good reason to me."

"How come?"

Alice took a deep breath. "Kissing...it's like a requirement, these days." She looked back up to Anthony's puzzled face. "How many dates do you go on with someone before you kiss?"

Anthony stuttered for a bit. "Ah, well, I-I'm not really the best example..."

"Most people. On average."

Anthony just stuttered some more, looking around the room as if the answer was written on the wall somewhere.

"I've done the research," Alice continued. "Over 80% of people usually say by date three."

Anthony nodded. "That sounds reasonable."

"Have you ever come to trust someone after three dates?"

Again, Anthony got fidgety, scratching at the back of his neck and not looking at her. "Like I said, I'm not really-" he chuckled "Never got to that point."

"Oh." Alice blinked and looked at her feet. She knew Anthony was a bit of a playboy, but she at least always imagined he had been somewhat dedicated to someone before. She shook the upset from her mind and refocused on the conversation at hand. "Well, I can tell you that I don't think I could ever trust someone that well after only seeing them three times."

"It's just a kiss, Alice," Anthony told her. "It's not like you're jumping into bed with someone." Which was a whole other statistical nightmare she'd been having.

"You're right. It is just a kiss. So would you kiss me?"

Anthony made a face that was half-frown and half-pout. "But it's your first kiss. It should be-"

Alice groaned and rolled her eyes. "I know! Everyone says that. Your first kiss should be special, with someone special. But guess what? I missed that window, okay? You have that kind of kiss when you're a teenager! Only I didn't, and so I need this one now."

"You didn't miss out on it," Anthony said. He reached out to touch her arm, then they both realized she was still half-naked under the towel, and each took a slight shuffle back. "There's still time."

Alice bit her lip to keep the frustration tears from falling out. "No, there's not!" She was tired of waiting, and she was tired of having this conversation. "How many people our age haven't been kissed yet, Anthony? One! Me!"

"Well, I'm sure there's more than-"

"And how many people, honestly, are going to wait weeks, maybe even months to kiss someone? Especially when there's so many other people out there who *will* kiss them?"

"Plenty. You just-"

"And!" Time to get to the heart of the problem. The one that was slipping out despite her best judgement. The one that Alice felt leaving her lips, each word increasing the heat of her skin. "How many people are going to want to keep dating someone who's awful at it!?"

Anthony stared at her, his head tilted slightly to the side. If she wasn't so petrified at what she had just said, she might have thought to continue ranting.

But they just stood there for a few seconds, each frozen in their own thoughts.

"You think you'd be awful at it?" Anthony finally asked.

Alice wrapped her arms around herself, condensing her body as small as she could make it. She shrugged. "I've never done it. I'm sure I would be. It's just like any other skill, and without practice...I'd be rubbish."

"So..." Anthony took a daring step forward, his eyes looking up as he thought, his voice languid. "What you're saying is.... you want me to... *teach* you how to kiss?"

Alice blinked, her body uncoiling. He was onto something here. It wasn't a first kiss because she liked him. It was practice.

"Research," Alice said, her voice a soft whisper. "For the book."

Anthony nodded at her. Their eyes met. An understanding passed between them.

And then Alice was very aware of her skin, and how much of it was not covered, and she flushed a hot red. "But not like this!" she practically yelled, making Anthony take that step back. "Sorry. I just, er..."

She gestured down to her towel and Anthony huffed a small laugh.

"Yeah," he said. "Best with clothes on."

Alice agreed, so she shooed him out of the room and got dressed.

*

Tony's leg bounced against the couch as he listened to the other line ring. Alice had had the good sense of mind to buy a burner phone when she had last gone to town. Tony had made a note to thank her for all the thoughts she had that he didn't. She really was always prepared in all the ways he wasn't.

No one picked up. Tony huffed and dialed again. He knew Sandra was cautious about unknown numbers, had to be in their line of work. But she should at least try answering the phone.

When she didn't the second time, Tony left her a voicemail. He placed the phone next to him and looked at the laptop on his stomach. He had no intention of actually doing anything for this presentation thing. But if he showed up completely empty-handed, Alice would know he hadn't tried. And he didn't want her mad at him, so he'd slap something together.

Not but two minutes later his phone was ringing.

"Should have just left one the first time," Sandra said as soon as he picked up.

"Should just answer your phone," Tony countered.

Sandra laughed. "Everything's alright, isn't it? Alice hasn't kicked you out yet, has she?"

"Yet?" Tony asked. Sandra just laughed again. "No, I'm still here. Actually, I could use some…" he looked over the edge of the couch, down the hall to the office door," ...help."

"You? Needing help? I'm shocked."

Tony rolled his eyes. "Why do I put up with you?" he asked.

"Same reason I do you." Because they were family. Because they were friends. "What do you need?"

"I need advice. About...girls."

Sandra sighed. "I told you sleeping with Alice was a bad idea."

"I-what? No!" Tony placed the laptop on the coffee table and sat up. "First of all, I am not sleeping with her, okay?" Not that he didn't want to. The very idea of being curled up around Alice made his heart skip a few beats. "And that's not...it's something else."

"Alright. Shoot."

Tony took a deep breath and thought about how best to explain it. Alice had been putting it off. It being the kiss she had asked him for. First, she had needed to get dressed. Fine, valid. But then she said she didn't want to forget everything she had thought about while he was helping her with the last task, so he left her alone to write. Then they had had onion in their dinner last night and she didn't want to offend him with bad breath. And then, and then, and then…

"Do girls like it or not like it when you kiss them by surprise?" Tony knew Alice was nervous. That was more than obvious. He knew that once she just did it, it would be fine. But should he just…do it for her?

"No," Sandra said. "We don't."

Tony frowned. "Then, uh, how…how should one go about…doing that?"

"*Is* this about Alice?" Sandra asked.

Tony closed his eyes and flopped back down. "It's a very long, private story. Short answer, yes."

"Look, if Alice doesn't want to kiss yo-"

"She does! Is the problem. She told me!" Tony sighed and opened his eyes, staring at the ceiling. Because he had never thought about it before. At least, not seriously. Sure, he had *dreamed* about kissing Alice; but who wouldn't? He didn't see it as an actual possibility until yesterday, when she had asked him for it.

"Maybe she changed her mind," Sandra suggested. And that was the answer that Tony feared. Because he had gotten excited. He had let himself hope. And now? Now he had to deal with the heart-crushing, aching pain that is not getting to kiss Alice.

"You're probably right," Tony agreed. Of course she was. Who was he kidding? Alice wouldn't want to kiss him. She was miles out of his league. Much too good. Much too pure for the likes of him. "Thanks."

"Tony…I'm sorry."

Tony sat up half-way, the horror of his demise replaced with confusion. "About what?"

"You really like her, don't you?"

Firsthand Research

Tony felt the blush on his face, happy to know no one was around to see it. He nodded. "Yeah. I think I do."

"Maybe it's time you get a different job," Sandra suggested. "It does you no good pining like that."

Tony glanced over at the laptop. Then shook his head. "Yeah. Probably. I gotta go, but thanks."

"Ton-"

Tony cut her off. He didn't need pity. Or a lecture. Or anything else she might give him. What he needed was Alice. But he could never have that.

*

Alice bit her lip and stared at the door. She clenched the phone tight in her hand and bounced a bit. The other line rang once, but she hung up immediately.

"Get a grip!" she told herself, walking in a circle around the room. "You cannot call your sister for advice on kissing!"

She shook her legs as she walked, waving her arms in the air to get rid of the nerves. They came back with a rush as her phone rang. She yelped in surprise and dropped it. Her sister's name stared up at her.

Alice groaned and picked the phone back up. "Sorry!" she said. "I was just, uh, trying to call someone else and accidentally hit your number."

"Really?" Katie asked. "Because usually when you call once and hang up it's because you're upset about something?"

"Wha-? I'm not upset! I don't do that!"

She could hear the judgment in the silence.

Alice bit her lip, shook her legs a few more times and just went for it.

"I'm going to kiss him! I am! I am! I am! I just can't!" She huffed and puffed, falling into her desk chair. Her arms and legs were growing weary from all the anxiety.

"Wow. So. We've moved on from never seeing him again, to having regular sex...to kissing?"

Alice rolled her eyes. "We are not having regular sex. And it's not like... it's just...Arrg! How do I do it?"

Katie laughed softly, away from the phone. But Alice still heard it. "Are you asking me how to kiss?"

Alice scrunched down in her seat, wishing she could hide from the world. "I just want to do it right," she mumbled.

Yes, Anthony was going to be teaching her how to do it properly. But the truth she had given him was true. She didn't want to be a bad kisser for whoever she ended up dating. And despite all logic telling her she would never date Anthony; she didn't want to be a bad kisser for him either. No. She wanted to be good. She wanted him to like it.

She wanted him to like her.

"I'm going to give you three pieces of advice," Katie told her. Alice sat up and grabbed her notebook. "Tilt your head. Close your eyes. And relax."

Alice frowned, setting the empty page back down. "That's it? Really?"

"Darling, that's all you need. Kissing is all about intuition. About changing in the moment, reacting to who you're with. It's practical."

Alice's frown deepened and she sank further in her chair. "It's going to be awful," she mumbled.

"You do this you know. You always hype yourself up for things, and then they turn out much better than you expect. I'm sure it will be great. And you'll be fine."

"I hope you're right," Alice said. "Because I don't know how I'll survive it."

"You will. And call me when you do. Because I want to hear everything."

Alice shook her head, rolled her eyes, and promised to do no such thing.

Chapter 12
'Sex' Lesson Six – Kissing

I'm ready now.

Tony gulped and looked at Alice, sitting across from him on the couch. It was the very same couch he had kissed her breasts on. So it seemed a little fitting, he supposed, to kiss her lips on it too. The words she had just told him were still ringing in his ears.

Alice had come out of the office, sat down, said *that*, then tilted her head and closed her eyes. Waiting. She was waiting for him.

And Tony had been sitting there not moving for what felt like hours.

Tony startled, realizing this. He scooted forward on the couch, right next to Alice. She had one leg folded under her, her side pressing against the cushions as she waited. Tony mimicked her posture so he could fit their bodies together better.

Alice jolted slightly when he reached out and placed a hand on her cheek. But she didn't move away or say anything else. Tony kept his palm against her face, brushing his fingers under the curls by her ear, getting a soft hold of her. He pulled, gently, and she leaned her body forward at his command.

Tony gulped and licked his lips. It was going to happen. She hadn't changed her mind. She hadn't decided she didn't want his help after all. He would get to kiss her. As part of his job.

He had to do it right.

Tony leaned forward and tilted his head opposite of Alice. He watched her face as they moved closer, just a breath of air apart. Alice's lips fell open a bit, one shaking ever so slightly. Her face twitched a little, here and there. Nervous twitches.

Firsthand Research

Tony very gently pressed his lips to Alice's shaking one. He pulled away quickly, just a gentle nip. The shaking stopped. Alice's face seemed to relax a bit, curiosity taking hold. Tony smiled. Alice had no idea how *fun* kissing could be. And what kind of an assistant would he be if he didn't show her?

Shuffling his body forward so they didn't have to lean so much, Tony continued to make quick, gentle touches to Alice's bottom lip. He alternated which way their heads were tilted, fingers moving Alice's head with ease. And he kept doing it until he got the reaction he was waiting for, until Alice's lips closed when he went in, trying to keep his dancing kisses close.

Tony chuckled softly, running his thumb over Alice's cheek.

"S-sorry," Alice said.

"It's alright." He smiled at her, glad she kept her eyes closed and couldn't see the adoration in his own. "I was waiting for that."

"You were?" Alice's eyebrows furrowed. Her eyelids twitched a bit but didn't open. "I was just...reacting."

"That's all kissing is," Tony told her.

He didn't want her thinking to get in the way of her feeling, so he leaned back in and nipped once more. And once more Alice tried to keep him there. So, Tony decided to give her what she wanted. He nudged Alice's lips open, slipping the bottom one between his own. He had had so many dreams about that lip. About how round and plump it was. About how *soft*.

Oh, it was positively divine. He sucked on it, enjoying the way the skin moved against his own, enjoying how the fat flattened and expanded with each movement. And he kept his eyes on Alice, watching as her eyebrows rose in surprise, but not distaste. Alice even let out a little moan, although Tony was sure she would never admit it.

That was alright. He heard it, and would remember it for life.

Alice, as a reaction, brought her own lips around Tony's upper one, mimicking his suck. Tony smiled and felt her smile back at him as they pressed their lips together.

"Quick learner," Tony whispered when they parted for air.

"It helps to have such a great teacher," Alice said.

They sat there, still close, still breathing on each other. Alice kept her eyes closed. Tony could just lean in a little bit and kiss her again and again until the end of time. But she had only asked for one. So, he took a deep breath and pulled back, his fingers lingering slightly on her face.

Alice also took a deep breath, then flickered her eyes open. A tinge of pink spread across her cheeks and she smiled, looking down at her lap. "Thank you," she said. "That was...lovely."

Tony's smile widened. "So, do I get a raise now?"

He worried, for just a moment, he maybe shouldn't have made that joke. But then Alice laughed softly and looked back up at him. "Perhaps I'll buy you some more clothes."

"Like a fancy suit," Tony suggested.

Alice nodded and laughed again. Then she licked her lips and bit the bottom one gently as her attention wandered.

"Have to go write?" Tony asked, leaning his head against the back of the couch.

Alice nodded. "And rewrite every other kiss scene I've ever done."

Tony chuckled. "I thought they were all pretty good in the past."

Alice stood up. "And now they'll be better." She raced back to the office, Tony watching her as she bounced away.

Chapter 13
Surprise Visit

"I am calling to give you fair and reasonable notice."

Alice raised her eyebrow, holding the phone to her ear. "Uh...okay? Should I be worried?"

"Very," Katie said. "Liam is on his way up to visit."

Alice startled, sitting up straight in her chair. "What? I told him not to visit while I was up here! I-I need time to write!"

Katie chuckled. "You mean you need time to kiss your new boyfriend?"

Alice started an argument, but there was so much wrong with that question she didn't even know where to begin. "When did he leave?"

"A few minutes ago. I'd hide your beau somewhere if I was you."

"He is not my beau!" Alice hung up and jumped to her feet. The city wasn't all that far away from the town, and Liam wasn't known for being a slow driver. She raced out to the living room. Katie was right; Beau or not, Anthony needed to hide.

"Whoa," Anthony said, hopping off the couch. "Where's the fire?"

"On its way. Liam's coming over to check in on me."

Anthony's eyes widened a bit. "Well, that can't be good."

Alice shook her head. "No. You have to not be here!"

"Okay, uh...where should I be?"

Alice rushed into her room, grabbing her backpack and emptying it on the bed. "Here, take the computer and some money and go to town. I'm sure there's a nice little bakery you can sit in for a while."

"Uh...I don't suppose you have, like, some kind of cover for the bikes?"

Alice stared at him, wondering what he meant. Then her attention drifted to the window. More specifically, the heavy sheet of rain falling outside. She deflated, dropping her bag on the floor. She couldn't very well send Anthony out into the rain like that. He was bound to catch a cold, if nothing worse. "Oh, dear." She glanced around the room. "We'll just have to hide you somewhere."

Anthony shrugged. "I could just hang out in my room with the door closed. Hide in the closet if I hear anything."

"That could work." Alice took a few deep breaths, trying to calm her heart from the rush of adrenaline in her body. Her family was going to give her a heart attack one of these days.

"Relax," Anthony said, rubbing her back a bit. "It'll be fine. Trust me, I'm a pro at hiding from crazy guys."

Alice glanced over at him. "I am unsurprised, but not eased of fear."

"You are definitely a writer." Anthony chuckled. He picked up the laptop and smiled at her. "I'll be in my room if you need anything."

Alice nodded at him. "I think I'll need a lot." She took a calming breath. "Don't get me wrong. I love my brother, but he can just be a bit...much."

"Yeah, family's like that."

"Is your family like that?" Alice asked. She had met them all, of course, through various events for her book. But she hadn't really gotten to know them like she has with Anthony.

"They can be." Anthony patted her on the shoulder. "Just holler if you need me to come out and take some heat."

Alice laughed and pushed him down the hall. "Thank you, but I think I can handle my brother just fine."

*

Tony was doing the exact same thing he would be doing if he was out in the living room. But, for some reason, doing it in his bedroom just made it not as fun. Perhaps it was the fact that he *couldn't* leave his room. Something about not being able to do things made you want to do them even more.

It also apparently made you really thirsty. So, Tony wandered out of his room to go get some water from the kitchen.

"What are you doing?" Alice hissed, hurrying down the hall to him.

"Getting some water," Tony said, gesturing to the glass in his hand. "At least I hope it's water."

"You're supposed to stay in your room."

"Only when Liam's here."

"He is."

Tony's eyebrows rose at the hiss, and then rose further at the sound of a door down the hallway opening and closing. He probably should have realized the bathroom door had been closed when he walked past it.

"Hide," Alice said, pushing at him.

"Where do you expect me to go?" Tony asked.

"Here!" Alice opened one of the tall pantry doors and shoved Tony inside. There wasn't really a lot of room, and parts of him refused to be crammed in there, even when he crouched down to try and fit under some of the shelves.

Alice gasped and turned, shutting the door on him, inside or not. He whimpered and bit his fist as his foot, caught in the crossfires, throbbed in pain.

Through the slit that the partially-closed door left, Tony had a front row seat to half of the kitchen and half of Alice. And the half that was Alice was the really good bit. And then the pain in his foot wasn't the problem anymore.

Tony tried to shift and adjust, get some pressure either on or off his groin for however long he would be stuck in there.

"So," Liam's voice said off-screen. "Seems like you're really settling in here."

"Oh yes," Alice said. "It's quite a lovely little place."

"I have to say. I'm a bit surprised you didn't get frightened and call me."

Tony rolled his eyes. Mainly because Alice had gotten frightened. And had smacked Tony in the face with a bat because of it.

"What can I say? I guess I'm growing up." Alice chuckled.

There was a small moment of pause, giving Tony the time to listen to his own heartbeat as he tried not to look at Alice's butt.

"Wouldn't you like to sit down?" Liam asked.

"Ah, no." Alice chuckled again. "I've been sitting down all morning. Could use some stretching actually."

And then she did start to stretch.

Oh, come on, Tony thought, every part of his body excited by the show being put on before him.

"You should try yoga," Liam said. "It's good to take a break between writing. At least every hour."

Alice stepped to the side, thankfully no longer stretching. She pushed one leg back against Tony's foot, either trying to hide it or shove it back in. And it certainly wasn't going to fit in at all. "I'll be sure to give it a shot."

"Good. It's important to keep your body active, especially since you sit at a desk all day."

"Yes, yes," Alice said, clearly annoyed. "So you've said before."

"I just want to make sure you're staying healthy. Can't have my baby sister getting sick."

Tony's leg spasmed, his foot kicking out against Alice's leg. She rebutted by shoving back against it. He hissed as pain traveled up his calf.

"Is everything alright?" Liam asked. Tony heard the chair squeak across the floor as Liam stood up.

"Perfectly," Alice said.

"I thought I heard something." Liam stepped over, appearing in view through the crack.

Alice shook her head, hair bouncing beautifully against her neck. "I didn't hear anything."

"Really?" Liam shifted, trying to look past her, but she blocked him with a mirrored move. "It sounded like a snake. Maybe I should take a look for you."

"No! That, uh," Alice chuckled. "That's alright. I, I bet you it was just…" she reached behind her, hand slipping through the crack. She opened and closed it a few times. Tony startled and looked over the shelves. He found a can of soda and popped it open, handing it up to Alice. "…a can that opened on its own!"

Liam frowned, taking the can from Alice, studying it. "You should get rid of the rest. If one's defective, they might all be. You could get hurt."

"I'll go to the store tomorrow and get some new ones."

"I could take you now," Liam offered. "Could fit a lot more in the car, and wouldn't have to carry it all back up."

Alice hesitated for a second. "That sounds lovely. I'll meet you out there, just have to grab my bag."

Liam nodded with a wide smile and turned to leave. Alice waited until the main door closed, then spun around, pulling Tony out.

"I'm so sorry, are you okay?"

Tony groaned as he stretched his limbs back out. "Yeah. I think you may have amputated my foot, but other than that."

"Just, keep that elevated while we're out, okay? I promise I'll try to get him to leave soon."

Tony shrugged. "Ah, take your time. I won't be going anywhere anyway." He pointed to his foot, laughing so she knew he wasn't being serious.

She gave him an apologetic smile. "I really am sorry. Please take good care of it, okay?"

Tony winked at her. "You're the boss."

Chapter 14
Sex Lesson Seven – Fingering

Liam and Alice had come back, and a few minutes of chatting later, Liam left. Alice retreated to her office to make up for all the work lost during his visit. And Tony returned to messing about, this time on the couch.

"May I borrow you for a second?" Alice asked, appearing suddenly over the back of the couch. He hadn't heard the squeak of her office door.

Tony yelped and snapped the laptop shut, lest she see his less than adequate presentation.

"Sorry," Alice said. "I didn't mean to startle you."

"That's okay." Tony placed a hand over his chest, trying to calm his heart. "What's up?"

"I need to see how something would work." Alice walked around to the front of the couch. "The way bodies would...er...fit together?" She cupped her hands around each other. "As you know, I left my artist mannequins at home."

"Sure!" Tony said, sitting up straight and placing the laptop on the coffee table. "Where do you need me?"

Alice pursed her lips and tilted her head, looking around at the space. "On the floor, if you please. Sitting against the couch."

Tony did as he was instructed. "Like this?"

Alice nodded and nudged his legs open with her foot until they were spread wide enough for another person to sit between.

Anthony held his breath as Alice settled down against him, back pressed against his chest. His muscles seized up in his attempt to not just wrap his arms around her and cover her neck in hickeys. He screwed his eyes shut to the image of how that would look.

"Is this uncomfortable for you?" Alice asked.

Tony wasn't really sure which aspect of comfort she was talking about. "Nah," he said, glad he was able to keep his voice under control. "How about you?"

"It's quite cozy, actually." Alice shifted a bit, her body moving back and forth against Tony's as if she were trying to settle into a chair. Tony had to turn his head to the side, biting against his lip. There was no way he couldn't not get an erection like this. "And you would be able to reach...things? Like this?"

"What things?" Tony breathed out.

"You know. Things."

Tony blinked his eyes open and looked down. Alice's head was resting against his shoulder, and she was staring up at him. He choked a bit, caught off guard by the beauty of her eyes. He cleared his throat. "Yeah. I could reach things."

"Good. Uhm. Thank you." Alice blushed and pushed herself up to her feet. Tony crossed his legs and placed his hands over his lap.

"Seems like Naomi and Malcolm are getting up to some fun," he commented.

Alice smiled. "Oh yes. Malcolm had a brilliant idea the other night."

Tony tilted his head, finding it hard not to return Alice's smile. "Yeah? What's that?"

"Well, because Naomi's never…" Alice gestured down and Tony nodded, following along. "They're going to start a little slow. And small." She chuckled a bit.

"Fingers?" Tony asked.

Alice nodded, seemingly happy with his correct guess. Then she bit her lip and looked down at her feet, fingers picking at each other. "Actually I…

I've never tried that. Well, I've *tried* but…"

Tony pushed himself to his feet, forgetting his indecency for a moment. "But?"

Alice glanced up at his face, her body hunching over a bit in embarrassment. "I've never had the courage to go through with it." She looked back down. "It's pathetic, I know."

Tony stepped closer. "It's not pathetic."

"I've just been scared. Of it hurting, you know?"

Tony knew. "Would it help if…if someone else…" He didn't want to say it, just in case it wouldn't help. The less he looked like an idiot right now, the better.

Alice's eyes bounced back up to him. "I…I mean…It'd be good for the, uh, the book."

Tony let out a soft chuckle. "Well, we can't keep the book waiting."

*

Alice fiddled her thumbs together, watching Anthony arrange the pillows into a little pile. They had agreed it would be more comfortable on the bed. And Alice stood to the side, pants already shed, watching. Anthony settled on the pile, pressing back a few times to test its structural integrity. Once he was satisfied, he smiled at her and patted the spot between his spread legs.

Alice did not tell her legs to move, but they did anyway, carrying her over and onto the bed. She had no awareness of her own actions as she sat where Anthony had instructed. Too tired from worry to hold herself up, she leaned back against him, both of them supported by the pillows behind.

"How's that?" Anthony asked, his breath low and hot in Alice's ear.

She shivered, even though she felt she was at risk of overheating. "It's fine," she tried to say. Only a little squeak came out.

"Are you sure you want to do this?" Anthony asked as he covered them with the blanket.

Hidden from the rest of the world, Alice could relax a little. She listened to Anthony's soft breaths, felt his chest move against her in the quiet of the room. She closed her eyes and nodded. "Yes," she said with a steady voice. "I want this.

"Good." Anthony's lips tickled against her ear as he smiled. "Anytime you want to stop, just say the word, okay?"

Alice nodded again, letting the full weight of her body press against Anthony. She moved now with each breath he took. She let her eyes close and leaned her head back against his shoulder. Maybe she could just fall asleep, and it would be over before she knew it.

Sleep was not an option as Anthony's hands drifted over her thighs. They slid around, hooking under her knees and pulling them up until her feet were resting against the mattress. The blanket slipped down a little, but he was quick to pull it back up.

Properly situated once more, Anthony's fingers traced a delicate line over Alice's panties before they dipped under the hem, sliding their way down to her labia.

Alice's breath hitched as one hand spread her open, warm fingers holding back the folds of fat as the other hand ventured in further. Alice bit her lip, tried to calm her breath as two fingers found and gently squeezed against her clit.

"You don't have to hold anything back," Anthony whispered, his voice miles away. "In fact, it's easier for me to make sure I'm doing it right if I can hear you."

Alice let her breath out in a shaky gasp. "Are you sure?" she didn't want to seem wanton, after all.

She could hear the smile in Anthony's reply. "I'm positive. I want to hear. If you'll let me."

And Alice couldn't stop herself even if she wanted to, not when a third finger circled around her clit, pressures of pleasure coming at her from three directions. She let her mouth fall open and a small moan that felt big escaped into the air.

Anthony hummed a pleasant note. "Yeah. Like that. That's perfect."

"That's what's perfect," Alice replied, nodding weakly to her lap.

Anthony chuckled, Alice's body moving with each jerk of his chest. "I wouldn't say perfect." The two fingers on the side released, the third one moving around in deeper circles. "But it gets the job done."

And Alice could feel it at work, a release of wet slipping its way out, readying herself for what came next. That didn't come for a while, not until Anthony had spent a good long time playing with her, teasing a finger at her entrance every now and then before drawing back and circling around her clit.

Alice gasped, clamping her legs shut around Anthony's hand. But it had been too late. She came, rocking against the fingers still pressed against her.

"I'm sorry," she whispered.

Anthony laughed and kissed the side of her head. If she wasn't so tired from the anxiety and the orgasm, she might have thought to comment on that. "Nothing to apologize for. In fact, it'll help."

Alice nodded and Anthony gave her a moment to rest, one hand smoothing over her thighs as the other kept a gentle pressure around her labia.

"I think I'm ready," Alice said after a minute or two.

"Think?"

Alice huffed and shook her head. "I'm ready."

Anthony's fingers resumed their original position, one hand holding her open, the other inching towards her entrance. His pinky slid further and further down, until it was right there, pressing gently.

"Any pain?" he asked.

Alice shook her head. Her hands grabbed fists of the sheets next to Anthony's legs, waiting tense for the moment to come.

The finger started to slide in. There was a little resistance, a tight pressure against the unfamiliar sensation. This was where Alice would usually chicken out and stop. But Anthony kept going, breathing hard as his pinky continued to move.

It was strange. Odd. Not painful, but certainly weird. Alice's muscles reacted to the intrusion by trying to push it back out, which only made the sensation heightened by the tightness around Anthony's finger. It was a little difficult to breath, but she managed.

"Talk to me," Anthony said. "How ya doin'?"

"Okay." Alice was surprised by how normal her voice sounded, compared to the insanity in her mind. "It's just a little weird."

Anthony's finger halted. "Does it hurt?"

"No, no." It started to move again. "It's just a little...unusual."

Anthony chuckled softly. "Yeah. I know what you mean. It's certainly something to get used to."

Alice nodded and closed her eyes so she could try to get used to it. Eventually the finger couldn't go in any further, and Alice's body seemed to sigh in relief as it started to drag back out. But then it was pushing back in, and she tensed. She could feel the sensation of the finger in her, but it didn't necessarily feel good. It wasn't bad, but this was supposed to feel good, wasn't it?

Anthony hummed, then moved his fingers, letting Alice's outer labia close so his other hand could play with her clit. And that, at least, felt wonderful. The pleasure of his fingers on her clit drew away the attention of the intrusion of his other finger. And before long, Alice could barely feel it at all.

"How's it going down there?" Anthony asked.

Alice opened her eyes, looking up into Anthony's. His pupils were blown wide, which should hurt, considering they had left the lights on.

"Going good down here," she said. "How's it up there?"

"Weather's just fine," Anthony said. He smiled and gently pinched against Alice's clit, making her jump in pleasure. "How many did you want?"

Alice closed her eyes again; she couldn't possibly talk about that while looking at him. The very idea. "I think just the one is fine for now." Especially since she didn't really see what all the fuss was about.

"You got it." Anthony continued his work, and Alice enjoyed it, resting against him without caution. "You know, you're really wet."

Any sort of comfort and relaxation Alice might have had was gone in a hot flash of a second. "I'm sorry."

"No, it's nothing to apologize about! It's a good thing." Anthony leaned his head against hers. "Means I'm doing my job right."

"Oh." Alice let herself relax a bit, but she was still a little on edge after that.

Then Anthony hooked his finger up a bit, bending it so the tip pressed hard against her walls. And it would have been an uncomfortable sensation, were it not for the blinding pleasure it drew from her.

Alice's body actually jolted up, her back arching, her breath stilling as she tried to comprehend what she was feeling. It was like nothing she had ever experienced before. Every minute movement from Anthony's fingers made her nerves fire alive with electricity.

"Breathe," Anthony said, sitting up to match her posture.

She pressed back against him, using the feeling of his breath to steady her own. It came out in breathy little moans that seemed to echo in the space between them. It only lasted a few seconds before she was coming again, feeling both legs and vagina closing around Anthony's fingers.

Anthony kept the pressure up as she crested and fell. Weak, she collapsed against him. Anthony laid back against the pillows as Alice caught her breath. He pulled his finger out slow and steady, a strange drag that left Alice feeling oddly empty, in more ways than one.

"That was…" Alice couldn't even find the word for it. She could try and sit for hours thinking on it and no word would ever come close to matching the experience she just had.

"Glad you liked it." Anthony pressed their heads together again and then his hands were slipping out of Alice's panties.

She frowned, despite herself.

"Ah," Anthony said. "That explains that."

Alice opened her eyes to see what he was going on about, and then quickly closed them before pulling the covers up over her head and rolling over Tony's leg to the other side of the bed.

Whatever mortification times ten was what she felt. It certainly explained why she had been so eager. So horny all this time.

Anthony laughed. "It's okay. Roughly 50% of the population does it, don't ya know."

Alice screwed her eyes even tighter. "I am so sorry," she mumbled out through the blanket. She could never face Anthony again. She couldn't face anyone. She would never see the light of day for as long as she lived.

"Hey. Really, it's fine." Anthony placed a hand on her over the covers. Hopefully not the one that had gotten so defiled.

"My blood is on your hand," Alice cried out, as if he wasn't aware.

"Among other things," Anthony added.

Alice sobbed and curled her body into a tight ball. Death would be better than this. Anything would be better than this. Maybe if she just lied very, very still, the ground would open up and swallow her whole.

"Look. A simple wash and it's gone." The bed moved as Anthony climbed off it. He didn't use the bathroom that was right there to wash his hands. Alice heard him move out of the room, heading to his own.

He was gone for a few minutes. And after about two of those minutes, Alice braved existence long enough to get up and lock the door. She simply could not face him again.

The door jiggled and Alice hid back under her blankets.

"It's really not a big deal," Anthony called out. He sighed. "Do you need any supplies or anything for it? Got all you need? I can run to the store for you if ya want."

What Alice needed was a swift and painless removal from the situation.

"It's not the first time I've had someone else's blood on my hand, you know. Granted, those were all under different circumstances."

Alice whined and curled up tighter. Shut up shut up shut up.

"I have a mom and a sister," he said. "And a sister-in-law, come to think of it."

Alice tried to wish him away, but it didn't seem to work.

"Come on out," Anthony continued. "I'll make us some hot cocoa and we can watch a movie or something."

"No, thank you!" Alice said.

"Ah, please?" Anthony sighed again. "It's really not a big deal. I promise." He didn't say anything else, and Alice hoped he had just gone away. Then he started knocking a rhythmic beat on her door. "I'm not leaving until you come out."

Alice groaned. She knew he meant it. He could be awfully stubborn when he wanted to be. "I...I have to clean up."

"Alright," Anthony said. "That's fair. Tell ya what, I'll go heat up some dinner and make coca. If you're not out in fifteen, I'm coming in after you." He laughed a bit and walked away.

Firsthand Research

Alice groaned and let a few minutes pass. Just when she started to formulate her plan to escape out the window and go live in the woods, Anthony started singing from the kitchen. It wasn't a song that Alice knew, but it sounded lovely from what she could hear. And Anthony sounded so at ease that she figured maybe it wasn't such a big deal.

They were adults after all. And Anthony was right. It wasn't like Alice was the only person who did that. Granted, most people didn't do it all over someone else's hand. But she wasn't going to think about that. No, she was going to clean up and go have dinner with Anthony as if nothing was amiss.

Chapter 15
The Interview

The rest of the week passed dreadfully slow. Tony managed to successfully get Alice out of the office for meals, but she refused to be seen else-wise. She claimed she had too much work to make up for and couldn't be distracted. But the flush of her face every time they were together told him that was a lie.

At least he could mess about and not work on his project as long as she wasn't coming around often. But he did eventually get bored enough to work on it a little bit. It was a little too good for his taste, but still shitty enough to fail. It would be perfect.

"Are you excited for tomorrow?" Alice asked. They sat at the kitchen island with an empty seat between them. They were having leftover pasta from the night before.

"Hm?" Tony asked, his mouth half full of a bite.

"Your interview," Alice reminded him.

"Oh yeah." Tony pushed the food around on his plate. "That."

Alice leaned over, placing a hand on his arm. "It's natural to be nervous," she said. "It's a big day. But I know you'll do amazing."

"I'm not nervous."

"I'd be happy to help you practice," Alice offered, smiling her bright smile at him. He's been missing that smile. "I know working on it ahead of time can really help calm your nerves."

"Ah, well, I don't have any nerves so…" Tony shrugged. The truth was, he really couldn't have Alice seeing all the 'hard work' he's put into his 'presentation'. She would know he was messing up on purpose, and then she would be mad at him. And he couldn't live if she were mad at him.

"It could still be helpful." Alice pulled her hand back and Tony frowned at the empty spot on his arm, now cold.

Tony had a feeling that if he didn't take Alice up on her offer, she would return to her office come the end of dinner and he'd spend another night alone. So, he figured a night spent in embarrassment and pain would be better than that, especially if the night was spent with Alice.

They finished up eating and Tony set the laptop up in the living room, giving Alice the completely thought through and very well put together presentation he had done. She understandably looked a little less than impressed when he was finished.

Okay, she was thoroughly unimpressed.

"That was...nice," she said. She shifted on the couch a bit, biting her lip as her hands wrung together in her lap.

"That's not what you really think, is it?" Tony asked. Not because he wanted to hear how shit his presentation had been, but because he didn't want Alice to feel she had to lie to him. They were friends, and friends didn't lie. Even though he lied about how hard he was working on everything.

"Well...perhaps I could offer just a few suggestions?" Alice asked, her eyebrows raised slightly, as if asking for permission. "Only, I know you worked very hard on this, and I wouldn't want to imply anything by it."

Tony crossed his arms, genuinely curious. "What would you be implying?"

"I don't want you to think that I think it's not good enough. I just think that if we worked together, it could be just a little bit better. For, er, insurance."

Tony chuckled softly, shaking his head. "You can just say it's shit." It was, after all.

"Oh, but it's not!" Alice bounced to her feet and crossed to him, grabbing his hands in hers. Soft and warm. Comforting. "You did your best to make this and therefore it is the best! I really didn't mean anything by it, I'm sorry."

Whatever guilt times 8000 was what Tony felt in that moment, looking into her pleading eyes, feeling the gentle pulse of her hands on his. She was apologizing for telling the truth, all because Tony had lied. He sighed, feeling completely fed up with his own antics.

"No," he said. "It, uh, you're right. It's awful. And I... I didn't really try." He bowed his head and looked at his feet, unable to meet Alice's gaze. He was scum. Worse than scum. And she deserved a better breed of friend.

"Oh," Alice said, letting out a relieved breath of air. "Thank goodness. You had me really worried for a second." She laughed, and Tony glanced back up, distrustful of her calm. "I just wish you would have told me you really didn't want the job earlier. I would have cancelled with Nate if you wanted."

"It's not that," Tony said. Then he snapped his mouth shut, cursing himself for saying anything at all. That was such an easy out, and he missed it.

"No?" Alice tilted her head. She was still holding his hands and his fingers twitched a bit in her grasp. "Then what?"

"Just lazy, I guess," Tony said with a shrug. "Didn't feel like doing it."

Alice squinted at him, her mouth forming into a hard, thin line. Tony gulped. He hated that look. That was a look that always preceded a lecture. And even though Tony knew he deserved one, he really didn't think he could handle it.

"Tell me why you really didn't do it," Alice said.

Worse than getting a lecture was having to talk about his *feelings*. Tony shrugged, unsure how to properly deflect the situation. It's not like he could just run away. Unless he didn't want to sleep in a bed that night.

Alice tutted and tugged on his arms, pulling him over to the couch. He let himself get pushed to the cushions. Alice left briefly and he eyed the door, wondering if sleeping out on the forest floor was really all that bad. When Alice returned, she had two glasses of wine and passed one to him before joining him on the couch.

"Trying to get me drunk?" Tony asked with a nervous laugh. He stilled his nerves and tried not to swallow the whole glass in one gulp.

"No," Alice said, sipping at her glass. "Just creating a more relaxing environment."

"So, yes." Tony winked at her. Apparently, he was incapable of turning it off. At least, when it came to Alice.

Alice placed a hand on his knee and, honestly, that wasn't fair. She gave it a little squeeze. "I'm your friend, Anthony. I hope you know you can tell me anything. And I promise I will treat anything you have to say with all the respect and kindness you've shown me." She smiled then; the sweetest, softest smile Tony's ever seen. And how the fuck was he supposed to look that smile in the eye and deny it anything?

"Alright," he said, shifting one leg under him so he could turn to face her fully. Might as well just get it over with. After all, Alice had been so open and honest with him concerning her own fears. It was only fair he returned the notion. "I'm six years old, okay?" Alice nodded, mirroring Tony's position. "Now, up until this point, I was the world's best student. Okay? I'm talking gold stars on all my drawings, perfectly spelled name on my little cubby. I was even a hall monitor in kindergarten."

Alice laughed. "That sounds adorable."

"Oh, trust me," Tony said. "It was. I do have pictures." He tried to ignore the way her eyes lit up at that. "Anyway, first grade seemed to be going on the same track, right? Front row, teacher's pet, the whole nine yards. Then, disaster."

Tony left Alice in a moment of suspense, taking a sip of his wine.

"Subtraction," he said, earning an amused gasp from Alice. He shook his head, remembering the pain of such a horrid subject. "I had addition down flat. I could add things in my sleep! But subtracting things? Oh no, that was a different story."

"It can be a difficult thing to get a hold of," Alice agreed with a head nod.

"I just couldn't get it. And then we had a test, which, if you ask me, is just something all schools should do away with. But we had 'em. And so I was up practically all night studying.”

“All night?” Alice asked.

“Well, until I fell asleep at my desk. I was only six. Anyway, I get up, and I go to school all baggy eyed and yawny. I take the test, feeling awful about it the whole time. And then…”

“Then?”

Tony sighed and closed his eyes, playing with the glass in his hand, already almost empty. “98,” he admitted. “8-5. It’s three, not four.”

“But that’s a wonderful score!” Alice said. Her hand was back on his knee, giving it another squeeze. Perhaps a little higher up.

Tony scoffed and shrugged. “Tell that to my father.”

Alice furrowed her eyebrows and Tony let out a little groan. He was back to regretting talking at all. He downed the rest of his glass.

“Grounded me for a week,” he said.

“Over a 98?”

Tony nodded. “Made me retake the test, too. And do extra homework every night to make up for it.”

“You’re joking!” Alice said. “You have to be! There’s no way someone could react in such a way to one missed question.”

Tony shrugged, because Alice was probably right. But he had been too young and foolish to see that. “Anyway, I just, uh, I figured why bother, you know?”

“But you tried your absolute hardest,” Alice argued. “He can’t have been so cruel.”

“You’ve met him, right? His policy is that if you aren’t doing something perfect, then you aren’t doing your best.” Tony winced a bit. He had heard it so much growing up, he forgot how funny it sounded to normal people.

"That's just awful thinking," Alice said, frowning, thoroughly offended on Tony's behalf. "Your whole family needs an attitude adjustment."

Tony laughed a bit. Just knowing that Alice was on his side seemed to be easing his pain a bit. Maybe the alcohol was just starting to kick in. "So, yeah," he continued. "I just kind of figured like, if I was going to get in trouble anyway, I'd rather not get in trouble for actually trying, you know." He shrugged, looking away. "I, uh, I just... I know I won't get the job."

"And you didn't want it to be because you tried and failed," Alice said. Tony nodded, not the least bit surprised that Alice knew exactly what he was feeling, when he was feeling it.

"I'm sorry," he said. He forced himself to make eye contact. "You did me a favor by getting this interview and I really just...fucked it up."

"Nonsense!" Alice patted his leg and leaned forward, pulling the laptop over to them. "We still have," she checked her watch, "about fifteen hours until you're due in. We can fix it."

There was such a determination in her eyes that Tony felt a little nervous. He hadn't planned on spending the night actually putting his thoughts in a cohesive presentation. But he also hadn't planned on being able to spend the night with Alice, which he preferred to pretty much any other kind of night. "I don't want to take you away from your work," he said. "I'm sure I can figure something out."

"I want to help," Alice said. "You've done so much for me, it's the least I could do."

Tony didn't want to remind her that everything he was doing for her was part of the deal of him staying around. He didn't want that to be true. If that wasn't true, then what they sort of had could be something kind of special. "Only if you're sure you're not busy."

"Trust me." Alice blushed a little and turned the laptop back on. "I've gotten plenty done this week."

*

Firsthand Research

Alice took a deep breath, sighing contently as she snuggled further under the blanket. Only it wasn't covering her properly. She muttered and grabbed for the edge, feeling it rather heavy as she dragged it up to her neck. It pulled away from her leg and she huffed, peeking out to see what sort of curled mess it had gotten into.

It hadn't gotten into a mess, but Alice sure had. The comforting pressure on her body wasn't a blanket, but Anthony, who was sprawled out on top of her snoring softly. And the hard pressure under her head wasn't her pillow, but the arm of the couch. They were a tangled mess of limbs laying out in the living room.

Alice gasped and sat up, unintentionally pushing Anthony to the floor. He yelled out and bounced to his knees, wild eyes searching for the upset to his slumber.

"We fell asleep!" Alice told him. She gasped again and looked at her watch. She sighed in relief, noticing they still have about an hour and a half before Anthony's interview time.

"Oh shit!" Anthony said, thinking the same thing she had. He shook the laptop awake and relaxed a bit when he saw the time. "Fuck, did we even finish?"

Alice sat up properly, smoothing down her hair. "I think, just about."

She looked at the wrinkled state of Anthony's clothes, and the thin, barely noticeable shadow of hair on his chin. They had spent hours working on the presentation. Anthony had all the basics, and the ideas and plans he had for the company were really rather thoughtful. He just needed a better way to organize it.

Alice stood up and stretched. "You go shower and clean up," she told him. "I'll call a taxi and finish up the last bit, okay?"

Anthony got to his feet, nodding as well. He looked at her for a second, eyes slightly squinted, searching her face for information of some sort. "Did we…" He looked over at the couch.

Alice flushed hot, suddenly in need of a shower herself. A cold one. "Goodness no!" she said. "You fell asleep on the floor." She chuckled nervously. "Silly."

"Huh," Anthony said. "Feel pretty good for floor sleeping."

Alice shook her head and shoved Anthony towards the hall. "Go now, we'll be late."

Anthony sauntered his way down to his bathroom and Alice let out a deep breath, failing to not watch him walk away. Truth be told, it had felt wonderful waking up with Anthony wrapped around her. Maybe it had just been that she slept in later than usual, but she felt so well rested, like she hadn't slept that deeply in years. She would never admit that out loud, of course. But it was certainly something to think about, and she considered getting herself a nice,

*

weighted blanket for home.

Anthony's leg bounced as they sat in the reception area. It was painted a calming tan color, and smelled like vanilla, with soft music playing from a stereo in the corner. One other person had been waiting when they got there and had been called in earlier as another person left. Now they sat alone with the receptionist.

"Relax," Alice said, placing a calming hand on his knee. "You're going to do amazing."

Anthony shook his head. "I'm not gonna get it," he whispered. "We should just go. There's no point."

"Shush," Alice said. She gave his knee a little squeeze and he jumped a bit. "You are going to go in there and rock that presentation. And they are going to be so taken with you that they'll have no choice but to hire you. Probably right on the spot."

"Alice," Anthony hissed, shrinking down in his seat. There was an adorable little blush on his face, and she chuckled.

Firsthand Research

"You'll be fine."

The door opened and the person from before them walked out, eyes wide and haunted. Anthony shivered. A few seconds later and the door opened again, the receptionist telling Anthony he could go in now.

"I'll be right here," Alice said, smiling at him as he got up. "Go get 'em!"

Anthony gave her a wary look and disappeared behind the door. Alice took out the notebook she had brought with her, hoping to get some work done while he was in there. Anthony had told her she should go walk around town or something, get some shopping in perhaps. But she wanted to be here to support him, even if she couldn't be in the room with him.

But writing didn't seem to be happening. She was too nervous, listening for any words or sounds she could hear from the other room, above the music. She nearly asked if they could turn it down, but that would have been taking things a bit too far. She spent the next 43 minutes staring at the door, flipping her pen around between her fingers.

When the door opened, revealing a gaunt Anthony, Alice jumped a little. She rushed over to him as he slumped forward, eyes staring at nothing, wide and unblinking.

"How'd it go?" Alice asked, rubbing his arm a bit, trying to get a reaction from him.

He shook his head slowly, still just staring straight ahead. Alice sighed and grabbed his arm in hers. "It's alright," she said as she led him back outside. "I'm sure you did better than you think." She patted his back and called a

*

car for the ride home. The whole time, Anthony just sat there, staring off into space.

It had been awful. Horrible. Horrendous. Tony's never done anything quite spectacularly as bad as that before. He had been terrible, stuttering the whole time, very aware of every uh and um he said. Which had been a lot. He had even drawn a complete blank at one point, skipping over an entire part of his presentation because he just could not remember what it had even been about.

All in all, he felt like shit.

"This'll perk you up," Alice said, sliding the bowl of ice cream before him. She sat next to him at the island, their arms touching a bit. That certainly perked him up a bit anyway. He eyed the ice cream, but his stomach was in knots, and he couldn't even think about eating it.

Alice placed a hand on his, giving it a slight squeeze. He finally found the energy to turn and look at her. She was smiling her soft smile. It was damn hard not to be happy looking at it, but Tony still only felt marginally better.

"Thanks for going with me," he mumbled. "Sorry you wasted your time on nothing."

Alice's smile dropped to a frown, and she lightly slapped his shoulder. "You stop that! Even if you don't get the job, it was good practice, and you should be damn proud of the work you did."

Tony nodded and looked back down at the counter. His phone buzzed to life in his pocket, vibrating against his hip with a not entirely unpleasant sensation. He let it ring.

Alice huffed and reached around him, digging the phone out of his pocket, her hands tickling him as she went. His body couldn't tell if he should react with laughter or arousal, so he just shivered at the mixed signals.

"Anthony Dawson's office," she said, answering the phone. He glared at her.

Alice laughed. "Hi, Nate. Yes, it's Alice...no, no, he's here. One second." Alice held the phone out to him, giving him a hard look.

Tony really didn't want to take the call, but he feared the pain and abandonment he might face from Alice if he denied her. He took the phone and held it limply to his ear. "Hi."

Nate chuckled a bit. "You sound chipper," he said.

Tony stood up and rubbed his face with a sigh, walking away from the island. "Give it to me straight," he said.

Nate laughed again. "When can you start?"

Tony squinted at his ice cream, imagining it to be Nate. "What?" Surely it was a joke. Tony had been awful. There was no way they were actually hiring him.

"You're hired," Nate confirmed. "Best presentation we saw all day, hardly even a contest."

Tony slid his gaze over to Alice, thinking maybe she had something to do with this. "Seriously? Me?" Alice sat up at attention, a sparkle in her eyes.

"You know the industry, Tony," Nate said. "And you have amazing ideas on how to work it. So, when can you start?"

"Uh...Monday?" Alice stood up with a clap, holding her hands to her chest.

"I'll send you some paperwork to bring with you," Nate said. He was quiet for a moment. "You know, I'm really glad I ran into Alice the other day. You're going to do great here."

Tony nodded and hung up, looking at Alice with wide eyes.

"Well? Did you get it?" she asked.

He nodded again, hardly believing it himself. After all that? All those ums and that whole missing section, he was the best? Either Nate had been lying, or everyone else had really been shit. Tony wasn't sure he could trust it, but then Alice smiled so wide, her eyes lit up with joy. For him.

Tony let out a little laugh, relieved and excited. He had never imagined getting a real job, let alone one he actually thought he could do well. He rushed forward, wrapping his arms around the one who had helped him get it.

Alice laughed, looking rather surprised and pleased. And, forgetting himself for just a moment, fueled by the good feeling of this prospect, and itching to chase after an even better one, Tony pulled Alice into a celebratory kiss.

Not even the shock in Alice's face could bring Tony down. He was on top of the fucking world, and he was never gonna die.

"Well," Alice said, clearing her throat with a blush. "I-I'm very happy for you, Anthony. I told you you could do it."

"I couldn't have done it without your help," he assured her, grabbing her hands in his. All he wanted to do was kiss her again, maybe curl up around her and just exist in her presence. But that wasn't possible, so he had to settle for looking deep into her beautiful eyes, memorizing the way they shone.

Alice pulled a hand out of his grasp and placed it on his cheek. This was new. "You are so much more capable than you know, my dear. And I hope this has taught you that."

"Yeah," Tony said, feeling all warm and squishy at her touch. "Thanks for, uh, well, for not giving up on me. Or whatever."

Alice smiled and chuckled. "I never will." She patted his cheek gently and sat at the counter. "Now, come eat your ice cream before it melts."

Chapter 16
Sex Dream - Riding

Alice had retired to her office after their healthy lunch of ice cream. Tony paced around for a bit, not entirely sure what to do with his time. He had way too much energy to actually sit and do something on the laptop, and it was too cold out that day to try anything outside. Clearly that only left him with one other option.

He entered his room, too wound up to realize his door didn't close as properly as he thought. He shed his clothes and slithered his way under the blankets, getting himself nice and comfortable in bed.

Tony closed his eyes and leaned his head back, letting his hand wander down as he picked any number of dreams he had to work from. Alice had been making an appearance in more than half these days, and it didn't surprise him when she showed up then.

She was wearing that lovely blue lingerie from the other day, all soft and smooth against her skin. She snuck into the room, biting on her bottom lip, looking a little shy.

"I hope I'm not interrupting," she said, half of her body hidden by the door.

"Not at all," Tony said, smiling back at her. "Come on in."

Alice blushed a bit and smiled softly before closing the door behind her. Tony's eyes were glued to her as she crossed the room to his bed. "I was hoping you could help me with something," she explained.

Tony leaned up on his elbows, smiling at her. "Of course. You know me; Always happy to lend a hand where I can."

"I was rather hoping you could lend more than just a hand…" Alice sat on the edge of the bed, reaching out and pressing a hand to the blanket over

Tony's crotch. Tony let out a soft moan, showing his appreciation for that.

"My body is yours to use as you please." Tony winked at her and laid himself back down, hands under his head, letting her have free reign.

"Any way I please?" Alice asked, fingers hooking under the edge of the blanket and dragging it down.

"Any way," Tony confirmed.

Alice smiled that sweet smile of hers at him and then got to her knees, pulling the blanket all the way off. Tony shivered a bit as the cold air rushed over him, but it was swiftly chased away by the heat of Alice's body. She straddled his lap, hands on his chest, looking down at him with adoration.

Tony let out a laugh. "Seems like Naomi is getting a little more used to things," he teased.

Alice chuckled softly. She let a hand trail down Tony's body, nails gently scrapping over his skin. "Seems like it," she agreed.

Tony hissed in pleasure as her hand wrapped around his dick, stroking it gently until it started to leak a bit of pre-cum. Tony managed to make eye contact, staring into the beauty of Alice as she rubbed his own sex over his dick. Then Alice smiled and shifted forward, and Tony had to close his eyes to keep himself from exploding.

Alice sat up slightly, using one hand to push aside the edge of her panties. The other hand held the base of Tony's cock, helping to guide it in. And she was so tight and hot and wet, and Tony felt like the breath was being kicked out of him as he sunk into her. It didn't help that Alice let out her own moan of delight in time with his.

"Fuck, Alice," Tony said. "You feel so good."

"Not as good...as you feel," Alice said. Barely even started and already she sounded wrecked.

Tony risked opening his eyes. She was as beautiful as ever. Her face was flushed, and her hair was a little wet with sweat, small curls stuck to her forehead as the rest bounced in time with her rocks. Tony's eyes scanned over the rest of her body, watching as each part moved and jiggled with every hop she made, a glorious symphony of dancing. And the noises she made; little gasps and huffs with each up and down that were true music to Tony's ears. He couldn't believe his own luck that he had such a vision of beauty in his life.

"You're gorgeous," he said, finding his own breath hard to come by.

"And you...are so...handsoooo—" Alice flung her head back, redoubling her efforts as her pleasure grew. She lost balance a bit as she reached up with one hand, easily undoing the little tie that kept her breasts contained.

Tony gulped as they bounced their way to freedom. She truly didn't know how wonderful her breasts were. So full and round and... *bouncy*. Tony couldn't help it; he had had those beautiful things in his hands before and he needed them there again. He pulled his arms around and reached up, sighing contently as he felt them squish and mold slightly to his touch.

"Ohh, Anthony," Alice moaned, her head still hung back. "That feels... wonderful."

Tony licked his lips and focused on massaging and tweaking her breasts, trying to keep his orgasm at bay. But feeling the weight of them move against his hands with each bounce Alice made did not help.

"Fuck, Alice, I'm...I'm close." He breathed hard, hoping to make the moment of joy last longer.

"Me too." Alice let her head flop back forward, looking at Tony with wide eyes and wider pupils. "Anthony, you make me feel so good. Oh, oh, please. Please, Anthony, please."

"Oh, Alice. Anything for you." Tony moved his hips up to match Alice's bounce, a slap of skin against skin as they chased their pleasures to their peak, calling out each other's names.

Tony came down alone, his hand and stomach covered with the come that he hadn't covered Alice with. He sighed, a little bit of guilt and loneliness creeping in as he shook free of his imagination. He heard a scuffle and his attention snapped to the door.

It was open, just a crack, and Alice was staring at him. His body went rigid, fear creeping into every inch of him, wondering how much she had seen, how much she had heard. Truth be told, he wasn't sure what had been said in the dream and what had been said in real life.

"I'm sorry!" Alice shouted, before scampering away.

Tony sighed and laid back down, free arm covering his face. Great. The last thing he needed was for Alice to catch him doing that, especially when it was her he was thinking about. Now she was just going to think that Tony only wanted her for sex, that she was just another wild fling of his he would move on from.

But the truth was, Tony would never move on from Alice. He had fallen in love with her words, and now he was falling in love with her.

If only she loved him back.

Chapter 17
A Car, a Diner, and a Revelation

Goodness.

Well, that had happened.

Alice stood with her back pressed up against the office door, staring at the wall but seeing only Anthony in her mind. Anthony nude between the sheets. Anthony moaning her name as he...as he…

Alice blushed and hid her face in her hands. She couldn't even think about it. It was too much. She didn't even know what to think. On the one hand, it had been rather flattering to be the object of desire. But on the other…

What did it even mean?

Did Anthony like her? Certainly not. At least, not in that way. He clearly admired her body; he had made that pretty obvious. But it wasn't entirely surprising. Anthony didn't care, as he said, about anything like that. He would probably have sex with anyone. And he was probably only thinking about Alice in that moment because of their current proximity to each other.

And maybe that kiss.

But Alice was most certainly *not* thinking about that kiss!

In fact, she shook it from her head and sat herself at her desk, determined to get back to work.

She would write out all of her frustrations. That was what she was good at, after all.

Only she kept seeing it. Kept hearing it. It echoed in her ears and refused to leave her alone. Anthony had said her name so...wonderfully. She had heard it, whispered down the hall as she looked for a little snack. At first, she thought maybe Anthony was in trouble or something, what with the sounds he was making. He could have been hurt!

But really, once Alice had seen he was fine (more than fine apparently), she should have just left. But...well...she had missed the grand finale last time. She just wanted to see what it was like.

For the book, of course.

It was a terrible breach of privacy and Alice was determined to make it up to him.

But *how*? That was the question, wasn't it? Alice pushed away from her desk and stared out the window. A simple dinner would not be a sufficient apology. And as much as she enjoyed cooking (especially with Anthony around), she couldn't afford the time to cook every night. She was already still so far behind on her work. No, she needed something else. Something big.

And she didn't even have to ask Katie for help with it.

*

Tony had started to get used to operating on a normal, non-nocturnal sleep schedule. Which would be good news for his new job. He really had an actual job now? But waking up to Alice cooking in the kitchen and waking up to the sound of a giant truck backing up right next to his room were two entirely different kinds of waking up.

Groggy eyed and curious, Tony tossed on his jammies and stumbled out to the living room. The door to Alice's office and room were both open, so she must be outside with all that noise. Tony puffed out his chest, wishing he had gotten something a little more intimidating than sushi for his wardrobe. After all, any kind of scum could be out there harassing his Alice.

Not that Alice was his or anything! Not that he didn't want that.

Tony shook the fantasy away and stepped out into the weekend, morning sun.

Alice was happily chattering away to one man, who looked the truck-driver type, while a second man was unhooking a car from the tow in the back. Tony let himself be distracted for a moment. Then he noticed the way

Alice was smiling at the driver, a familiar twinkle in her eye. Not on his watch!

"What's going on out here?" he asked. He stood next to Alice and wrapped an arm around her shoulders. Then he remembered that she really, honestly, wasn't his. But it was too late. His arm was already there. And it didn't move.

"I've gotten you a present," Alice explained. Tony looked back at the car, now sitting perfectly in the driveway, eyes wide.

She didn't.

"You are a very lucky man," the driver told Tony. "Most expensive gift my girl ever got me was a pair of shoes."

Tony chuckled nervously, still too tired to process what was going on properly. It was too early for this kind of thing.

"Oh, no, we aren't-" Alice started. But the second man joined them before she had a chance to argue the point.

Tony stood still, arm around Alice, staring at his gift as Alice went about and signed papers and took keys. The men said their farewells and then drove off, leaving the two of them standing there in silence.

Alice fiddled with the keys. "Well? Do you like it?"

"No!" Tony stepped closer to the car, finally letting go of Alice's shoulders. "I mean, yes, but...*no*."

Alice shook her head. "No what?"

Tony turned, his wide exasperation now facing her. "You can't buy me a car." As if that was something that needed to be explained.

"Oh, but I did." Alice leaned forward, giving him a little knowing look. "I do have quite the successful line up of books on the market."

"I didn't mean you can't. I mean you *can't*."

"Why ever not?"

"It's too much!"

"Too much?"

"Clothes and food are one thing but…" Tony sighed and turned back, gesturing to the car with both arms, "a car?" he shook his head. "It's too much."

"Well, you need some way to get to work every day," Alice offered. She shuffled her feet and looked down at her hands, nervously picking at the keys she held. "And…and I just thought…Well, I just…I just wanted to apologize for, er, the, um." She glanced at him briefly, then looked up, "the other night."

Tony had thought they silently agreed to never talk about that. After all, they hadn't brought it up as they ate dinner. They even managed to sit together on the same couch and watch a movie without bringing it up. Not that Tony didn't think about it non-stop. Not that he didn't long to reach out and touch her while simultaneously flinching every time she came too close to him. "You don't…I mean…there's nothing to apologize *for*." If anything, he's the one who should be apologizing to her.

"It was an invasion of privacy, and I shouldn't have…watched…" Alice gulped and looked at him, head turned slightly, blushing.

And Tony got it. But still. *A car*? Was she crazy? Was he really in love with such a… such a… such an angel? Tony sighed, running a hand over his face and through his hair. "A loan," he compromised. Alice gave him a questioning look. "I'm paying you back."

Alice opened her mouth, ready to argue. Then she sighed and nodded. "No interest!"

"Thank you." Tony held a diplomatic hand out to her and she shook it. "Probably gotta get back to work, huh?" Tony asked, trying to avoid having to talk about the incident any further.

"Well." Alice looked up at the sky, bright blue with lots of fluffy white clouds. "It is the weekend. And the weather is so lovely. And really, we should make sure it works…"

Tony grinned at her. He opened the passenger side door. "Hop on in."

Alice gave him a smile that held back a laugh. "Do you perhaps want to change first?"

"Yeah," Tony said, looking down at his outfit. "Probably."

Damn. That was supposed to have been cool. And the sushi ruined it.

*

Anthony drove a bit too fast, in Alice's opinion. But even though she chided him on it, she found it quite thrilling, and at a few times it was hard to stifle a laugh in exchange for a displeased groan.

Anthony knew the area around here much better than she, and he took them down an old back road, trees on one side, open farmland on the other. It was brilliant and beautiful. And watching Anthony smile and light up his eyes was just the icing on the cake.

If Alice let her imagination wander, which she was known to do, she would think of Anthony reaching over and holding her hand as he drove. And if she let her imagination run truly wild, he would reach over and hold her thigh instead, giving it a little squeeze with every turn and bend. Alice closed her eyes, letting her imagination loose as the open window blew a lovely chill over her face. Her hair would be a mess after this, but she didn't mind. It was likely to be the last reasonably warm day of the year, and she was determined to enjoy it.

"Hungry?" Anthony asked, interrupting the image of his hand creeping higher and higher on Alice's leg.

Alice blinked her eyes open, smiling at the color of what leaves remained on trees. "I could eat," she proclaimed.

Anthony flashed a smile at her. "I know this great place not too far from here." He laughed softly. "Used to sneak out at night and grab a midnight snack there. Never seen it in the day, come to think of it."

Alice imagined a younger Anthony, climbing out of a window, probably meeting up with some guy or girl to have a 'snack' with. She wondered what would have happened if she knew him back then. Would he have noticed her, talked to her, befriended her? Would he have been the one to whisper in her ear, encouraging her to break a few rules, live a little on the wild side? After all, they were young, that was what they were supposed to do.

Or would he just have been another in a long line of guys Alice never had the guts to admit she liked? Or one on the slightly shorter list of guys who turned her down, never even speaking to her after the months of courage she took to build up to it?

"Hopefully it's just as good now as it was then," she said.

Anthony nodded, his smile never faltering.

As they pulled into the parking lot of the diner, Alice fished out the little mirror she had in her purse. She ran her fingers through her hair, gently knocking loose the tangled curls without creating a frizz. It wasn't perfect, but it would do. It wasn't like she was going to run into anyone she knew in there.

"Looks the same," Anthony said, hands in his pockets as he looked the building over.

"I've always enjoyed diner food," Alice told him as he held the door open for her. "I've never met one to disappoint yet."

The diner had a seat-yourself policy and wasn't terribly crowded, despite being the perfect time for that. Anthony led Alice over to a booth on the right, not in the corner, but just next to it.

"It's very cozy in here," Alice said. She picked up the menu on the table and looked it over.

"Oh yes!" Anthony shouted. "Still have it." There was a miniature version of a jukebox on their table. Anthony dug in his pocket, producing a few coins. "Anything you want to listen to?" he asked as he popped the coins in the top.

Alice shook her head. "Whatever you want."

Alice, deciding she would try the French toast, looked out at the regular crowd at the bar up front. A man sat with his hat on the seat next to him. A woman in a sunflower dress did a crossword puzzled while sipping at her coffee. And at the other end a very familiar face wore an apron and refilled the cup of a man there with his kid.

Had Alice been alone, she would have beat a hasty retreat. She did not want to deal with that, and she hoped against all hope that someone else would be their server that day.

"You alright?" Anthony asked.

Alice gulped and laughed back the panic. "Perfectly fine." She tried to blink her eyes to a normal size, but evolution kept them peeled wide.

Anthony quirked an eyebrow at her, but thankfully said nothing. Unthankfully, he said nothing because Daria had appeared, filling their mugs with coffee before readying a pen and pad. Alice bowed her head, hoping the locks of her hair would properly hide her face.

"What can I get you?" Daria asked with a small sigh.

Anthony waited a beat, then said, "cheese omelet for me," when Alice didn't speak up.

They both turned their attention to her.

"French toast," she said in a voice that was both a whisper and much too high in pitch. "Please."

"Sure thing."

Daria walked away and Alice let out a sigh of relief that she hadn't been found. But she certainly couldn't spend the whole meal scrunched down with her hair blocking her face. People were liable to think she had been kidnapped or something.

Anthony leaned over the table as Alice brushed her hair behind her ears. "I'm gonna go ahead and ask this again, just to check, but...you alright?"

Alice bit her lip and wondered how much to tell him. "I went to school with her," she whispered, Anthony leaning closer to hear. "We didn't exactly end on good terms."

"Shit." Anthony fell back in his seat. "You wanna leave?"

Alice smiled at him. He was so considerate like that. "No, no. I'll be alright. Thank you."

Anthony smirked a bit and leaned back over, watching the rest of the diner as he whispered. "You wanna order a lot extra and then skip out on the bill?"

Alice laughed and gently kicked him under the table. He sat back with a grin. "No. But thank you for the offer."

The little jukebox on their table binged, and a new song started to play throughout the diner. Anthony started to dance in his seat. At least, he tried to dance. Alice would exactly call whatever he was doing *dancing*.

Anthony's dancing, and Alice's enjoyment of it, was cut off by a foreboding voice.

"Tony." The person belonging to the voice was on the shorter side. Beneath their own apron they had a... unique sense of style. "Didn't expect to see you around here again."

"Bree!" Anthony greeted. He leaned back against the booth, arms spread over the top of it. "Finally took over the family business, eh?"

Bree looked over at Alice, expression a mix between disgust and amusement. "See you're still up to your old ways."

Alice blushed, both for being mistaken as Anthony's date and for knowing it wasn't as ridiculous as she thought—that other people could see it. However wrong the sight may be.

"Oh no, no," Anthony said. He gestured to Alice. "Alice and I are just friends." There was a bitterness to his voice that she pretended not to pick up on.

Bree scoffed. "Sure." They turned to Alice, leaning down on the table. "You're too good for him," they said. Then they tossed Anthony a glare. "Get out while you still can."

Anthony just laughed them away. "Ah don't listen to them. They never liked me."

Two plates clattered to the table before them. "I knew it."

Alice looked up at Daria, cursing that she didn't notice her coming. Didn't properly hide. Daria placed her hand on her hips, an amused smirk on her face. "Alice *Follick*. What are you doing in a dinky place like this?"

"I think it's rather charming," Alice said, perfectly deflecting the question.

Daria chuckled. "Rumor is your books aren't doing so hot anymore." She smiled, an unpleasant sight. "Must be why you've turned to such… *unsavory* means of income."

"Ah, well, uhm." Alice cleared her throat, very aware of Anthony staring at her. As if waiting for something. "Thank you for our food." She picked up her silverware and busied herself with cutting her toast.

Daria scoffed and rolled her eyes before skulking away.

It was quiet for a moment as Alice prepared her breakfast. She reached for the syrup bottle, but found it pulled out of reach by Anthony, who was still staring at her.

"What the fuck was that?" he asked.

"Can I please have the syrup?" Alice stood up and reached for it again. Anthony pulled it closer to his chest, waiting for an answer. Alice huffed, determined not to give him one. She reached over the back of her booth, grabbed the syrup from the empty table behind them, and then gave Anthony a look of victory as she poured it over her toast.

Anthony squinted his eyes and pulled his plate over. He continued to just stare at her as they ate. And Alice tried to look anywhere else but at him.

"How is your omelet?" she asked. He shook his head, chewing slowly as he kept up his intense gaze.

Alice huffed again. He was really being quite childish. She reached into her bag and pulled out her notebook and pen. Seemed like she would be getting some work done this morning after all. She barely saw Anthony's hand as it shot out and pulled the notebook over. He held it to his chest like the syrup, giving Alice a challenging look.

Alice frowned at him. "Give me back my notebook."

"Answer my question."

Alice glared at him and shook her head. "It wasn't anything."

"Alice." Anthony leaned closer, eyebrows high on his face. "You are one of the cleverest people I know. I alone thought of like, ten great comebacks to that. What happened?"

"Not everything deserves a witty response," she informed him.

"Well, that sure as hell did!" Alice looked down at the table, unable to meet his eyes. Because he was sort of right. "Are you...scared of her?" he asked.

"No," Alice whispered. She felt quite foolish and figured this really wasn't the best of places for this conversation. But at least there weren't too many people around. "I'm scared of being her."

Anthony gave her a questioning look and gestured for her to continue.

Alice sighed and shifted in her seat. "I just...I suppose I can understand where she's coming from. You see, she's also a writer. And... she's really not terrible at it. And there's just such a huge amount of luck that goes into being published that, well, it's understandable to be a little jaded when someone you know has made it and you haven't. And I very well could have been unlucky enough to be passed over and stuck somewhere...charming."

Anthony twitched a smile. "That wasn't jaded. That was like, openly aggressive. Besides," Anthony leaned back and waved a hand towards the bar area. "Don't feel too bad for her. She did this to herself."

"Oh, did she?"

"Yeah." Anthony shrugged. "She was querying the same time you did." Which made sense. They had graduated together. Anthony laughed. "You should have seen it, Alice. I mean. I see what you were saying about the writing not being bad but, she was awful."

Alice sat up a bit straighter, curious. "Oh?"

Anthony nodded, pleased with himself. "I remember her. She was unagented, like you." Alice nodded, remembering well the troubles with all that and how she was very glad there were still companies like Nana Jan's that accepted unsolicited manuscripts. "Only, unlike you, she told us exactly why she didn't have an agent in her query letter."

Alice sighed and shook her head. Mistake number one. They had learned about that in school. "And what reason did she give?"

Anthony bit back a laugh and checked to make sure Daria wasn't around. "Something along the lines of how they don't know anything and clearly are just turning away anyone they aren't friends with or whatever."

Alice stared at him with disbelief. "You're joking?"

Anthony shook his head. "I'm not. She sounded like she believed she was god's gift to writing."

"I can't believe you remembered that? It was years ago."

"Well, it was, to date, the funniest submission I've ever seen." They shared a soft laugh. "So, ya see? She was never gonna make it with that kind of attitude. You both have talent, but you," he pointed at Alice, "have the grace, charm, and personal awareness required to actually succeed at, well, any job really. So don't feel bad for her. And certainly don't let her antagonize you unanswered."

Alice nodded. Anthony was right. She did have a tendency to be a bit of a pushover. She decided that the next time Daria did or said anything, she would do or say something back.

"Anything else for you, has-been?" Daria asked a few minutes later, giving Alice the perfect opportunity.

Alice took a deep breath, puffed out her chest, and froze. She tried to think of a good comeback, then just any comeback at all. But it was as if all words had just flown out of her brain. She shook her head, feeling too mortified to be upset. Daria rolled her eyes again and slapped a check down on the table.

"Sure you don't want to just run out on the bill?" Anthony asked, thankfully not mentioning Alice's blunder.

"No, no," Alice said. "That wouldn't be very nice."

"Oh, well, don't give her a tip!" Anthony exasperated as Alice placed some money on the table.

"Easier than asking for change," she lied.

Anthony shook his head at her, and they climbed out of the booth. Hand on the door, Alice remembered the English vocabulary. She spun around, nearly knocking into Anthony behind her. She pointed a finger at Daria and said, "At least I've been!" then practically ran out of the diner.

Anthony laughed as he unlocked the car and held the door open for her.

"I know," Alice said. She buried her face in her hands. "That wasn't exactly witty." She really was much better at writing these kinds of exchanges.

"No, no," Anthony said as he started the car. "That was brilliant, and I'm proud of you."

Alice smiled. She was a bit proud of herself. Sure, it hadn't been much of an insult, and she was certain Daria wouldn't think twice about it. But Alice had said it. She hadn't let the fear hold her back, and that was a major achievement.

"At least the food was good, huh?" Anthony asked. He grinned at her, and they shared a laugh.

More than just the food that been good that morning, Alice figured.

Chapter 18
Sex Lesson Eight – Vibrations

"Hey Alice," Tony called out, shutting the door with his foot. "Package for you."

He stared at the small box in his hand, trying to suss out what it could be. The return label was pretty generic, which didn't help much. He gave it a little shake, but there was no sound that came from it.

Alice hurried down the hall to him. "Ah! Thank you." She took the box from him and rushed into her bedroom.

Tony blinked at the spot where the package had been only a second ago. That kind of reaction could only mean one thing.

"Looked a bit small to be lingerie," he said with a smirk as he softly knocked his knuckles against the door. "What'cha got in there?"

"Nothing!"

Tony chuckled. She was awfully cute when she was flustered or embarrassed. Doubly so when both.

"Just wouldn't want you to get stuck on anything else," he said. He leaned back against the door, arms folded before him. "I know I have a job job now, but, well, I am still your assistant."

Alice didn't respond and Tony furrowed his eyebrows, wondering if maybe she had escaped through the window. Then the door opened and deposited Tony on the floor, a thump to his back knocking the wind out of him.

"Oh dear!" Alice knelt next to him as he rubbed his head.

"Ow."

"Are you alright?"

"Yeah, I'm-what's that?"

Tony knew exactly what the thing Alice held in her hands was. He's seen 'em before. Truth be told, he had always wanted to try one out with someone. But he couldn't *say* that. Certainly not to Alice.

Alice looked at the device in her hands, gasped, and held it behind her back. "What's what?" she asked.

Tony leaned up on his elbows and craned his neck to peak around to her back. "Naomi and Malcolm getting a little saucy, are they?"

"Actua-YES!" Alice jumped to her feet, face a lovely shade of red. "That's correct. The, uhm, well, I've skipped ahead to the end, and um, yes. This."

Alice held the device back out, matching remote in hand. Tony stayed on the floor and looked up at the vibrator with a sparkle in his eyes. It was just a clitoris simulator. But still. The idea of remote controlled *anything* in the bedroom really got him excited. He had to play this smooth, couldn't let on how much he wanted this. So, really not much different than all their other lessons.

"Need any help?" Tony asked.

"Oh! I, well..." Alice sat on the edge of the bed looking down at the device. "I-I think I'll be alright. But, um, thank you."

Tony deflated, his shoulders dropping a bit. He tried not to sound too disappointed. "If you're sure." He sat up, stretched a bit, then stood. "I'll be right out there." He pointed to the living room. "If you need me."

Alice nodded and Tony shut the door for her as he left. He thought about leaving it open, but unlike *some* people, he wasn't going to go around snooping on others during their private sexy times.

Tony chuckled to himself and sat down, mind already running through all the scenarios going on behind that door, especially the ones that could involve him.

The door opened not even a minute later.

Firsthand Research

"I need you."

*

Alice bit her lip as Anthony studied the device she had handed him. She figured she should have her pants off or something, but he hadn't actually said that, and she wasn't about to go getting naked unless it was necessary.

"You have any lube, by chance?" Anthony asked.

Alice furrowed her eyebrows at him. "N-no? I...it, it doesn't go in does it?" Alice panicked and grabbed the box, checking over the back. She had specifically gotten it because it *didn't*.

"No, it doesn't." Anthony took the box from her, saying 'you can trust me'. And she did. "It just still needs some for being there, otherwise it could hurt."

"O-oh." Alice didn't know that. But it made sense, now that he mentioned it. "Uhm...Well I suppose we'll just have to try it out later." She grabbed for the vibrator, but Anthony pulled it back, tutting at her with a sly grin.

"Wait here."

He disappeared and Alice let her legs shake. She had originally bought the toy just for her. Being with Anthony had awakened something in her and she felt a lot more... *needy* these days. But Anthony was just helping her with the book, it wasn't like she could just go around asking him to get her off whenever she wanted. But letting Anthony think this was for the book...well, that worked out in her favor doubly so.

"Here we are," Anthony said. He returned with the device and a bottle of lube in hand.

"That's not old, is it?" Alice asked. She watched as Anthony popped it open, already pouring some out on the curve of the device. She could imagine him grabbing it from some secret teen-hood stash somewhere.

"Nope. Brought it with me."

"You...you were getting kicked out and you packed *lube*?"

Anthony shrugged and winked at her. "You never know, right?"

Alice shook her head and shuffled around nervously. "Uhm, so do I, er, need to be…" she gestured to her groin.

"No," he said. He stepped closer, the heat of his energy calming her nerves. "I just need to get in there to set it up. You'll actually need everything on to help keep it in place."

"I see." That was what she had needed his help for. She didn't know how any of this worked, and asking him was just much quicker than looking it up online.

"Is it alright if I go in?" Anthony asked.

Alice blushed and turned her head with a nod. Anthony undid the button of Alice's jeans and pulled down the zipper. She felt fog in her breath as he reached in, sliding a hand under her panties. One finger, wet with lube, rubbed around her clit, making her whimper softly.

Anthony smiled, and Alice nearly thought to playfully slap him for his cheek. But then he was removing that hand and replacing it with the one that held the device. It was long and curved, with a bent bit near the top that would settle against Alice's clit. Anthony's fingers spread her open a little bit, fitting the vibrator in place. It was a little unusual, but not bad.

"How's that?" Anthony asked, pulling his hand away a bit, making sure the device was settled properly.

"Good," Alice told him. Better if his hand stayed.

"Any pain?"

She shook her head. Anthony re did her pants for her and then grabbed the remote off the bed. Alice hadn't really thought of him actually controlling the device. But now that it was an option, she was looking forward to it. After all, he knew things. More than she did. He would know how to make it work properly.

"We're gonna go through the speeds and make sure everything works, okay?" he asked. Alice nodded. "Just let me know if anything feels off."

Alice nodded again and Anthony pressed a button. Alice gasped, feeling the little device come to life between her legs. She was now very glad for the lube Anthony had been so thoughtful to remember. It was a teasing pressure, certainly something that she couldn't get off on. But it felt good all the same.

"Good?" Anthony asked. "Not moving around where it shouldn't or anything?"

"No, it's...wonderful."

Anthony pressed a second button and the vibrator kicked up in power, rocking against Alice in a way that had her eyes popping a bit. She reached out and grabbed Anthony's arm to steady herself. He grabbed her back.

"Off?" he asked.

Alice shook her head. "No. It's good. Sorry." She went to pull her arm back, but Anthony just gave it a squeeze, keeping it in place.

"No worries," he told her. "Another?"

Alice nodded. They worked their way through the different speeds and settings, Alice moving closer to Anthony with each one until she was practically leaning against him. And he checked in after every change, making sure she was okay. Finally, Anthony worked her back down to the lower setting, expertly knowing not to turn it off after such stimulation.

"I think it's all in order," Alice managed to say. She straightened herself with a little resistance from Anthony.

"Glad I could be of help." Anthony held the remote out to her and Alice stared at it. Now that she had considered Anthony controlling it, she couldn't think of anything else.

Anthony slowly pulled it back, raising an eyebrow at her. She looked him in the eyes, and they didn't need words to know this was something they both wanted. Even though neither of them would admit it.

Firsthand Research

"You should probably get back to work then, huh?" Anthony said, smirking a bit as he flipped the remote in his hand.

Alice couldn't fight a smile of her own. This, she decided, was going to be fun.

*

It was only torture if the other person wasn't enjoying it. And judging by the not-so-stifled moans coming from the office, Alice was certainly enjoying it. Right now, she was being allowed a small break. A minute or two of a lower setting. After all, she had just managed a full twenty seconds on high without coming. She deserved a reward.

Well, a bit anyway.

Anthony chuckled to himself and turned up the power again, not too high. Just enough to get that little squeak reaction from her. Loud enough to be heard through the door. He could only imagine her face right now. All flushed and beautiful. Mouth hung open in pleasure. Eyes closed because how could she possibly be writing through all of this?

It was glorious.

*

Alice's fingers flew across the keys of her typewriter. There were too many mistakes to count but it didn't matter. She had so many things to write down it wasn't funny. She had never had the chance to write while actually feeling the pleasures of the body. And this was the perfect opportunity.

Every touched nerve and bumped pleasure was another word in her arsenal. The sentences she wrote weren't even coherent, or in order, or in any way trying to be part of a scene. She just wrote down what she felt. Touches, vibrations, exhilaration. And among it all: Anthony.

Anthony who was controlling the device between her legs. Anthony who knew when to back off just before she crested, and when to pick up the pace when things started to get boring. Anthony who always kept her guessing and never cycled the same way twice. He was brilliant, amazing, fantastic, and

163

Alice would just have to switch the name around in the edits.

She had managed to get through a longer bought of high vibration, and Anthony had dialed back. She sighed, relieved, as she regrouped and focused on the last sentence she had felt. Then the vibrator kicked back up and Alice squeaked.

She slammed a hand on her desk and squeezed her legs together, begging her body not to come. Not yet. It was too soon. It had been nearly half an hour, but it was too soon. She needed more. She had so many more thoughts and experiences to write out. She needed the time.

Alice held her breath and stood up a bit. "A-Anthony," she tried to call out, but it was just a huffed whisper. If he just went back down a bit, she could get her body settled again and keep going. But he seemed intent on making her orgasm right then and there.

Alice gave in. She flopped back to her chair, leaned against it and pressed a hand between her legs, forcing the vibrations deeper against her body. "Anthony," she said again, because it felt so right.

"Anthony!" she shouted as she came, because who else on god's green Earth could ever make her feel this way?

"I'm right here, Angel," Anthony said.

Alice jumped, her body a molten mess from the orgasm and the shock. Anthony was leaning against the door frame, smirking at her. He toyed with the remote, slowly lowering the speed as Alice's heart rate climbed down. When the device was finally off, Alice realized how much of a mess she must look.

"I, uhm…" She wasn't sure what to say. "Thank you," she decided. "For the help."

Anthony opened his mouth, closed it, looked her up and down, then licked his lips. He let out a soft huff of a laugh. "So, we're even now, right?"

Alice blinked at him, then remembered her past sins. She felt a wave of awful embarrassment, but then again, he was right. He had intruded on her personal space and watched her come, all while calling out his name. So they *were* even now.

She smiled at him, brushing the sweat soaked hair from her face. "You're still not paying me interest on the car."

Chapter 19
Rumors Only Grow

New day. New job. New me.

Tony scoffed and relaxed his body. He wore suits pretty often, especially with all the parties his family threw. It wasn't like he was uncomfortable in them, but it felt different today. Because he had to actually *try*.

Tony adjusted his tie, glad he could still remember how one worked, and stepped out of his room. Alice was in the kitchen, not cooking, but wrapping something up in a paper towel.

"I figured you would be too nervous to eat right now," she said, smiling at him. "So, I packed you some breakfast for later." She pulled over a small lunch box and placed the towel in it before zipping up. "And I made you some lunch."

Tony stared at the bag, feeling like he was a kid heading off to school. "You didn't have to do that."

"It's your first day! I can't very well have you going around forgetting to eat." Alice's smile brightened and she slid the bag over to him. "Are you all prepared?"

"As prepared as I can be, I suppose."

Alice walked around the counter, standing before him. She fidgeted for a moment, and Tony wondered if he was forgetting something. He glanced down to make sure he was wearing his pants, and felt Alice's arms around him, holding him in a tight hug.

"I am so proud of you," she whispered, "and incredibly happy. And I hope you have just the best of days."

If Tony's brain wasn't already so focused on the anxiety of his first day of work, it would have been on overdrive trying to keep himself all together after that.

The hug probably lasted a little longer than it should, but neither of them mentioned it.

"I hope you have the best of writing days," Tony told her. He picked up his lunch bag, wondering what she had made for him.

"I'm sure I will, free of distractions." Alice laughed and Tony wished he didn't have to go. He wanted to stay with that laugh and that smile forever. But being late on his first day would probably be pretty bad. So, he grabbed his briefcase, nearly thought about kissing Alice on the cheek, remembered himself, and left.

*

An office. A desk. A phone. Tony had it all! And he loved it, sitting down in a space made just for him. It almost made him forget about the work he would have to do. But then he saw a blinking light on his phone alerting him that he already had a message. Guess he was hitting the ground running.

"You liar," the message started. Tony had forgotten he had given Sandra his work number. Now he regretted it. "You big fat liar. You better call me."

Tony sighed. He certainly could not start his first day of work by making a phone call to his sister. He would start it, apparently, by talking with Nate. Which was just fine, he figured, as his boss walked through the door to Tony's office.

"You sly dog."

Tony smirked. "It's why you hired me."

"Do you even know what I'm talking about?"

"Something good, I hope."

Nate laughed a bit. "Check the news."

Tony turned to his computer. "Er, which one?"

"Any of 'em."

Tony opened up his favorite news site and thanked his lucky stars he wasn't drinking anything, for surely he would have spat it out all over his screen and then spilled it out all over his lap. He's seen his name and picture in the news plenty of times. But nothing quite this heart-stopping.

"Has famed romance writer Alice Follick finally found love?" he read. Then he leaned over, studying the picture of him and Alice at the diner, smiling at each other over their shared meal. He continued reading the actual article. "Alice Follick was seen fawning over Anthony Dawson of publishing house fame this past Sunday. *Fawning*? She wasn't fawning. Does it look like she's fawning!?" He turned his monitor around.

Nate leaned over his desk and studied the screen. "If anyone is fawning here, it's you." He laughed.

"I do not fawn," Tony informed him. *I pine relentlessly.*

"Either way, you've got yourself a keeper." Nate winked at him.

"But...we aren't dating!"

Nate looked between Tony and the picture on the screen. "Do you guys know that?"

Tony growled and grabbed his cell phone, standing up. "I have to-" he wanted to say go deal with this. But he was at work. Could he even go deal with this?

"Go on," Nate said with a smile. He stepped to the side and gestured to the hall. "Can't keep your lady waiting."

Tony pointed his phone at Nate as he slipped past. "She is not my lady!"

But she was the best friend he had and the best thing he had going on in his life, so he hurried down the hall, hiding away in the stairwell as he dialed her number.

"Ah," Alice said. "I was wondering when I'd hear from you. Are you okay?"

"Am-? Am *I* okay?"

"That is what I asked."

Tony barked a laugh and slid down against the wall, sitting with a hard thump. "Are you?"

"I'm perfectly alright, yes."

Tony furrowed his face and tsked a bit. "Do you...did you see the news today?"

Alice hummed a no. "I've been very good at keeping distractions to a minimum. Why? Has something happened?"

Something had, but Tony was curious now. He sat up a bit. "Why were you expecting a call from me, then?"

"Just waiting to hear how everything is going over there. Any big projects yet?"

Tony could probably distract her long enough that she would never find out, but she should probably know. He hung his head, resting his forehead against his knee. "You should check the news."

He heard the tick of the laptop in the background. Then a soft gasp. He clenched his eyes shut.

"I'm so sorry," he mumbled.

"Oh dear," Alice said. She sighed, huffed, muttered a bit, then sighed again. "Well. I suppose we should run some interference, hm?"

"I'm sorry," Tony apologized again. Because he couldn't stand to be the cause of a problem for Alice. He was supposed to be making her life easier, not more complicated. "I'll do whatever we need. I'll call every news company and yell at them until they take it all down."

"I'm afraid it's a bit too late for that," Alice said. Tony thought he heard the hint of a smile in her voice, but he must have heard it wrong.

"Then I'll shake the memory out of everyone's mind!" he sighed. "I'm so, so, sorry.

Alice laughed. "Anthony, relax. This is not my first time at the rodeo. I can't shake hands with someone without the world thinking we're dating or working together on a new project. I have had my fair share of rumors."

"Yeah," Tony said, slouching down further. "But this one was my fault."

He heard Alice huff and could imagine the little pout on her face. "Oh. I see. So you hired someone to take pictures of us while we were out at the diner, then?"

"What? No! Of course not."

"Then I'm sorry, dear. But I really have no idea how this is your fault."

Tony ran a hand down his face. "I-that's not-you know what I mean!"

"I'm afraid I don't. This is the fault of whoever took that photo and decided to put the rumor out there." She paused for a moment. "Probably Daria."

Tony growled. "I'm gonna kill her."

"You will do no such thing. In fact, what you should do is be more worried about yourself."

Tony scratched his head. "Uh, I'm sure that's true. But why, exactly?"

"Think about it. You and Nate have already seen it so early. Nana Jan will probably see it soon, if she hasn't already."

Tony let that sink in. "She's gonna kill me."

"I won't let her!"

"She'll kill you, too," Tony reminded her. That, at least, he could properly feel guilty about.

"She can't possibly. You have a job now, remember? In town? If anyone asks, you got the job, we ran into each other, and went out for a brunch? Completely innocent. She doesn't need to know about you staying at the cabin. As far as anyone is concerned, you've never set foot in it!"

"Wow. That...is a really good lie." He was always proud of Alice, but in that moment, he was proud in a way that surprised him.

"I told you," Alice said, her voice echoing his pride. "This is not my first time at the rodeo." They shared a soft laugh. "Now stop worrying and get back to work."

"Yes, Ma'am!"

*

Alice hung up the phone and let out a deep sigh. She really had had her fair share of rumors. But it had been so long since she's actually been out and about, that she didn't really remember the protocol for it all. She hummed and looked through her phone contacts. She was pretty sure she had a publicist still...he'd probably be glad to finally have some work to do.

A knock slammed on the door and Alice jumped, her fingers spasming over her phone, opening a random app. She shook her head and steeled herself, peeking out into the hall, staring at the door. The same harsh knock pounded, the wood actually moving against the frame.

Alice would have been terrified, already ready to call the police, had it not been for the voice that called out to her. "Alice! Open up!"

Alice gulped and did just that. "Liam! I assume you've seen the news..."

Liam pushed past her, his face dark as he looked about the room. "Where is he?"

"Anthony is not here," she told him.

Liam scoffed and started checking rooms, Alice trailing after him, hoping he wouldn't start digging in drawers in his search. "You expect me to believe that? This is his family's place, of course he's here."

Liam started down the hall, and Alice knew that if he looked in Anthony's room they would be found. And it would be very hard to dissuade the rumors if he knew they were living together.

"Liam, please!" Alice grabbed his arm and pulled him to a stop. He huffed and studied her. "He's not here, I swear." He hardened his glare. "He got a job in town and is staying at a place there, okay? There is no need to overreact."

"No need? I'm not going to just stand around here while that sleazeball takes advantage of my little sister."

Alice moved her hands to her hips. "First of all, Anthony is not a *sleazeball*. Secondly, you may not have noticed, but during your war on guys not good enough for me, I have grown up. I don't need your protection."

Liam adjusted his stance with a huff. Alice readied herself in case she had to block him again. "I know his type, Alice. He's never been with someone for longer than a week! He takes what he wants and then he leaves."

"So?"

"*So*? Maybe you don't care about your heart, but I do. And I won't have him breaking it!"

Alice softened a little. She did appreciate where he was coming from. It was nice to have support, someone who cared about your wellbeing. But it became a problem when said care turned violent.

"Anthony will not break my heart," she explained, using her calming voice. "He can't. We're just friends."

Liam scoffed. "Well, the two of you were being very *friendly* on Sunday."

"Really, Liam." Alice frowned at him, utilizing her best disappointed face as she crossed her arms over her chest. "You can't believe everything you read on the internet."

"It's not what I read. It's what I saw." Liam dug his phone out of his pocket and showed Alice the picture that's been posted all over the place.

They really did look like a happy couple in love. And Alice let herself blush for a brief moment, thinking of such a thing with Anthony. But then she remembered who was standing before her and she shook her head. "It looks like two friends having lunch to me."

"I know that look." Liam zoomed in on Anthony's face. Alice tried to deny it, but there was something in his eyes, she had to admit. He did look at her like she hung the stars. "It's a look that says he wants to… *defile* you."

Alice let out a breathy laugh. "Liam, do you even hear yourself right now?" She shook her head. "I am the last person in the world that Anthony would want to defile. If he were to actually 'defile' anyone."

"I know what I see." Liam huffed and placed the phone back in his pocket. "Just friends or not, you aren't seeing him ever again."

"Excuse me?"

Liam pointed a finger at her. "You are not allowed to see him!"

Alice raised her eyebrows, strengthening her stance. "You can't tell me what to do."

"Yes I can. It's my right as your older brother." Liam crossed his arms, challenging her.

Alice frowned and pointing to the door. "Leave." She tapped her foot against the floor, waiting.

Liam startled. "What?"

"You are not welcome here, and I want you to leave."

Liam's expression melted, his body deflating a bit. Alice almost felt a little sad, but then Liam snarled a bit. "I'm going to find him," he warned. Then he, thankfully, left.

Alice let out the breath she had been holding with a shudder, her body shaking a bit from the adrenaline. She had never spoken that way to anyone before, let alone her family. It was a little bit thrilling, and a little bit terrifying. Anthony, it seemed, was certainly having an influence on her.

Chapter 20
Sex Lesson Nine – Blowjob

It had been a day. And that's all that could be said about that. Tony and Nate had spent the time working through his first campaign together, Nate helping him with all the specifics of how their office operated. And Tony had even stayed late to put everything together for a presentation later that week. But he couldn't properly assess everything going on while Alice and the rumor were in the back of his mind.

He half expected Nana to be at the cabin when he arrived. So he was very pleasantly surprised to find Alice there alone, sitting on the couch, pen between her teeth as she studied the laptop screen. Pages were spread out haphazardly around the table, cushions, and even floor.

"In other news," Tony said with a smirk. "Hurricane Alice has swept through the area, leaving total destruction in its wake."

Alice startled and looked at him with wide eyes. Then she glanced at the clock. "Anthony! You're late!"

"Busy day," he explained. He dropped his bags on the chair, picked up a few of the pages, and deposited himself on the couch next to her.

"Oh, sorry about the mess." She hurriedly tidied up her piles. "Just needed to move a few things around."

Tony waved her off. "No worries."

"So." She turned to her side, tucking one leg under her as she faced him. "How did it go?"

"Busy," Tony repeated. "But I don't wanna talk about that." He leaned over, grabbing her hand, loving the way its warmth felt under his own cold. "How have you been?"

Firsthand Research

"I told you I would be fine." She rolled her eyes but smiled. And she didn't move her hand away. But she also didn't hold his back. "I have someone to handle that."

Maybe he should move his hand.

"You know a guy, huh?"

No. She didn't seem to mind.

"He's very good at what he does."

But the longer he kept it there, the more awkward it became.

"He better be. Wouldn't want to have to kill him for you."

Alice chuckled and looked down at where their hands touched. Damn. He should have just moved it away. But then she placed her other hand over his. Tony was very, very aware of his heart beating hard in his chest, always in Alice's direction. Maybe they should just let the rumors be true.

"Alice-" "Anthony-"

They shared a laugh.

"Go on," Alice said.

"No, no, you first," Tony insisted.

They stared at each other, each too stubborn to back down in their polite patience. Then Alice blushed and dropped her head. Her fingers picked at Tony's hand a bit, a surprisingly enjoyable sensation.

"I know you've had a long day," she started. "And I wouldn't want to add to your plate any. But, well...I was wondering if you could help me with something? For the book?"

Tony smiled at her. She truly didn't know how effective her shy adorableness was. Or she did know and was a mastermind at manipulating him. Not that he minded being manipulated by her. He quite enjoyed it, matter of fact.

"Anything for the book."

"Oh, good!" Alice stood up, Tony's hand falling out from her hold. She disappeared into her room for a moment then reappeared holding something in her hand. Something long and oblong shaped. She sat back down and held it out to him. "You have experience, yes?"

Tony gingerly took it from her and looked it over. "I do have one, yes."

"I mean with, er, *pleasuring* it."

"I do have one," Tony reiterated with a laugh. Alice huffed at him. "What would you like to know?"

Alice's face darkened, a lovely red spreading out over her cheeks. "How to...well...how to, uhm…" She gestured to the dildo, telling Tony nothing. He shook his head and looked at her expectantly. She dropped her head again and mumbled, "oral."

"Ahh," Tony said. "Not to brag, but I have been told I'm pretty damn good at it."

Alice looked up at him through her eyelashes. "Could you teach me?"

Tony grabbed her chin with soft fingers and urged her head up, looking her right in those beautiful hazel eyes. "I'll teach you anything you'd like."

Alice let out a shaky breath, blowing warm air over his hand. "I'd like," she said.

"Then call me professor."

"Oh? Will I be graded?"

Tony chuckled. "Absolutely."

"I'd better pay very close attention, then."

Tony held the dildo up between them. "This shall be a hands-and mouth-on lesson."

Alice smiled at him a bit, her body relaxing slightly. "I'm just not sure of the proper, er, techniques? And the internet wasn't being very helpful."

"Oh, it rarely is." Tony gripped the base of the dildo and leaned closer, so she could get a better look. "Step one, the tongue."

Alice's eyes widened as Tony stuck out his tongue. He pressed it to the dildo just above where his fingers were holding it, let it spread out as he licked his way up, maintaining a steady gaze on Alice's face. When he got to the tip, he flicked his tongue over the edge of it as he finished the languid process.

"Tongue," Alice said, her breath shaking her words. "It...licks."

Tony bit his lip but couldn't stop the laughter from bubbling out. "I have never been more convinced that you are a dirty, dirty plagiarizer."

Alice huffed and gently shoved his shoulder a bit. "I'm still learning this; it'll be better once I have time to process it all."

"Ready to process that?" He turned the dildo around, so the underside was facing her, and held it out.

Alice jumped back a bit, eyes wider. "I, what, now?"

"No time like the present."

"I don't..." Alice hunched down a bit, her attention bouncing around the room. "I'm not sure I... could..."

"Participation is 50% of your grade," Tony said. Not to pressure her, but just to give her that extra little push he knew she needed.

Alice licked her lips, and Tony couldn't stop staring at the shine of them. He nearly missed Alice shooting forward, quickly licking a trail up the dildo in the blink of an eye. "There. Done."

Tony chuckled and shook his head at her. "I'm afraid in this instance, speed is not the answer."

"Could...could you not look while I do it?" Alice asked, turning a bit, hiding her beautiful face behind her hair.

Firsthand Research

"How else would I know you were doing it right?"

Alice was quiet for a moment. Tony knew what he wanted her to suggest, but he also knew he was not that lucky, and he certainly didn't have enough karma stored up to cash in for it.

"I'm more than happy to just keep showing you," he told her. "But I think you'll be able to write it better having done it yourself."

Alice turned slowly, bothering her bottom lip between her teeth. "You, uh, wouldn't have to look if you could...feel it. Right?"

Tony studied the object in his hand. "Alas, science has yet to come so far."

Alice rolled her eyes. "I meant…" she huffed. "As you said...you do... you *have one*."

Tony had never died before, but he was pretty sure that's what it felt like. "I...do."

"Maybe I could…" Alice gestured to his lap. "While you weren't looking? O-only if you'd want, that is."

Oh, I want. I so desperately, desperately want. "Anything for you." He shook his head. "The book, I mean."

Alice glanced at him, a spark of life returning to his body as their eyes met briefly. "I think it would be the best way for it. And-and you could still show me on the, er, that."

Tony nodded, all too eager for exactly that to happen. But he was the one supposed to be in control here. He had to keep calm, cool, and collected. For Alice.

"Here, wouldn't want you to hurt your knees any." He shifted over and laid back on the couch, resting up against the arm so he could still see her. Not like he would be watching when she *performed*.

Alice shuffled after him, nestling herself between his legs, hovering over his groin. Her hands shook as she reached up to his belt, then stopped. "I, uh."

Tony smiled at her and reached down, gently pushing her hands out of the way. She blushed and looked down as he fished himself out, unsurprisingly hard as a rock already.

"Should I...?" Alice looked between his face and his dick, as if unsure where her attention should be focused.

Tony covered his eyes with his free hand and smiled. "Step one, tongue!"

He felt warm, shivering fingers grab the base of his cock, perhaps a little too tight, but he didn't mind. How could he, when the wet, warm texture of Alice's tongue was pressing against him, dragging up, a soft friction leaving behind a wet trail? And she had been paying extra close attention, he noted, as she flicked a bit just under the head. He didn't even realize he had moaned until he heard the echo of it coming back to him.

"Good?" Alice asked.

"A-plus," Tony told her. She chuckled, and he deemed it safe to look again. "Okay. Step two. The swirl."

Tony brought the dildo to his mouth and tilted his head down so Alice could see. He stuck his tongue out again, this time rolling it around the tip. He folded it around the underside, flattened it over the top, and pressed hard along the sides. He really was good at this.

"Should that be slow as well?" Alice asked.

Tony closed his eyes, mainly because he couldn't look at her nestled between his legs like that, face framed by his thighs, without spontaneously combusting into flames. "It's good to vary the speed a little. Keep me on my toes."

He felt Alice's fingers on him again and held his breath. He's had a lot of blowjobs in the past, but there was something so very different about this one, and not just because he was coaching. Realistically, there was nothing different about Alice's tongue and mouth than most others. And yet there was. As it mimicked Tony's motions, swirling around his cock with deliberate, if sometimes misplaced, pulses of pressure, it felt like something magical, like something unreal. And if he wasn't being stimulated to all hell and back again, he might have tried to figure that feeling out.

"That's good," he said. And as he heard his own voice, he knew he was in trouble. Only on step two and already a wreck. He wasn't sure *he* would last much longer. Thankfully, Alice was a beginner, and he wasn't going to try and show her any advanced techniques.

"It's interesting how it actually gets harder to do the longer you go on," Alice commented, ever reminding him they were doing this for research. "Like, I think the saliva makes it harder to keep control."

It's also what makes it super fucking hot, Tony thought. But he said, "Yeah, it can get a little messy. But sometimes that's more fun." He winked at her, and she smiled, tucking her head down a bit. "Now, the third step I like to call the lollipop."

Alice snorted and held a hand to her mouth as she laughed.

"Don't laugh," he teased. "It's a very effective maneuver. See, you just, pretend like it's a lollipop. Best tasting one you've ever had. And you just gotta, suck all the flavor right out of it."

Alice kept laughing, but nodded, watching him intently. Tony brought the dildo back up and very seductively placed his lips around the head, just the tip resting against his tongue. Alice shifted, her legs squirming together. He quirked an eyebrow at that and then closed his lips, sucking on the head of the dildo like it really was the most delicious lollipop ever.

"And don't be afraid to get your tongue involved too," he mumbled around the object in his mouth as he did just that. Of course, it was always better on a real dick. They at least had a taste, and not the manufactured silicon taste of toys.

Alice nodded and watched for a few seconds longer. Tony noticed that one of her hands had disappeared, pressed down between her legs. He didn't mention it. He just closed his eyes, laid his head back, and waited.

Soft. Her lips were so fucking soft. It really wasn't fair. He had never had something so smooth and gentle on him before, and he had to remember himself before he bucked his hips up, chasing the warmth of what surrounded him. He grabbed a fistful of the couch and held his breath as those soft delicacies pressed around him, pressure pulling as Alice sucked. If he had a soul, he didn't anymore, for surely she just pulled it right out from him.

He swore he saw stars, too, as Alice put her tongue in play. And it really, super wasn't fair. Alice wasn't allowed to be that good at her first time. Sure, it wasn't technically the best. It was a little bit sloppy, a little out of sync, a little jerky on the pace. But it was bloody brilliant! Tony thought her jerking him off was fantastic, but this? This was on a whole other level. And he felt he was on a different planet.

Only, no matter what planet his mind was residing in, his body was still on Earth, still comfortable under the weight of Alice's body, still clenching every muscle as the wave of pure pleasure started to crest.

"Oh fuck!"

Tony reached down, eyes popping open as he grabbed Alice's hair and pulled her head back. He was a bit late, a nice glob of come landing on her chin as the rest fell down to his shirt and pants. And then he realized he was holding a fist full of her hair.

"Sorry!" he said, releasing her. He grimaced at the glob on her chin, dripping around the curve of it. "Uh, here, let me get that for you." He wiped his thumb over it, clearing the majority of it away, but also just smearing it more. "Fuck."

He sat up a bit, frantically looking for something he could clean her up with. He stilled at her touch, hands on his arm, soft, warm.

"Anthony," she said, "It's alright."

"Is not," he argued. Here he was, supposed to be the one with all the knowledge and experience, coming on her face like a teen who couldn't keep it in his pants. It was embarrassing. And she probably didn't appreciate it.

She smiled at him, however, her eyes soft and warm. "It really is." She patted his arm and then sat up. She grabbed a tissue from the box on the table to the side and properly wiped herself off. "It means I'm doing my job right, right?" She raised her eyebrows at him.

"I thought it was my job," he countered.

Alice smiled, coy. "I can't properly write Naomi doing this if I'm not good at it myself, yes? And so that," she gestured to the mess on his clothes, "Must mean I'm good."

"You're better than good," he told her. She handed him a tissue and he cleaned up what he could. "You were brilliant."

Alice looked down, smiling and blushing in that infuriatingly cute way she did. "You really think so?"

"Wouldn't have done that if you weren't," he reminded her.

She laughed a soft laugh and licked her lips before looking at him. "You should go change. I'm going to clean up and start dinner."

"Don't have to rush away to write down all your findings?" Tony asked.

"There's time for that later. For now, I'm hungry."

Tony didn't go there.

Chapter 21
Totally not a Date Take Two

"It's *real.*"

Alice looked up from the sink, watching as Anthony rubbed his fingers over the check in his hand. She smiled at him, knowing well the feeling she had gotten when she got her first paycheck. Granted, it was only for a few dollars but, hey, you have to start somewhere.

"Yes, dear," she said. "It's real, and you earned it."

Anthony's head slowly looked up to meet her gaze. "*Did I, though?*"

Alice huffed and turned off the faucet, placing her freshly washed lettuce on a towel to the side. She wiped her hands dry and placed them on her hips. "Absolutely. You worked very hard, and you should be proud of what you've accomplished."

Anthony frowned a bit and looked back at the check. "I *guess.*"

Alice rolled her eyes and shook her head at him. She could see how he felt like that. His first campaign had yet to start running, so it was easy to feel like nothing had really been accomplished. But Anthony had done so much. And not just for work, but personally. He's grown a lot in the last few weeks, and Alice thought he deserved every penny, and perhaps more.

"So, what are you going to buy with your first paycheck?" she asked, returning to the task of making dinner.

Anthony hummed and watched her work. She caught the brief glimpse of a smirk on his face as she turned to finish cooking. "I'm taking you out," he declared.

Alice felt the blush creep over her face, her skin feeling tight and dry. "What?"

"Dinner," Anthony explained.

A date?

"Wh-why would you do that?" Alice swallowed, but her mouth and throat had become quite dry at the prospect. Why did she feel so much more flustered over a date than she had over any of their lessons?

"Because," Anthony tapped his fingers against the counter, "I can't really cook. Unless you want cereal. I make a mean bowl of cereal."

Alice needed to turn back to the island and get the rest of her ingredients, but she couldn't let him see her like that, so she just kept her face by the steam of the stove. She had to clear her throat to talk properly. "Why would you want to cook anyway?"

"I wanna do something nice," Anthony explained. "You're always doing nice things for me, ya know? And, well, you got me this job, so-"

"I did not get you this job," Alice said. She summoned the courage to look back at him, hoping the red on her face could be seen as just the heat of the stove. "You worked very hard, and are very talented, and *you* got this job."

Anthony nodded but didn't look like he fully believed her. "Well, you got me the interview anyway." That she would give him. "And I just, I dunno, I want to thank you. For... everything."

Alice's face relaxed, her skin no longer on fire, her muscles no longer tense. It wasn't a date, just a thank you. In the same way she had been thanking him for all his help with her research. She was relieved, if not a little disappointed. She might have enjoyed a date with him. But this certainly wasn't a date, so she could relax and enjoy herself properly.

"Well," she said, grabbing the ingredients she needed. "I think a dinner out sounds perfectly lovely. Thank you."

Anthony smiled again as she turned back to the stove. But then she heard the frown in his voice as he spoke. "What if it happens again?"

"What if what happens?"

"Another headline," Anthony explained.

Alice stilled, the spinach in her pan turning a bit soggy as it over-cooked. "Well, we'll deal with it the same way we did last time."

"I don't…" Anthony sighed. "Maybe I'll just order something in."

"Nonsense. We are not going to hide away in here because we're afraid of some rumors." However, Alice had to admit that if something did get out, Liam and Katie would both become impossible to deal with. Katie had, after all, phoned just after Liam had left to call Alice a liar. One time only, huh?

"Are you sure?" Tony asked.

Alice smiled. "I'm positive." She wasn't going to let the world or her family stop her from living life. And a nice dinner out with a good friend was just the kind of night she needed as she moved into the last few scenes of her book. "We're going to go out, and we're going to have fun!"

*

Tony sat back on the bed, ticking his tongue as he waited. He heard Alice moving around in the closet, and he kind of hoped she would ask him to come in and help her out as he had before. But he really had started to run out of all his luck. It was bound to happen eventually.

"What about this?" Alice asked, stepping out into the room.

Tony tilted his head and looked at her. She was wearing a white blouse, with a little puff around the sleeves, tucked into a simple black skirt that went down to her shins. He scrunched his face up a little.

"No?" she asked. Tony shook his head and she huffed. "Well, I am beginning to run out of options."

"What about that dress off to the side?" Tony asked. He craned his neck to see it better.

"Oh, no," Alice said. She stepped over, blocking Tony's vision with her body. "I couldn't. It, er, it doesn't fit."

"Then why did you bring it?"

Alice chuckled that nervous chuckle of hers and turned around, closing herself back in the closet as she changed once again. Tony checked his watch, glad they had started this an hour before their reservation. She never answered his question.

"Alright, it's either this or I'm wearing jeans."

Alice emerged again. This time she sported a blue button up shirt laying gently over a pair of tan pants that seemed to have a permanent wrinkle to them. Tony squinted, looked at the pants, then looked at Alice.

"Jeans it is!" she declared. She threw her hands in the air in defeat and turned back to the closet.

Tony jumped up and raced over, beating her to the door, holding it open. "C'mon," he said, leaning over her. "Just try it on."

"It doesn't fit," Alice insisted. She crossed her arms and challenged him. Tony never was one to back down from a challenge.

Smiling at her, Tony reached behind him and felt around for the dress in question. He pulled it off the rack and held it up to her. So that was the real problem. The dress was an off-white top, sheen in places where it didn't count, with slits running down the sides from the shoulders to the elbows, allowing the perfect peek of skin to show through. It was attached with a small bow to the skirt of the dress, a tan and white tartan style that rose to well above the knees. And with a neckline that swooped down below the collarbone, Tony knew exactly why Alice didn't want to wear it.

"Doesn't fit," Alice said again, her voice shy and uncertain.

Tony held the dress closer to her, tilting his head. "Looks like it would fit to me."

"Well, looks can be deceiving."

Alice snatched the dress out of his hand and ducked under his arm, stepping into the closet. Tony frowned and let her close the door. He wandered back to the bed and plopped down, trying to imagine what Alice would look like in that dress. You'd be able to see the delicious curve of her thighs, the smooth texture of her skin, the delicate structure of her neck. She would look divine, especially with a necklace, gold, draped around her, something like a jewel fitted right between her breasts.

The door opened and Alice started to say something, but just kind of squeaked a bit. Tony sat up, his head spinning. Not because he had sat up too fast, but because the image he had just made in his head was nothing compared to the reality of it standing before him.

Alice was *beautiful*. The dress hugged her curves in all the right places and left just enough to the imagination. It was, obviously, something a little outside of her comfort zone, given the way she was hunched over a bit, arms scrunched forward, fingers picking at the hem of the skirt. But even in a non-confident pose like that, Alice was an image of pure beauty.

"See?" she said, not looking directly at him. "It...it doesn't fit."

"What are you talking about?" Tony asked. He surprised himself with how easily he found he could talk. "You look..." he struggled to find the right word, sputtering and mumbling because no word had been invented that described it.

"Awful?" Alice suggested. "Trying too hard? Not dressing for my body type?"

"*Stunning*," Tony offered. It wasn't the perfect word, but he wanted her to stop saying such terrible things.

Alice frowned and turned to look in the mirror that hung on the back of the closet door. "You're lying," she said.

"I'm really not." Tony stood behind her, itching to reach out and touch, to place hands on hips, run fingers over arms, press legs to legs. But he held his hands behind his back and resisted the urge. He looked at Alice in the mirror as she did. "You're beautiful."

"You're just saying that." Alice relaxed a little, her shoulders no longer hunched, her head held a little higher. With every bit of confidence, she looked even more amazing in the dress.

"I'm telling the truth," Tony argued. Alice turned around to frown at him. He couldn't hold it back anymore, reaching out to gently cup her cheek. "You always look beautiful." He dropped his voice to a whisper, feeling an electric heat between them, like the last time he had helped her pick out an outfit. "But in that…" he let his gaze wander, drinking in the full sight of her. "…You're the most beautiful woman in the world."

"Is that what you tell all your dates? It's a very good line."

Tony's attention snapped back up. Alice was looking down at her feet. Tony had told a lot of men and women a lot of things. But this one he meant. He moved his hand from Alice's cheek to her chin, lifting her head back up.

"This isn't a date," he reminded her. Then he shrugged with a smile. "What reason would I have to lie?"

Alice pouted a bit and turned back to the mirror, studying herself. "You-you're sure?" she asked. "I... I look okay?"

"Better than okay. Perfect. Amazing. Wonderful."

Alice bit her lip and hummed and hawed for a bit. "Well, I suppose...I suppose I *could*. I-I have been meaning to wear it for a while now…"

"You are free to wear whatever you want," Tony said, stepping away. "But I meant what I said." He held his hands out to her. "Stunning."

*

Alice let Anthony talk her into wearing the dress. She still felt a little... exposed. But only because she's never really worn anything like this before. Not because she didn't want to. She did want to. But surely she *couldn't*. Dresses like that weren't made for her, despite the sizing it claimed to be. But it was much too late to change, she knew, as Anthony drove them into town.

Anthony, on the other hand, looked quite handsome in his suit, tailored perfectly to his waist. It fit him in neat lines that accentuated all his sharp features. Not that Alice was noticing his features, certainly not.

They were dining that night at a relatively new little bistro that had set up in town. A classy location that Nate had suggested to them. A valet attendant parked their car, and Alice shivered a bit in the fall air as they entered. She should have brought a jacket, but none had matched the dress.

Anthony's jacket would match, however…

The interior of the restaurant was quite romantic, and little groups and couples sat close together at small tables, talking in soft voices. Alice watched them as they waited to be seated, always on the hunt for book material.

A small group of people at a table near the door laughed. Alice was certain that someone had just said something funny and unrelated to their arrival, but she fidgeted and gently tugged at the bottom of the dress' skirt, covering as much as she could.

And then there was Anthony's hand on her back. A warm pressure a little lower than should be allowed for a not-date. But comforting. And she let that pressure guide her through the tables to their table near the back. And it didn't matter if anyone looked at them. Because Anthony thought she looked stunning, and maybe his hand on her back could convince them all to think the same.

They sat down and Alice finally allowed herself to relax a little, now that she could hide her legs under the table. All thoughts of how she looked flew out the window as she studied the menu, eyes lighting up. They had quite the wonderful selection, and she was very thankful to Nate for the suggestion.

Alice placed her order and looked at the soft glow of the lights, the waiters in their fancy dress, the diners in their fancier dress. It was all so alluring and charming, and the music played at just the right level to create a soft buzz that wouldn't overpower softer conversation. She felt a spark of inspiration and reached for her purse, only to remember she hadn't brought her notebook with her.

Because she knew this would happen and she didn't want to be rude when Anthony had made such a lovely gesture. So she pulled her twitching fingers back and smiled at Anthony as he finished placing his own order.

"You alright?" Anthony asked once the waiter had gone.

Alice nodded and hummed a yes. "Perfectly fine."

Anthony scoffed and made a show of looking at Alice's hands. "You're twitching."

Alice placed one hand on the other and willed them to calm themselves. "Am not," she said as the words she itched to write ran through her head on a loop.

Anthony smirked and reached into his jacket, pulling out a pen. He handed it, and a napkin, over.

"I'm terribly sorry," Alice rushed out, grabbing the pen and napkin. She scribbled like mad, certain that she wouldn't be able to read what she wrote later on. But at least she would get it out. "Just a minute."

"No rush," Anthony said. She glanced at him, and he had a look of pure adoration on his face. Most people scowled at her when she wrote in public, especially somewhere fancy like this.

With a slight blush, Alice finished the writing she had come up with and sighed in relief, finally able to think of something else again. "Thank you." She handed the pen back to Anthony and shoved the napkin in her purse.

"So, how is the book coming along?" Anthony asked. "Haven't had an update in a while."

"Very well, very well indeed." Alice smiled and straightened in her seat. "Only a few more scenes to write left. And then the first round of editing." She shook her head. "But we don't have to talk about that."

"I like talking about it," Anthony said, a relaxed smile on his face. "Makes me feel special, you know. Getting all the sneak peeks before it goes out into the world."

Alice chuckled at him. "Well, I'm very glad to have the extra set of eyes. I really don't think I would have gotten this far without your help. And if I had, it certainly wouldn't have been any good."

Anthony's smile only grew. "Don't sell yourself so short. You're an amazing writer, and you would have been just as well off without me."

"Don't sell *yourself* so short," Alice countered. "You have been very helpful, and you make an excellent teacher."

Anthony laughed. "Alright, we'll compromise. We're both fantastically amazing in every way and we make one hell of a team."

"I'll toast to that," Alice said, raising her glass. Anthony followed her motions, and they clinked glasses, each taking a small sip of wine.

They settled into a small silence as they stared at each other. They did make a great team. And Alice was certainly going to miss having him around after this was all over.

"Still haven't heard from Nana Jan?" Alice asked, trying to keep her mind off the loneliness and worry that thought caused her.

"Nope. Figure your publicist told her the story you told him and she let it go."

"Still. If she was looking into it at all, she'd find out you joined with a publishing house." Alice sipped at her wine again. "Might not like that."

She watched Anthony gulp and look about the room. "It's fine. I'm sure it's fine."

She wasn't convinced.

*

"It's raining," Alice announced.

Tony frowned and turned in his seat, watching the rain fall outside. He hadn't even noticed it over the sound of the crowd around them. "Looks like a storm," he muttered.

Alice made a soft noise and then cleared her throat. "Perhaps we should order dessert to go," she suggested. "Make it back before it gets bad."

Tony spun back around. Alice looked worried, her eyes scanning along the windows as the rain picked up in speed. She bit on her bottom lip and picked at her fingers. Tony didn't want to leave. They had been having such a wonderful time. Talking had been easier than he expected, and they hadn't had any awkward silences or hiccups in conversation. And they had laughed and smiled and enjoyed their time. And he didn't want it to end.

But, more than that, he didn't want Alice to be uncomfortable.

"Yeah," he said. "Sounds like a good idea to me."

Alice smiled, relaxing a bit in relief. Anthony tapped his fingers against the table as they waited for their desserts, studying Alice with a soft intensity. He nearly yelled at Nate for suggesting this restaurant. After all, this wasn't a date, and he was trying oh so very hard to not be obvious.

But then again, Alice had said yes. And she had worn the dress he suggested. And she had laughed and talked and enjoyed herself.

Maybe it was a date?

But Tony wasn't sure how to *ask* if it was. He certainly didn't want to assume it had been if it wasn't. But if it was and he went about acting like it wasn't, then he was a jerk, and he'd probably loose Alice forever.

Not like he had her or anything. But it would be nice if he-

"Are you okay?"

Tony blinked, realizing he hadn't done that for a few seconds as he just stared at Alice. He sat up with a blush, clearing his throat. "Uh, yeah, sorry. Was just thinking."

"Oh? Anything I should worry about?"

Tony opened his mouth, hoping he would just vocalize his thoughts with ease. But anything he would have said was cut off by a loud roar of thunder that seemed to shake the restaurant a bit. And Alice jumped. And their bill was coming out. And it really wasn't the time, so Anthony shut his mouth and shook his head.

"It's nothing. Let's get home."

They waited by the door as the car was brought around. Tony couldn't tell if Alice was shivering because of the cold or the worry over the storm. He figured he'd offer his jacket either way.

"A-are you sure?" Alice said, gingerly taking it from him. "I wouldn't want you to be cold."

Tony shrugged. "I'm fine. I don't get cold easily. Besides, it's raining." He gestured to her dress. "Wouldn't want to ruin your outfit."

Alice smiled at him and blushed, draping the jacket over her shoulders. It would be too small to properly wear, of course, but it would keep some of the rain and chill out.

Tony didn't miss the way that Alice twitched or jumped as the storm ragged around them in the car. She held tight to the door handle with white knuckles at every wind that swept past.

He was surprised she was still in one piece by the time they arrived back at the house. "Wait here," he announced as he shut off the car. "I'll go grab an umbrella."

"No thank you," Alice said, hurriedly.

Tony frowned. "No need to be all independent and modern," he joked.

"It's not that," Alice said with a slight roll of her eyes. Then she blushed and looked out at the dark, dark sky. It lit up with a flash and she shivered again. "Uhm...I just, I don't want to be alone..."

Tony's face softened. She was really scared. "I understand. C'mon." He hoped out and ran around to her door, opening it for her and holding a hand out. She grabbed it, grip tight, and they ran inside together, a pair of soaking messes breathing hard once the door was closed.

"Thank you," Alice whispered. They were still holding hands, crowding together for warmth. "I know it's a little, well, childish but-"

Tony placed a finger to her lips, stilling her. She radiated warmth, even as she shivered in the cold. They were still holding hands. "It's alright. Storms are a perfectly valid thing to be afraid of."

Alice stepped a little closer, not that there was much space left between them anyway. Then there was a loud crack of the storm outside, and they were plunged into darkness. Alice yelped and jumped forward that extra bit, pressing herself against Tony.

He chuckled softly and wrapped one arm around her. And only one. Because they were still holding hands.

"Hey," he whispered. "I have an idea." Alice nodded against him. "How about we get some dry clothes on, and then we can watch a movie or something on the laptop until the storm's over?"

Alice nodded again. Her voice was soft when she spoke. "I like that idea."

"Okay."

Hands still held, they walked down to Tony's room, using the light of his phone to lead the way. After grabbing his pajamas, they walked back to Alice's room, both fitting inside the closet to change. Back to back, they finally let go of each other's hands, both with a little hesitation.

There wasn't a heat in the room as they stripped, dried, and dressed. This wasn't a sexually charged moment, just a moment. A moment of one friend being scared and another being there for them.

Whether or not the dinner was a date didn't matter. They were friends before anything else. And that's all he needed to know.

"Would it be awfully weird if we watched in here?" Alice asked, shuffling nervously by the door. "Only, there's no blinds in the living room and, well…"

"Already on it." Tony smiled at her and pulled the blinds down as she climbed onto the bed. They settled against the headboard, a blanket draped over their legs to keep them warm. And warm they were, as Alice pressed herself against Tony, watching him turn the laptop on.

"I never properly thanked you for diner," she said. "It really was lovely."

Tony smiled and turned his head, catching himself just before he kissed her forehead. "Glad you liked it. Up until the storm bit, of course."

There was a brief moment of silence. And then, "This isn't half bad, either," as Alice leaned her head on his shoulder.

Couldn't argue with that.

Chapter 22
Sex Dream – Victorian Boob Job

The storm raged on outside as Anthony led Alice up to the barn. Her dress was soaked at the top, the bodice turning sheen around her chest. And the skirt was positively covered in mud from running up the street. They had just been trying to go for a nice walk around the gardens and out of nowhere, a storm.

"Well," Anthony said, laughing a bit as he closed the door to the winds behind them. "That was something."

"I'm ever so glad you were there with me," Alice said. She looked around and deemed a nearby block of hay a suitable seat. "I'm not sure what I would have done out there alone."

Anthony leaned up against the door and smirked at her. "Well, I'm not sure your family would approve my being here." He pushed off and sauntered over to her. "What *would* they say?"

Alice looked up at him with wide, innocent eyes. Then she glanced down to her dress, pressed wet to her skin. "Well, I'm sure they would have something to say about the state of my dress."

Anthony's gaze followed hers, eyes turning hungry as they took in the sight. And what a sight she was. "Well, we certainly can't have anyone seeing you like *that*."

Alice hummed in agreement. She pushed her chest out a bit, fingers toying over the top of her bust. "We really should do something about it, don't you think?"

"Let me help," Anthony said, stepping closer.

"How gentlemanly of you."

Anthony's fingers were long and dexterous. Alice was certain he could untie any number of dressings, blindfolded, in just a few seconds. But he took his time undoing each knot with a calculated slowness. And as he pulled each string loose, he was sure to look in her eyes, tongue running over his lips to match the gentle tug.

Alice let out a soft sigh as the last tie was undone, releasing its hold on her breasts. They fell free, pushing the rest of the fabric open. Her nipples hardened as the cold blew over the wet. She shivered with delight.

"There," Anthony said. He took a step back and studied his handiwork. "Much better."

"Oh, yes," Alice agreed. She pulled a little bit at the bodice, opening it wider. "I'm sure they'll have no trouble with us being together like this." She leaned back a bit, supporting herself with her hands behind her, really pushing her chest out there. She giggled at the way Anthony's eyes opened.

"Then again," Anthony mused. "Wouldn't want you to get cold…"

"I am so awfully chilly," Alice agreed. She leaned back further, lowering herself to her elbows. "If only there were someone around to keep me warm…"

The slick of the rain on her skin was starting to dry, but there was still a soft sheen that shone in the gentle light of the barn. Anthony licked his lips and pounced forward. Alice laughed as he landed on top of her, his legs disappearing in the folds of her dress as they laid back on the hay. It pricked and poked at her back, but she didn't care; not when Anthony was kissing her neck in that way that made her toes curl.

Alice moaned softly as he sucked and bit at her skin. "Oh, my," she said, trying to catch her breath. "Certainly can't be caught like this."

Anthony growled softly and pushed himself up, staring down at Alice with quite a primal expression. "Then we'd better be quick."

Alice smiled and reached up, running her fingers through his hair, wet and soft. His eyes closed and he hummed in delight. Alice chuckled and reached between them with her other hand, fumbling around for the button on his pants. Anthony let her try for a few seconds, then got to his knees as she continued to struggle.

Alice sat herself up a bit, arranging her bodice and retying part of it in such a way that her breasts pressed together quite nicely, creating a perfect area for Anthony's dick to nestle in.

"Fuck, Alice," Anthony breathed as he got himself out.

"Do watch your language, dear," Alice chided. She slid down, lowering herself so her chest was properly aligned with Anthony's groin. Hay stuck to her dress as she moved. "I am a lady with such sensitive ears."

Anthony chuckled and grabbed her breasts in his hands, giving them a squeeze before he gently pulled them apart, sliding his dick between them. He released, letting the skin and muscle and fat mold around him with a delicious moan.

Alice grabbed Anthony's waist, then smirked and slid her hands back, grabbing a tight hold of his ass. He smirked back at her, grabbing her sides as he shifted his hips back and forth.

Alice laughed a low tone and pulled Anthony closer, feeling up his butt as she urged his movements faster. There was something so sinfully delicious about the way he slid against her skin, wet from more than just the rain. And the way he moaned, muttering out her name between gentle gasps and sighs.

"You are positively beautiful, my darling," Alice told him.

Anthony smiled, his eyes sparkling with how wide his pupils were. "Not nearly as beautiful as you." He winked.

Alice blushed and bent her head a bit, the perfect image of a demure young woman. A demure young woman with the stable boy's dick pressed between her breasts, but still.

"I love you," Anthony whispered, his hips stuttering as he got close.

Alice moved her hands back to his waist, squeezing him tight. "And I love you," she said.

Firsthand Research

Anthony groaned and tipped his head back, eyes closing as he came. Globs of hot come fell on Alice's chest, coating her skin in a new type of slick. And it excited her.

"Never loved the rain so much," Anthony said with a chuckle. Alice nodded. "But now…" he smirked and lowered himself, sliding down, hand sneaking back to find the hem of her dress.

Alice laughed, opening her legs, inviting him in.

She blinked and was no longer tickled by hay. She was nestled in a bed, curled on her side, an alarm blaring in the distance. Someone next to her moved and mumbled. Alice gasped and reached over, half-laying on Anthony as she grabbed for her phone.

"Terribly sorry," she said as she turned the alarm off.

"S'alright," Anthony mumbled. He reached up and held Alice to his body.

"Oh," she said. The memory of her dream flooded back to her, and she blushed, very aware of Tony's body, hot and soft, beneath her. She cleared her throat and successfully managed to wiggle out of his hold. He was already asleep again, thankfully.

Alice didn't even remember falling asleep. She remembered curling up next to Anthony as they watched a movie, trying to ignore the storm outside. And then…that dream…Alice shook her head and looked over at Anthony.

She should wake him up.

Or at least get out of the bed.

But…it was awfully warm under the covers. And if Anthony was going to sleep in, well, she saw no reason why she couldn't, too.

Chapter 23

The Morning After...and the Day After That

Alice woke back up with a crick in her neck, and an Anthony under her body. She hadn't meant to fall asleep *on top* of him. She tried to roll herself away, but, at the first sign of movement, Anthony tightened his hold, pulling her back to his body.

Alice wouldn't lie. It felt nice. Just as it had felt nice to wake up on the couch with him laying on her. Something about being so close to Anthony was just...nice. He was warm, without being hot. And he was flexible in such a way that he could have all of his limbs around her without either of them being in any pain. Alice closed her eyes and imagined what it would be like if she could wake up like this every day.

"Oh, uh, sorry," Anthony said. Then the limbs surrounding her fell away and Alice rolled onto her back, pulling the covers up over her chest as the memory of the dream came back to her. She could still feel the heat of his... well, of *that*.

"Sleep well?" Alice asked. She looked over at him, then quickly back at the ceiling. The way his hair was messed up, all tossed about, and with his eyes-half closed and face soft; looking at him too long was asking for trouble.

Anthony stretched out beside her, and they should probably both be concerned with how un-concerning waking up in bed together was. "Like a rock," he said. "How about you."

"Good. Had a weird dream." Alice shut her eyes and cursed herself. Why did she say that? He didn't need to know about her wild fantasies!

Not that she had fantasies about him, of course.

"Oh?" Anthony turned on his side, propped up on one elbow and Alice couldn't *not* look at him. "What about?"

Alice gulped and cleared her throat. "Don't remember what. Just that I was a fancy Victorian lady," she admitted. And there was absolutely no reason to go beyond that.

"Ya know what," Anthony said. "Must have been something we ate, 'cause I had a weird dream last night too."

"Did you?" Alice shuffled up and sat against the headboard. Something about being a little more vertical made the situation feel less intense. "Anything good?"

Anthony matched her movement, and they sat comfortably with their arms pressed together. "I fell into this giant piranha tank, right? And I thought they were going to eat me, you know? But then they all turned around and looked at me with these biiiiiig cartoonish-like smiles. And then…"

"Then?"

"They started singing *It's a Small World.*"

Alice laughed, and Anthony smiled. "That is an odd dream," she said.

"Must 'ave been the wine," Anthony suggested.

"Must have," she agreed.

"So, got a long day of writing ahead?"

Alice nodded, but she thought about a day spent just like this instead. A day spent in bed with Anthony. A day filled with naps and cuddles, maybe a few kisses here and there. But that was just a daydream. In reality, she really did need to get back to work.

Anthony nudged her gently in the side. "How about a mean bowl of cereal to get you started?"

She smiled at him. "Sounds perfect."

*

Tony didn't, on the whole, enjoy waking up. Every morning he got out of bed was another morning he had to live with himself. And he wasn't all that great of company. But waking up with Alice in his arms? He couldn't think of a singular moment in his life where he felt more joy.

Then he woke up the next day alone in his bed, and he was back to wishing he could just stay asleep. Well, really, if he was wishing for things, he might as well wish that this thing between him and Alice was more than just a seasonal fling for book research.

He's never wanted more than a fling before. But now, that was all he wanted.

And he wanted it with Alice.

Tony's phone rang and he groaned. Didn't people know not to call him so early on the weekend? He was a working man now. He needed to sleep in on his days off.

"What?" Tony answered. He would have just let it go on ringing, but then he would never get back to sleep.

"Someone's cheery this morning," Sandra teased.

"And getting cheerier by the second. What did you want?"

"I'm coming up for lunch today."

Tony rolled onto his back and rubbed the bridge of his nose. "Funny, I don't have you on my schedule."

"It's important," Sandra said. "Can't wait."

Tony hummed. "Should I be scared?"

"A little." His eyes popped open, sleep officially chased away. "But don't worry. I'll explain when I get there."

"Fine," Tony grumbled. "But you better not say anything about me and Alice."

"But, Tony, I thought there was no thing about you and Alice.

He hung up on her laughter.

*

Alice flitted about in the kitchen, trying to decide what she would make for lunch. Anthony was being very unhelpful, sitting at the counter, hand in his chin, watching her.

"You don't have to make *anything*, Angel," he said.

"She's a guest in our house," Alice informed him. She paused for a second, rehearing Anthony's sentence in her mind, purposefully ignoring the repeat of her own. "Angel?"

"What?" Anthony asked. "Don't like it? I think it's fitting."

Alice gulped and tried to calm the blush in her cheeks. "I didn't say I didn't like it. I just...why?" It wasn't the first time he's called her that, but this time was so out of the blue.

She looked over her shoulder and Anthony shrugged. "I dunno. Why not?"

Alice couldn't think of a good reason. She could think of several, but none of them were enough to actually say out loud. Maybe, all combined, they would make sense. But she felt a little silly even considering sitting down and listing out the long line of reasons he shouldn't be using a pet name for her. So, she returned his shrug instead. "Why not."

Anthony smiled at her, and then someone knocked on the door.

Alice startled and decided that she would have to make something quick and easy, like a few sandwiches, for lunch. Anthony pulled back his sleeve and frowned at his watch. "Someone was breaking the speed limit," he mumbled.

He slumped off his chair and went to go let her in. Sandra was panting, as if she had run all the way over here instead of driving.

"Goodness, is everything alright?" Alice asked as she poured Sandra a glass of water.

"Phone calls all the way up here," Sandra explained. She thanked Alice and sat down at the island, chugging nearly the entire glass. "Everyone is kind of losing it right now."

"Everyone who?" Anthony slipped into the seat next to her. It's been a while since Alice saw the two of them together, and she forgot just how much they really did resemble each other. Not so much in their looks, but their mannerisms.

"Everyone on the board," Sandra clarified. She took a deep breath and downed the rest of her glass. "Nana is freaking them all out."

"She's not sick, is she?" Alice asked, wringing her hands together.

"No, but she may be losing her mind a little."

"Thought she already lost that," Anthony said with a laugh. Sandra kicked him gently. "What's she done this time?"

Sandra opened her mouth then paused, glancing quickly at Alice. She could take a hint.

"How about I go order us something delivered," Alice suggested. "Pizza good for everyone?"

"Pizza's perfect, Angel," Anthony said. And Alice and Sandra both gave him a look, each wildly different. "What?"

Alice cleared the lump in her throat and shook her head. She hoped Sandra would just let it go. After all, they didn't need any more fuel to the dating fire. She left them to their business and went to the computer in the office to order their lunch.

She really didn't want to eavesdrop. It wasn't nice. And she knew better. And she had been told time and time again to *not* do that.

But she couldn't help being a little curious.

After all, they were talking about Nana Jan, and that meant they were probably talking about the company. And being a writer for said company, Alice sort of had a right to know what was going on.

Firsthand Research

She crept to the door and pulled it back just a slight bit, wincing as the small creak ran out. Luckily it seemed like the two didn't hear it, continuing right on with their conversation unaware of the third party listening.

"She can't *do* anything," Anthony said. "I mean...what *is* she going to do?"

"I'm not sure," Sandra replied. "She didn't say. She just told us she was coming up with a plan of action. And now everyone's calling *me* about it."

"You want me to help field some calls for you or something?"

"No, Tony. I want you to be *careful*."

"Of what?"

Sandra sighed with the kind of exasperation only Anthony could give you. "Nate's company is on the list. First one. I wouldn't be surprised if all the rest were just to cover up that this is *personal*."

There was a pause in the conversation and Alice held her breath. What was this list? What was Nana Jan planning to do with Nate's company?

"She wouldn't," Anthony said after a minute. Then there was another, shorter pause. "Oh my god, she *would*."

"Be prepared for anything. I'll try to get more information out of her, but I suspect she knows I'll tell you. I have no idea what she'll do."

"I can't believe she would punish Nate because of me! I mean, isn't going out on my own and getting a job what she wanted from me in the first place!?"

"I don't think that meant going and working for a rival company."

Alice heard Anthony slam his hands on the counters. "What did she expect? Publishing is the only occupation I have any experience in at all!"

They were quiet for another moment, and Alice wished they would talk again, to drown out the never-ending list of thoughts that were racing through her brain. Nate was her friend. She had gotten Anthony that interview. And it was because he got hired that now Nana was going to do something to Nate's company. It was her fault.

"I'm not letting her get away with this," she heard Anthony whisper, just barely audible down the hall.

"There's not much you can do."

"I can fight. Nate can fight! We won't go down easily!"

Sandra sighed again, softer this time. "I don't think it's a fight you can win."

"We can. We will...We *have to*."

Alice swallowed the lump in her throat and clicked the door shut, returning to her desk. She probably shouldn't have listened in to that conversation. For many reasons. But, at the very least, Anthony was going to handle it. He had said so. No matter what Nana Jan threw their way, he would fix it.

Because he wasn't alone.

No, he had Alice. And they would work through all of this *together*.

She nodded, secure in that knowledge, and decided to get a little bit of work done while she was exiled from the kitchen. She was working on a particularly stubborn scene, and she could use a little forced isolation to get herself through it.

But her isolation didn't last long, as only a few minutes later Anthony was knocking on her door, gently pushing it open.

"Everything alright?" Alice asked, trying to look innocent, trying not to give away that she knew everything wasn't.

"It will be," Anthony said, his smile only half-formed on his face. "Sandra actually had to run, apparently the company just can't survive without her. On a Sunday."

"Oh," Alice deflated a little. She hadn't really spoken with Sandra much in quite some time and had been looking forward to catching up. "Well, more pizza for us!"

Anthony chuckled and nodded. He stepped up to the desk, paging through the papers spread about. Alice settled back in her seat and stared at the screen, wondering if she should try to work until lunch, or just give up for the day.

"Huh," Anthony said, in a slightly playful tone. He tsked. "I can't believe Naomi would cheat on such a guy like Malcolm."

"What?" Alice looked at him with a scrunched-up face. He was smirking, and he showed her the page in his hand. She gasped, adrenaline coursing through her body. He had found the pages she had written while they were testing out the vibrator. The pages where his name had slipped into nearly every paragraph the way he had slipped into her life. All she could do is stare at him with wide eyes.

Maybe, if she was really lucky, this was all just a terrible dream.

Anthony chuckled a bit, which did little to ease her mind. "Caught red handed."

Alice gulped, sinking into her chair a bit, like a child being scolded. "I'm sorry," she mumbled, even though she wasn't entirely sure what she was sorry for. It just felt like she ought to be sorry about something.

Anthony's smirk fell, his own face twisting in confusion. "There's nothing to apologize for," he said. He sat the paper back down. "I'm the one who's sorry. I shouldn't be snooping."

"No, it's okay, it's just…" Alice wasn't sure if explaining it would make the situation worse or better. But she figured it couldn't really get that much worse, so she might as well just tell him. "Well, when I was writing, a couple weeks ago, back when we were, uh, when I was testing out the…"

"Yeah." Anthony nodded, saving her from having to actually vocalize what they had done.

"Well, it's just that…Well I wasn't exactly thinking straight, you know and well…" she swallowed hard, unable to formulate the words needed to get across how embarrassed and sorry she was that she had put Anthony in like that. "I'm fixing it in edits."

Anthony, at some point, had stopped looking at her and was studying the piece of paper. "So, you write like this when you're getting off?"

Alice bit her lip and nodded. "I know it's not exactly *good*, but-"

"It's amazing," Anthony interrupted. "I mean, yeah edits for sure but like... wow." He picked it back up, and Alice wished his eyes would stop scanning over it the way they scanned over her sometimes.

"Y-you really think so?"

Anthony nodded. His eyes slowly drifted over to her as his smirk reclaimed its place on his face. "Ya know, I could help with that. If you wanted."

Alice blinked in confusion. "Help with what?"

"I could help," Anthony didn't clarify. "Ya know." He shrugged and looked pointedly at Alice's lap. She brought her legs together, pressing them closed.

"I know?"

Anthony chuckled and his smirk turned to a genuine smile as he placed the paper down once more. "I could get you off while you write."

"I, uhm, well, that is…" Alice looked everywhere in the room but at Anthony. How could she look at him after a proposal like *that*?

"It would certainly help the book," Anthony added.

Alice finally settled her eyes on his. "It *would*," she agreed, the small bit of panic that had been rising in her chest falling back down. "But," she licked her lips, "You're not exactly my assistant anymore."

Anthony huffed and crossed his arms. "I said I would help you with this book, and that's what I'm gonna do. So if it's not done, I'm not done." He patted the pages spread out on the desk. "Now, let's get to work!"

Alice felt a smile creep on her face, but she wasn't sure why. Anthony just...always made her smile. "Very well," she said. She held her hand out and he pulled her to her feet. "To work we shall get!"

Chapter 24
Sex Lesson Ten – Oral (Take Two)

The living room was the best place for it. Tony adjusted himself on the floor, making sure the pillow was properly supporting his head. He didn't need to get a kink in his neck from this. "Alright," he said, "I'm ready." He patted the edge of the coffee table, resting just over his forehead.

Alice fidgeted, standing next to him. She had changed into a skirt as Tony set the space up for them. She tugged at the hem, already resting below her knees. "Are you *sure*?"

Tony sighed but smiled. "I'm positive."

"I... I don't want to hurt you…"

"You won't. I promise."

Alice's eyes did a tour of the room before looking at him. "I could crush you."

"You can't. Physics."

Alice knelt down. Tony was just a few short movements away from the world's finest delicacy. If she would only get a move on…

"You've done this before, right? You're sure it works."

Tony reached over and placed a reassuring hand on her thigh. "I've done this before. It works. And you won't hurt me."

Alice gulped and bothered her bottom lip between her teeth. And all Tony could do was think about getting that lip between his own teeth. Maybe it was time for another kissing lesson.

In the blink of an eye Alice started to move, swinging one leg over until she was straddling Tony's face. She was still kneeling all the way up, the vision of Tony's dreams still too far away, but at least now he could see it. He hummed a pleased note and placed both hands on Alice's thighs, rubbing them gently.

"Is this okay?" Alice asked.

"Gonna need you a bit lower," Tony told her.

He felt her shake a bit, but then she sat back some. The skirt dragged up as she moved, revealing inch by inch the skin of her thighs as the material bunched up in Tony's hands. "Here?"

He could probably crane his neck up to reach, but where was the fun in that? "Biiiit more."

Alice gulped and then lowered herself so that she was sitting nearly on her feet. Her vagina was just a breath away. And what a lovely breath it was.

Tony squeezed the thighs under his hands and gave a tentative lick out. Alice jolted as his tongue met her lips, grazing over the curved edges ever so gently. He chuckled. "I don't hear much work going on up there."

A few seconds later and Alice started typing, her fingers seeming to fly across the keys at a speed he was sure no one else could match. He smiled to himself and pressed a tighter lick to the same path. He couldn't decide if he should be nice and let her write, or if he should make it his personal goal to get her so distracted that she couldn't write.

But he had time to figure that out as they went. For now, he was just going to enjoy his job.

Plump was the best word he could use to describe Alice. All of her. And her vagina was no different. Lovely, thick folds of fat protected her inner labia, and he licked them wet before turning his head to gently suck on them. Alice shuddered, gasping as her fingers stalled for a moment. Then Tony began to mold the fat around between his lips and she began typing again with renewed vigor.

Truth be told, Tony was glad Alice had agreed to this. He hadn't really had the time to enjoy this, all the way back when they made their agreement.

He only had a few minutes then, and he needed to devote that time purely to Alice. But now? Now he had some wiggle room. Now he could let himself enjoy it, feeling a tight pressure around his pants as he licked and sucked. And he hadn't even breached the surface yet.

Tony pulled back, licking his lips, savoring her taste. "How you doing up there?" He soothed his hands over Alice's thighs. They were shaking a little. He wasn't sure if it was from pain of position or pleasure, but he knew that either way they wouldn't be able to keep this up for as long as he wished.

"Good," Alice said, a rushed-out huff of breath as she typed. Tony couldn't wait to see what she was writing up there.

But he would have to wait. He still had work to do.

Tony pulled one hand away, slipping it up under the skirt. He slid his other hand around, resting it on the small of Alice's back, to help support her in this new position.

Alice let out a little moan as Tony's fingers followed the trace his tongue had made. She felt so good to touch, all of her. Soft, warm, mesmerizing. He tested the waters, pulling his fingers apart, pushing back the outer labia, revealing her to him. And she was beautiful.

Tony held her open as he stuck his tongue back out. He prodded gently at her clit, making her legs shake more as she moaned. He kept a similar pressure and rhythm going against it, up and down in soft pulses, each one accentuated by Alice's delicate voice from above.

She really was an angel.

Then he moved lower, keeping the pace and rhythm, pressing to all the sides of her inner labia. Then, one short, shallow press to her entrance.

"Yes," Alice moaned. And Tony did it again. "Yes," she cried. Three more jabs in quick succession. "Yes!" She demanded.

Tony pulled her down a bit, pushing up on his shoulders for a better angle. He wiggled his tongue inside her, pressing the walls open as he rhythmically fucked her. And she moaned in time with each thrust, her fingers powering across the keyboard like there was no tomorrow. And if there was no tomorrow, they would go out with a bang.

Tony let the outer labia close around his lips, using his thumb to reach in and play with Alice's clit instead. He let it match the pulsations of his tongue, but in opposition. For every press of this thumb to her clit he dragged his tongue out, and for every forward burst of his tongue, he moved his thumb away.

Alice cried and shook, her legs trembling as he pleasured her. He could hear it in her voice, feel it in the way her muscles moved. She was close.

Tony backed off, pulling his tongue out and downgrading the rotation of his thumb to a gentle whirl. Because he didn't want this to end. Like this, despite being able to hear the sound of the truth in the form of Alice's keys clicking away, it was easy for him to pretend. Pretend that this was his new reality, that this was simply part of what he did in his everyday life for the woman he loved. It could be part of his husbandly duties.

Wait.

Did he just say *husband*?

"Anthony," Alice moaned, in the most delightful manner. And he startled. Husband or not, this was his duty right now, and he'd better get a move on.

"Sorry, Angel" he muttered, before going back in. This time he swapped his tongue and fingers around. He let one finger ease its way in, careful to make sure there was no resistance. But as soon as he had pressed against the entrance, it was Alice who bucked down, eagerly accepting him.

As he moved that finger inside her, he took to kissing around every inch he could reach. He desperately desired to bite down on the loveliness of those thighs that straddled him, but he couldn't reach properly, so he settled for sucking once more on Alice's outer labia, all the while eyeing up where he truly wished his lips to be.

"Anthony," Alice moaned again. She was closer than close now. Tony stuck his tongue back between the folds of fat and pressed it against her clit.

She squeaked and her legs closed, nearly squishing his head between them as she rocked back and forth, taking all the pleasure from his finger and tongue that she deserved.

And as Alice moaned Anthony's name, pressing so wonderfully all around him, he came too. He hadn't even noticed the build of his own pleasure, his dick rubbing against his pants as he worked. It surprised him, that sudden release, that rush of endorphins and tingling over his body. He sighed out against Alice, making her shake even more.

Tony knew Alice needed to rest. She couldn't sit like that much longer, especially not after that. So, he slid down, pulling himself free and rubbing at the ache coming untouched had caused. He knelt up behind Alice and grabbed her arms. "Here," he said as he pulled back gently. "You should sit."

Alice nodded and weakly managed to get her legs out from under her, sitting with them under the coffee table as she leaned back against Tony. "Thank you."

Tony smiled to himself. A job well done.

Three knocks sounded against the door, and they both froze.

"Who is that?" Alice whispered.

Tony gulped, feeling his mouth going dry despite how wet it was. "Maybe Sandra came back for some reason?"

The knocks pounded again.

"I'll go check," Tony volunteered.

"No wait," Alice hissed. She grabbed his arm and held him to her. "What if it's Liam? Or Nana? Look at the state we're in!"

"We can't just not answer."

"Why not?"

Tony opened his mouth to respond, but she had a point. They could just be not home. So, they sat together, staring at the door, waiting.

Then Alice's phone rang.

"Well now, who is that?" She picked it up and stared at it, the number unknown. She shrugged and answered, "Hello?...Oh! Oh yes! I'm so sorry, we'll be right there." She hung up and leaned further into Tony's embrace, laughing.

"What?" Tony asked, finding it hard not to laugh with her.

She leaned her head back, face flushed, smile beautiful. "Lunch is here."

Chapter 25
Plans Led Astray

Tony's cheek still burned. He had driven all the way to work with his windows down, trying to will the cold air to remove the soft tingling sensation on his skin. But all it did was mess up his hair and chill his bones. When he sat down at his desk, his cheek still burned from where Alice had kissed him.

Tony raised a hand up to touch gently at that sacred spot. Alice had been weird all morning. She had kept giving him looks as he was getting ready. And she kept trying to insist that he let her make a lunch for him, an act he had refused her since that first day. Then she had trailed after him to the door, playing with the hem of her shirt as if she had something to say. But she didn't say anything. She just leaned up and placed a kiss right on his cheek.

Then she had blushed, said, "I'm sorry, I don't know why," and escaped to her office to hide.

Tony didn't know why either. And he spent his morning with his work ignored as he tried to figure it out.

*

"You're very lucky," Alice mumbled to the piece of paper sitting on her desk.

She thought writing long-hand might un-stick the last few pages she had left to write. So far, it wasn't working.

"You've already got him," she continued, staring at the one word written down: Naomi. "He's already married you! You know he's into you and you're just self-conscious." Alice frowned and slumped down in her seat.

Naomi *was* lucky. She didn't have to sit around and wonder if Malcolm liked her. Of course he did. He wouldn't have married her if he didn't, right? She didn't have to worry about kissing him on the cheek. She was allowed to do that. Alice, on the other hand, wasn't.

What had she been thinking?

Well, she had been thinking that she knew Anthony was going to be having troubles at work, and that he would shoulder it all with strength and bravery, all to save Nate's company. Her friend's company. And Alice wanted to show him how much she appreciated that.

But what possessed her to think Anthony would appreciate a kiss on the cheek, she didn't know.

Alice sighed and spun around in her chair. She held her phone in her hand. She really needed to get this book finished. The first draft deadline was swiftly approaching. And Alice had never had to ask for an extension before.

But then Anthony walked into her life. Smacked into it, rather. And her obsessive thoughts and worries about him were concerning and distracting. Sure, his knowledge and... practice help had certainly improved her writing and pace, but now everything was dragging, and Alice needed to get a grip!

Then her phone rang.

"Are you reading my mind?" She asked Katie, who she had been planning to call.

Katie chuckled. "I haven't heard from you in a while. I just wanted to check in and make sure you're okay."

Alice fiddled with the arm of the chair as her feet rocked it side to side. "I'm okay."

"No brother-related murders, I hope?"

Alice let herself chuckle. "Not yet." She licked her lips and waited for the silence to settle.

"Well," Katie said. "Glad to hear everything is okay."

Alice groaned. She was really going to make her start it all, wasn't she?

"Or is it?" Katie asked. She was.

Alice sighed. For some reason she felt like she was going to cry, like pressure was building up and only turning the valve in her eyes could release it.

"I don't want it to end," she admitted, making her voice as small as she felt.

"What?"

"This." Alice gestured to the room, not that Katie could see it. So she tried her best to clarify. "This house. This book. This *thing*."

"With Anthony?" Katie asked. Alice pouted. "Well, perhaps it doesn't have to end. The thing, I mean. The book probably needs to get finished up."

"But once the book ends the Anthony thing ends." Alice whined a little. "Why can't I just write it forever?"

"You'd run out of money?" Katie offered.

Alice spun back around in her chair and scowled at the offending blank pages before her.

"You should tell him how you feel," Katie said, slowly, like she was approaching a wild animal. And Alice figured her love life was quite skittish enough to warrant it.

"I can't," she said. For all the reasons she couldn't explain.

"He won't laugh at you," Katie said. "And I really don't anticipate him turning you down."

"He'll stop being my friend." Alice bit her lip, but her tears escaped anyway. She didn't want to lose Anthony, in any way. She liked him, romance or not. But if she told him that she would prefer romance between them, he would run off and leave her without a friend, and Alice couldn't stand for that to happen again. No, no. It was much better to hide her true feelings and just be happy as his friend, wondering for the rest of her life what it would be like to be more than that.

Alice didn't realize she had been vocalizing that out loud, and she gasped, throwing a hand over her mouth. She screwed her eyes shut and cursed herself. She should just hang up now before she gets her entire leg in her mouth.

"Oh, Alice," Katie started. Then she seemed to think better of it and swallowed back whatever comment she had. "Anthony Dawson may be a lot of things, but an abandoner of friends he is not."

"But, I mean, you know, we weren't really *friends* before. Friendly, yes, but…" Alice groaned and rubbed at her eyes that wouldn't stop leaking. "Once I leave here, we'll go back to that. And I can't stand it."

"I don't think that's true. He's got a new job now, and a new life perspective, it seems. I have a feeling you're going to be stuck with him for quite some time, however daunting that may be."

Alice didn't think that thought was very daunting at all. She quite liked that thought, matter of fact. She wanted Anthony around her, and she wanted him there for as long a time as she could get. Which is exactly why she very much could not tell him how she felt.

"You're probably right," Alice said. She sniffed away her tears and cleared off her face. "Thanks for the pep talk."

Katie chuckled. "I know you don't believe me, sis. But have some faith and hold out. You'll see."

Alice nodded weakly and hung up. She would see. She'd see the same old outcome, so she would simply avoid it as much as possible.

She straightened up and grabbed her pen.

Naomi had Malcolm.

Lucky indeed.

*

Sometime around lunch, Tony's skin had settled down. He had then managed to get some work done, which was good, considering that they had a presentation due next week. The fruits of Tony's labor were starting to bloom. And better than all of that, Nate hadn't mentioned anything about Nana Jan waging war on them.

So Tony stepped out of the office that night, a smile on his face, ready to head back home and have dinner with Alice. Maybe, if he was feeling up to it, he could coax an answer from her about that kiss that morning.

"Good evening, Anthony."

The voice struck a chill down Tony's spine, pulling an involuntary shiver from his body. He turned around slowly, pinching his own hand, hoping it was a dream. Or, more accurately, a nightmare.

But no. Nana Jan was standing right before him, hands folded overtop the handle of her umbrella, using it to support herself. Tony gulped.

"Nana! Er, hi!"

"Walk with me," she said. And she left him no choice. She turned on her heel and strode in the direction opposite of Tony's car.

Tony shivered again and trailed after her.

"Got a job," he said, hunching over himself. He shoved his hands in his pockets.

"So I've heard," Nana said.

And then they didn't speak again until she led him into a tea shop, where a table had already been procured, hot tea waiting for them.

Tony sat down across from her and fiddled with the silverware on the table. He bit his lip and squinted at her. He didn't live off her money anymore. He didn't work for her company. What was he so scared of? He straightened up. "I know what you're planning." Maybe not the specifics, but still. "And I'm going to stop you!"

"You're not going to do anything," Nana said, stirring the cup before her.

Tony scoffed. He crossed his arms and leaned back in his chair. "And you're not going to get away with this ridiculous take over scheme. I'll make sure of it."

"Such a shame." Nana tapped the spoon against the cup, an irritating ringing sound that Tony knew all too well. She took a small sip and nodded. "Alice had such wonderful potential."

Tony's face fell, his body slumping into his seat. Maybe he did still have something to be afraid of. "What is that supposed to mean?"

Nana let out a small smirk, seems to run in the family. "Oh, well, imagine what the papers would *say*. An esteemed romance writer, caught up in such a mess. A runaway love affair with the grandson of her… ex… publisher?"

Tony's jaw dropped, then clenched tight. "You wouldn't dare!"

Nana chuckled softly. "You have a choice, Anthony. Either convince Nate this is a battle he cannot win, or watch as Alice's career is destroyed."

Tony let out a scoff, if only to hide the panicked gasp. "Wh-why would I even care?"

Nana's smile only grew. "Oh, Anthony. There's no use trying to hide it. I know you've been staying at the cabin. And I know there was nothing innocent about that breakfast the two of you had."

Tony felt his blood boiling, and he knew his face was turning a deep red that matched his anger. "I can't believe you would be so cruel. No, actually, I can believe it. You *would* ruin Alice's life just so you can be the 'best' publishing house in the world."

"Oh, no." Nana set her cup down, turning it ever so slightly so it aligned properly with the rest of the dishes on the table. "*You're* going to ruin Alice's life, *unless* I remain the best publishing house in the world."

Tony's jaw began to shake, and tears threatened his stinging eyes. It was all his fault. He should have known. He ruined everything he touched, and how much had he touched Alice? Too much. He had ruined her life just as he had ruined his own. And the only way to save it was to betray his friend and throw away the only thing in his life he was ever actually proud of.

Nana pushed her chair back. "You won't be without your own reward," she added. "You've proven yourself more than capable, and there will be a position for you at the company. You can have your old life back."

But he didn't want his old life back. He wanted this new life. This new life he should have known would never last. He should have never let himself have it in the first place.

Nana got to her feet and patted him on the shoulder as she left. "Something to think about."

*

Tony slumped home, feet dragging him up to the door of the house. At least he had the night. He could think and plan so that when Nana presented the offer to Nate he could, possibly, have some kind of secret option C that solved all his problems.

"I really don't think you have anything to worry about," Alice said as Tony entered. Nate was sitting at the kitchen island, and Tony's body froze in the doorway. "This just means you're doing good, doesn't it?"

"Too good," Nate responded with a halfhearted chuckle.

Alice caught a glimpse of Tony and smiled. "Anthony! I was worried about you!"

Nate turned in his seat, frowning. A thick stack of paper sat on the counter before him.

"Sorry," Tony said. He moved towards them without really thinking about it. "Uh, ran into someone, got to talking, you know how it is." He fell into the seat next to Nate, eyes glued to the papers.

"Are you alright?" Alice asked. She started to reach out for his hand, then stopped, pulling back to twiddle her fingers together.

"Yeah." Tony tried to gulp, but his mouth was too dry. "What, uh, what's that?"

Nate slid the stack over to him. "A headache."

Tony didn't need to read it to know what it was, but he pretended.

"Nana Jan is trying to buy out Nate's company," Alice explained. "And if he doesn't, well, it doesn't exactly *say* it, but…"

Tony knew the but, and he knew exactly how it would all be worded within that stack.

"Nate came to ask for my opinion," Alice said. "But I think perhaps you can be more help to him. Right?" And she was looking at him with upturned eyes and raised eyebrows. Hopeful. She had hope in him. Badly misplaced hope.

"You had this all day?" Tony asked, pointedly ignoring the look on Alice's face. He didn't want to see what it would become. "Why didn't you say anything?"

"I didn't want to worry anyone," Nate said. He gave Alice a look. "Not until a decision was made, anyway."

"But Anthony knows how Nana Jan works," Alice said, returning his look. "And surely he can come up with some plan of attack. Right?"

Nate sighed. "Well, since the cat's out of the bag, what do you think?"

Tony gulped and leafed through the papers again. He couldn't stand to look at either of them, his two friends. Not while he betrayed them as such. "I think you'll never get a deal as good as this," he whispered. "And... She does have a lot of... ammunition…" Tony closed his eyes and groaned. He couldn't believe what he was saying, what he was doing. But he couldn't let Alice's life get ruined, no matter if it ruined his own. And Nate's. "You'd be a fool to turn it down."

"You...you really think that?" Alice asked. And Tony could hear the hurt in her voice. He kept his head down and nodded.

"It's just as well," Nate said, taking a deep breath. "Who doesn't want to retire so young, hm?"

"Nate, no." Tony glanced up, watching Alice grab his arm. "Look, just, don't make any rash decisions, okay? I'm sure you can fight this, and win! You have me, and Anthony! We won't let her do this to you."

They both looked at Tony, who winced and looked away.

"Have you, anyway," Nate said with a soft chuckle.

"Just, think about it for a few days, okay? Promise? Promise you won't do anything, at least not without me."

"I promise." Nate grabbed the stack and stood up. "Thanks for the help." Then he left, and all Tony could feel was a cold, sickly weight in his stomach.

"Anthony?" Alice asked. She placed hand on his arm, and he pulled it away. He didn't deserve her kindness. "What happened? Are you okay?"

"I have to, uh, go work on something." Tony slid out of his seat and slumped down to his room. He didn't even deserve that room, but he certainly had no energy to go find somewhere else to sleep.

So, he would leave in the morning.

Chapter 26
Sex Lesson Eleven – Positions

Alice had been up pretty late thinking. Thinking about Anthony and Nate and Nana Jan. Something had to have happened to Anthony between the time Sandra was over and the time Nate was. He wouldn't just change his mind over this whole affair like that.

Something, or perhaps someone, had gotten to him. But he had certainly seemed in no condition to talk last night. So Alice worried away the night and fell asleep on the couch, having gotten no work done.

And then the door was opening, and she shot up, adrenaline forcing her awake.

Anthony stood by the door, wincing. He had a bag slumped over his shoulder, and the sun was much too high in the sky.

"Where are you going?" Alice asked. She rubbed at her arms, a little chilly from her slumber.

"Uh, work?" Anthony said.

Alice squinted at him. "Work? Bit late, isn't it?"

"Slept through my alarm," Anthony said. He stood by the door, not looking at her.

"Why do you have all your stuff, then?" Alice sat up fully, blinking away any last remnants of sleep. She would need her full mental capacities this morning, it seemed.

Anthony sighed and dropped his bag to the floor. "Knew I should have gone out the window."

"You're not just leaving."

Anthony spun around. "I can't stay, Alice. I'm sorry."

He looked miserable. Not only like he hadn't slept, but also like he had seen a ghost. Or was a ghost. Or would be one soon. His eyes were highlighted by dark circles, and his skin was sunken and wrinkled.

Alice patted the seat next to her on the couch, but he didn't move. She frowned, hugging her arms over her chest. Of course. Anthony wouldn't want to sit next to her.

Anthony scooped down and picked his bag back up. "Good luck with the book," he said. "It'll do great, I know."

Alice watched as he turned, placing the key to his car on the table by the door. He couldn't walk to town; it was much too cold. Besides, the book wasn't done. He couldn't leave until it was. And Alice didn't want him to leave.

"But I need help!" she said, Anthony half-way out the door. He looked back at her. "With the book." She gestured to the paper mess around her.

She could see the conflict clear on Anthony's face. He wanted to leave, because he had failed Nate, but he wanted to stay so he wouldn't fail her.

"I can't finish it without you," Alice continued.

Anthony's face twitched into a sort of half-smirk. He took a step back inside. "Ah, c'mon. Don't sell yourself so short.

"It's true!" Alice assured him. She stood up, since he wouldn't sit down with her. "Without your expertise, the ending will fall flat. It'll deflate and be miserable. Surely you don't want that to happen, do you?"

Anthony twitched out another little smirk that Alice might have called cute, under different circumstances.

"Certainly can't have that," he said. He stepped fully into the house and Alice let out a sigh of relief. She felt like she could finally breathe. "My job here is yet to be done."

"Exactly." Alice smiled and walked up to him. She took his bag from him with little resistance. "Now, you start looking over these pages for me, and I'll go put your stuff away."

Anthony nodded and Alice smiled at him again before rushing off to return his belongings to his room. Honestly, what was he thinking? Just running away like that. Something had happened and he was going to run instead of deal with it.

Alice scoffed. And Katie thought he wouldn't run away from her if he knew her true feelings.

Anthony was settled on the couch, a handful of pages on his lap, lips pursed slightly as he studied them. He shifted, lifting one leg up with a furrowed brow. He tried to move it to the side, but it didn't quite go that way.

"Yeah, I don't, I don't think legs bend that way," he told her.

Alice gingerly sat down next to him, waiting to see if he would move away. She watched him maneuver his leg about. "Hm, you're right." She sighed. "But then, hrm, how could I…?" She lifted her own leg, trying to work out the puzzle herself.

"Here, like this?" Anthony turned on his side and hitched his leg over Alice's.

"Huh, that could work," Alice said. And she liked the weight of his leg on hers. And she wanted more of his weight on her, more of his warmth. "Do you suppose, I mean, would it be alright if we…figured out some more, er, positions?"

Anthony smiled, and Alice was so glad to see him looking better, much more like himself. "It's why I'm here."

"Here, look at this one." Alice leaned forward and grabbed another scene, making sure to keep Anthony's leg where it was. She handed the pages to him and toyed with the idea of putting her hands on his thigh. Surely that would be inappropriate.

"Hm, I mean, it technically works. But it might get a bit uncomfortable after a while. Here." Anthony turned to face her, moving his leg back. Alice was suddenly very cold. "Can I show you a better way?"

Alice nodded, perhaps a bit too eagerly. "Please!"

"Lie back," Anthony instructed, and Alice did just that. "So, legs up like this." And he grabbed her calves, raising them up as he knelt down between her legs. "See, legs hooked under the arms works, but around the waist is much more suited for long-term." Anthony guided Alice's legs back until they were wrapped around his waist, ankles crossed over each other. "Plus, it gets a deeper angle."

"Deeper angle," Alice repeated. She looked at the awkward curve of Anthony's back as he held himself up to look down at her. "That can't possibly be more comfortable for you."

"Well, it is when done properly." Anthony lowered himself, placing his hands on the couch cushions beside Alice. And as he did, his hips pushed forward, rubbing their groins together and lifting Alice's own off the couch a bit.

And it felt *good*. So good that Alice had to bite the inside of her cheek to hold back the moan that nearly squeaked out.

"See?" Anthony said. His face was right before hers now, breath hot on her skin.

Alice couldn't really see, not with how her vision was going blurry at the closeness of Anthony, her heart racing a mile a minute so close to his own chest she was sure he could feel it. But she could certainly feel.

And, apparently, Anthony could feel it too, as his breath hitched right before his hips jerked, pushing the two of them closer together.

"Ah," he said. "Sorry. Must just be reflex." He laughed and tried to pull away. Only Alice's legs wouldn't let him go. *She* wouldn't let him go.

Anthony pushed back up a little, looking down at Alice with a half-raised eyebrow.

"Uhm," Alice tried to think of something, but no words came to her, and she still wasn't moving her legs. "I just, I figured while we were here, we could, uh, make sure it's, er...adequate! For long term...usage."

Anthony blinked at her for a second then melted into a smile. "You're right. We gotta make sure it's right. For the book."

"Of course." Good to see that they were on the same page.

Anthony lowered himself down again, turning his head so he could rest it against Alice's shoulder. And then he was moving again, in that sinfully delicious way, pressing them together, rocking into Alice. And Alice didn't even try to stop the moans that elicited.

It shouldn't feel as good as it did. After all, they were wearing all their clothes, and nothing was pressing against where it really counted. But oh, how it still sent tingles of electric joy up and down Alice's spine, pooled hot desire in her stomach.

She had no idea how much time was passing, just that it was passing too quickly, and that she was running out of time, and that if she didn't do something soon it would all be over.

So, with every push from Anthony, Alice's legs clenched tighter, squeezing him closer, urging him to move faster, harder, more, more, more. Urging him to never leave that spot.

"Alice, fuck," Anthony whispered. And then she felt something hot and wet spread between them. And then she was moaning, adding her own mess to that spot.

They lay there together, breathing hot and heavy on each other's necks as the stick between them grew cold.

"Long term," Alice said, "Check."

Anthony laughed and moved to pull away. But still Alice's legs held him, even as her muscles grew weak and tired. Anthony just looked at her with that half-raised eyebrow.

Firsthand Research

She knew they needed to clean up and should probably not still be attached now that the 'research' was over. But she needed to be certain that, once she let go, Anthony would not try to run off on her again.

"Not until 'the end'," she told him.

Anthony smiled softly. "Not a page before."

Chapter 27
Third-wheelin'

"Alright," Tony said. "Spill it."

Alice jumped and looked over at him, eyes wide and innocent as if she hadn't been glancing at him every five seconds, opening her mouth and then closing it again. "Hm?"

"I know you want to tell me something, so just say it."

They sat comfortably on the couch, arms nearly touching. Every now and then Alice would reach for a page, and they would touch. Tony thought about shifting to the side a bit, but he was enjoying the mold the couch had made of him, and he leaned his head against the back.

"Well, it's actually something I'd like *you* to tell *me*," Alice said. She put her red pen down and fidgeted her thumbs together.

"Ask away."

Alice stared at her hands for a few seconds then took a deep breath. She straightened her spine and stilled her hands. Not looking at him she said, "I'd like to know what happened to change your mind."

"Change my mind?" Tony rolled his head to the side, staring at her. "About leaving?" He chuckled. "I didn't think I was that forgettable."

"No, not *that*." Alice shook her head and glanced over at him. "About Nana Jan."

"Huh?"

Alice sighed and turned to the side to face him, pouting a bit. "I, er, well I know it wasn't very proper of me but I well, uh, I happened to... overhear your conversation with Sandra on Sunday."

"So, you eavesdropped?"

Alice ignored him. "You were all ready to fight and win Sunday, and then last night you just, well, you gave up. And I... I'm sure something must have happened. So please tell me."

Tony stared at her big, beautiful eyes. Normally he couldn't say no to her. But for as powerful as her charm was, Nana's intimidation was twice as strong. He shook his head.

Alice reached over and grabbed Tony's hand. "Tell me what happened?" she urged." Please?"

Tony smiled at her with all the softness he could muster. "I want to, but I can't."

She pouted. "Well, why not?"

Tony tilted his head, eyes unable to stop from wandering over every feature of her delicate face. "Because you'd do something stupid."

"What if I promised *not* to do anything stupid?"

Tony smirked and gave her hand a squeeze. "I know you. You'd do something stupid."

His eyes finally found purchase on hers, lost in the soft green of the morning light reflecting in them. "I know you, too," she whispered. "And I don't want you dealing with this all alone."

Tony took a deep breath and straightened himself, staring out at the window. A portion of the shade was bunched up, revealing just a sliver of the bright world outside. But however bright that world may be, it was easily overshadowed by the thoughts running around in Tony's head. And maybe Alice was right, maybe it would be easier to just talk about it, at least.

"You have to promise me you won't do anything stupid," he said.

Alice sat up a bit, much too excited for the news she was about to receive. "I promise. Only smart choices from here on out." She patted his hand and waited.

Tony closed his eyes and smiled. He had to buy himself a few courage raising minutes. "Nana stopped by yesterday," he admitted. Already a weight felt lifted off his chest. Breath came a little easier and he found talking wasn't as hard as before. "She made some very large threats."

Alice's face puffed up a bit and she slapped her hands on her knees. "I knew it! I knew she must have said something to you." She hoped to her feet and started pacing a bit, back and forth before Tony's feet. Well, I can assure you, no matter what she threatened, it's nothing we can't deal with."

Tony took a deep breath. "She threatened to cut you lose," he said. "And not just that but drag your name through so much mud that you'll never work in this town again!" Tony flared his arm out in an attempt at humor, but his voice fell a little too flat for it.

Alice frowned at him. "Why would she threaten me?"

Tony shrugged. "Because you're Nate's friend. I guess she figured he'd cave knowing you were on the line."

"She is not getting away with this. She can't lose me if I lose her first!" Alice slammed a fist in her open palm, determination clear in every movement.

"And that's the stupid thing I thought you were going to do." Tony rocked himself to his feet, probably standing a little too close to Alice, but who's counting? "Alice, we can't let her do that to you."

"Well, I'm certainly not going to let it happen to you!"

"You have to," Tony whispered. He reached out, gently touching Alice's arms. "I know you want to help your friends, and that's what makes you so wonderful. But this time, Alice, you gotta let us take the fall."

Alice huffed. "Why?"

"Because Nate and I... our lives, our work, they're nothing compared to you." Alice opened her mouth to argue, but he cut her off. "You can't deny it. I've seen firsthand the effects your books have had on the world, Alice.

The people who have gotten the strength and courage to go after what they want, to love who they love. I mean, remember when Blue and Black came out?" Alice nodded, sitting down, eyes wide. "Do you even know how many people left their abusive partners *because* they read that book?" Alice shook her head. "Dozens. Hundreds, even. Alice," he knelt before her, urging her to believe the truth of his words, "what you do, what you write, it inspires people. And nothing Nate or I will ever do will even come close to that. It's not right to take you away from the world."

Alice's face fell, her hands folding together in her lap. "I... I didn't know all that."

"I know." Tony sat down next to her. "You focus on the next book, on getting more of your stories out there. And trust me, that's good. But your impact is so much larger than you realize. And you have to let this happen."

Alice looked at him, eyes watery and more of a blue shade now. "But I don't want it to happen."

Tony nodded, because he didn't want it to happen either. "There's no other choice." He reached up, gently wiping away a tear that dared to fall on Alice's cheek.

Alice's jaw quivered but she nodded, closing her eyes to the tears that would follow after the first. "We have to tell Nate," she croaked out. She sniffed and cleared her throat. "He has a right to know why this is happening."

Tony agreed with her, but that didn't make the prospect of telling Nate any easier. At least he knew Nate would be on board with the decision. Neither of them want Alice out of the business or hurt in any way. "I'll tell him."

"We will," Alice insisted. She grabbed his hand, and hers was cold. Tony figured his wasn't much warmer.

They stared into each other's eyes; a pain shared between them. And for as much as Tony hated to see Alice hurt, she had been right. He did feel a bit better having talked about it. He didn't have to face this alone... Maybe he didn't have to face anything alone…

"Alice–"

His phone rang, the confession caught at the back of his throat. He groaned as Alice's hand slipped away from him. "It's Nate," he announced.

Alice sniffed and wiped her face clean. "Put him on speaker."

"Tony here," he answered, setting the phone on the table before them.

"You don't sound sick," Nate said.

"Uh, I'm...not?"

Nate chuckled. "Then you better have a good reason for skipping work today."

"Uhhhhh," Tony looked to Alice. "I didn't think I still had it?"

"I'm not going to fire you for telling the truth, idiot. And the truth is, I'm going to need you to make sure everything goes well next week."

"*Next week*!?" Alice said.

"Oh, hey Alice. Yeah, next week."

"That's so soon." Alice grabbed Tony's hand again, warmed by the fire of the fight.

"Yeah, well, sharks swim fast," Nate said with a half-hearted chuckle. "Anyway, I expect your hooligan of a roommate to be in tomorrow to go over things."

"He'll be there," Alice assured him. "I promise. And Nate…"

"Yes?"

Alice took a deep breath and glanced at Tony, who nodded. "I'm sorry."

Nate chuckled. "You can't help that Tony's a coward."

"Hey!"

"It's my fault," Alice blurted out. She gulped. "It's my fault Nana Jan is doing this."

Nate was quiet for a moment and Alice was close to drawing blood with how hard she dug her nails into her skin. Tony couldn't stand to see her this way. After all, this *wasn't* her fault. She was just a part of the equation. An equation that would never have needed solving if he hadn't been involved.

"She's lying," Tony said, cutting off whatever Nate had started to say. "It's not her fault, it's mine."

"But I'm the one she threatened!" Alice argued.

"She threatened you?" Nate asked.

"She wouldn't have had to threaten you if I wasn't living here," Tony argued back.

"Wait, when did she threaten you?" Nate asked.

"Well, where else are you supposed to go? You're saying it's my fault for being nice and accommodating you?"

"Guys! Hey!"

"I'm saying it's not your fault at all!"

"Hello?"

"It has to be someone's fault!"

"And it's mine!"

A loud, low-pitched whistle put a stop to their arguing. They both looked to the phone, and Tony felt a bit of shame rising to his cheeks.

"You're both idiots, you know that right?" Nate said. They looked at each other and nodded. "This is business," he continued. "It's no one's *fault*. If it wasn't Nana Jan, it would have been someone else. If it wasn't my company, it would have been another. The world, believe it or not, does not revolve around the two of you. So shut-up and tell me when she threatened you."

Alice cleared her throat and leaned towards the phone a bit. "Do you want us to shut up or tell you?"

Nate let out a groan and Tony couldn't help but smile a bit. That was the Alice he knew and loved.

"It was just business," Tony told him. "Nana Jan said she'd stop doing business with Alice if we didn't stop doing business with everyone else."

"Can she actually do that?" Nate asked.

"I'm afraid she can," Alice said. "And Anthony won't let me take her up on it!"

"You shouldn't," Nate said, before Tony could. "Alice you'd be ridiculous to leave there, especially in bad blood."

Alice huffed and crossed her arms. It was a real shame that Nate couldn't see the look on her face. "I don't know why you're both under the assumption that I wouldn't do well without her! My books are good, aren't they? Wouldn't they be just as good anywhere else?"

"Your books are amazing," Tony told her. "But there's more to it at play than just good writing."

Alice squinted at him, because she didn't understand the inner workings of publishing the way the two of them did.

"Tony's right," Nate said, and Tony smiled. "For once." He scowled. "There's a lot Nana Jan could do to you, and a lot she does for you. You leaving is not an option."

"You two are infuriating," Alice mumbled.

"Listen, don't worry about it, okay? I'll make sure Tony gets me a billion dollars, and I'll go buy my own island or something. It's okay, really. I promise."

"She could pay that," Tony said. And he did know all the right buttons to push.

Alice frowned and deflated against the couch. She had such a perfect pout on her face that, given any other situation, Tony would call it cute. But it was a pout of true upset, and all it did was add to the weight of guilt in his stomach.

"I'll look over the papers again today," Tony told Nate, picking the phone back up. "I'll have lots of good fuck-with-Nana ideas tomorrow."

Nate laughed. "I'm sure you will. And I look forward to hearing all of them."

Tony hung up and shoved the phone back in his pocket. He settled down on the couch and stared at Alice, who was just pouting down at her lap with her arms crossed. He reached his elbow over and nudged her gently. "Hey."

Alice didn't respond, which was concerning on a multitude of levels.

Tony frowned and leaned forward to grab a stack of pages. It was the second to last scene, freshly written last night. One more to go and she'd be done. Tony scanned over the page with a frown.

"Alice, you realize like, half of this is missing right?" he asked. Alice looked over at the pages. "Unless you decided last minute to make this more of a fade-to-black kind of book."

"Nothing sounded right," Alice said. But she didn't sound like herself. "And I don't think it ever will until I... do it."

"Right."

Alice shifted to the side and Tony winced at the question he knew was coming. Rather, he winced at the answer he knew he'd have to give.

"I don't suppose... well, you are quite experienced... and I do have, er, protection..." Alice started, but never seemed to finish.

Tony sighed and tore his attention away from the paper. He might have changed his answer if Alice didn't look like a deer who had just watched another deer get run over and was now caught in the headlights herself. If she had had the hopeful, pleading look, with the upturned eyebrows and the biting of lips, Tony wouldn't have been able to turn her down.

"I don't think we should," he whispered, but it sounded so much louder in his head.

"Oh." Alice's shoulders dropped and she sighed. She lowered her gaze to the couch between them, a space that had not been there before.

"I'm not saying your first time has to be magical and special and perfect," Tony continued. He wanted to reach out and cup her face, but something told him that time had passed. "But at the very least it shouldn't be for book research."

Alice kept her head down but looked up at him. "You're probably right." She sighed and sat back against the cushions. "I suppose I'll just have to come up with something that sounds vaguely reasonable."

"Here's a wild idea," Tony said. "What if you were the one doing the fucking? Would that be enough practical knowledge to write it? Ya know? Like, get the opposite perspective at least."

Alice huffed a soft laugh, which was less than he was hoping for, but still good.

"I know you're an expert at sex, Anthony. But I fear you may have missed a biology class or two. I'm not exactly... equipped for that."

Tony shrugged. "They make strap-ons."

Alice gave him a look. "I have enough trouble finding a guy that would want to have sex with me. And you want me to start looking into girls that would let me... do *that*."

"Doesn't have to be a girl," Tony mumbled, though the image was trying to make a claim on his brain. "Could be a guy."

"Right. I can't find a guy to fuck me, but I'm sure there are just dozens lining up to let me fuck them."

Tony's brain stalled for a second as he processed Alice's use of the word fuck. And the restart must have knocked something loose in his brain because before he could stop himself, he was saying, "I'd let you fuck me."

Alice was quiet for a moment and Tony just stared at the pages on his lap. There was no way he could possibly look at her. He could only imagine the look on her face.

"Really?" Alice asked. Which was not the response he had been expecting.

He risked a glance up, but Alice only looked confused. She wasn't offended or horrified or scandalized like she looked at all his other propositions before eventually giving in. She looked, dare he say, intrigued.

Tony figured, fuck it. After a week he'll probably never see her again. Might as well go out with a bang. "Yeah. I mean, it's not like I haven't done it before." He smirked at her. "Not like I won't do it again."

Alice's lips parted slightly, and he longed to lunge forward and capture them up in his own. "I... I... you would do that? For... me?"

Tony's eyebrows furrowed a little. The words *for the book* crept up in the back of his throat, but he never said them. "Yeah, Alice," he said instead. "For you."

Alice's bottom lip quivered a bit and they looked into each other's eyes. Alice gulped. "Well, only if you're sure."

Tony swore the rest of the world melted away until there was only Alice in his vision. "Positive," he said. "Until 'The End', right?"

Alice blinked, and the world came flooding back as she looked away. "Yes. Until 'The End'."

*

She hadn't expected him to *show up*. When Alice had called and left a message to her editor, she expected a phone call back, not a man in a finely pressed suit knocking on her door.

"Quinton," she said, a slight waiver to her voice. Something about him always seemed to put her on edge. She wasn't sure if it was the thin cut of his suit that radiated *professionalism* or the way his smile always seemed to have an unusual number of teeth showing, but something just always made her nerves flare up when he was around. "What are you doing here?"

"You called me," he said, stepping into the room. "And when my number one client calls, I come running."

Alice chuckled nervously and glanced down the hall to where Anthony was in the bathroom. She was pretty sure everyone knew by now, but if she could stop the truth from snowballing, it would be helpful.

"Well, uhm, please do come in." Alice stepped to the side and held the door as he walked in. "Can I get you something to drink?"

"Nothing for me, thank you. But what I would like to know," he pointed at her, "is what's got you in my mailbox sounding like a frightened little kitten."

Alice frowned at him. "I did not sound like a frightened kitten," she argued. But she had winced when she left that voice mail. It didn't exactly scream confidence.

"Something is off," Quinton said. "And I'm here to help."

Alice glanced back down the hall and caught the sight of Anthony scurrying into his room. He must have heard them talking. Alice gingerly sat down at the kitchen island and gestured to the seat next to her. "I was hoping I could just pick your brain about the whole publishing work industry stuff."

"You're not thinking of changing jobs, are you?" Quinton sat in the chair, opening his blazer with a practiced flourish. "Usually, it goes the other way."

Alice chuckled. "No, I'm not. I just had a few questions about some things I wanted to ask. Nothing that important."

Quinton settled down in his seat with his hands folded before him. "Ask away."

"Well, uhm," Alice shifted uncomfortably in her own seat. "Do you know anything about what's happening with Nate's company, and the others?"

"Nothing specific. Just that a lot of changes and buyouts are going on. Lots of new clients and all that. Don't worry," he flashed her that too-toothy smile. "You'll still always be the top of my list."

Alice smiled back at him because it felt wrong otherwise. "I appreciate that. I don't suppose you know of any particular reason she started all of this?" Alice was hoping she could pinpoint the reason for this move. Maybe if she could discover the source, she could fix it and reverse it all.

Quinton shrugged. "Business, as far as I know. A few too many companies getting a bit too big."

Alice frowned. She was dreading that answer. "Well, what would happen if someone were to oppose it all. From the inside, that is."

"No one would."

Alice resisted the urge to roll her eyes. "But *if* they did."

"Let me put it to you this way." Quinton leaned forward. "Nana Jan is like a bullet train. Try and get in her way, and you won't survive."

Alice's frown deepened. "Not even if they were someone who sold a whole lot of books?"

Quinton sat back, eyeing her up with scrutiny. "What are you planning, Alice?"

"Nothing. Yet. Just... gathering all my options."

Quinton continued to study her. Then he took a short breath, a bit like a gasp. "Have you ever heard of an author by the name of S.T. Haywood?"

Alice ran through the long list of books in her mind, but no such name came up. She shook her head.

"He was the second most brilliant writer I've ever worked with." Quinton winked at her. "Published three books with us, all of which were the biggest hits of the year."

"I've never heard of him. What happened?"

Quinton leaned forward again, closer, encroaching on Alice's space and showing too many teeth again. "He tried to stop the train."

Alice gulped and shivered involuntarily. "Oh."

"I know you want to save your friend's company." Quinton stood back up and rebuttoned his blazer, signaling the end of their conversation. "But Nana Jan has locked on to the target. And I'd really hate to see you shot."

Alice nodded weakly and watched him walk out the door. She had been hoping for a better source of information, and perhaps she would have had more to say if it had been over the phone. She deflated against her seat. She just knew there was something she could do. Some piece of the puzzle she was missing that would solve all their problems.

"You promised not to do anything stupid."

Alice jumped and spun around, spying Anthony lurking in the hallway.

"That wasn't stupid," she informed him. "That was smart. I'm gathering intel."

Anthony laughed and joined her at the island, sitting where Quinton had been, removing all oppressing feelings from the air. "Let it go, Alice. There's nothing you can do."

"I don't believe you," she said. "There is something. I just haven't thought of it."

"Well, why don't you think on it while you finish the last chapter, hm?"

Alice scowled at him. "No, no. I need all functioning mental facilities to work it out."

Anthony chuckled. "Isn't your deadline the end of the month?"

Alice stilled and glanced over at the calendar. He was right. She only had two weeks left. And if she wanted any sort of round one edits to be done, she really should get a move on.

"Fine." She slid off her seat and pointed at Anthony. "But I will figure out a solution to this!"

Chapter 28
Sex Lesson Twelve – Pegging

Tony laid on the bed, all ready and prepped. Work had been difficult and a headache, but the over-night special package he had ordered was waiting for him, and it put him in a good mood. He figured Alice wouldn't want to know more of the details than necessary, especially considering certain aspects wouldn't be entirely relevant to her story. All Tony needed now was a little fingering to open himself up for the main event.

Alice watched with a steady eye as Tony poured a glob of lube on his fingers. "Now, technically the vagina makes its own," he told her, finding that the narration helped break the hot bubble between them. "But even then, it's a good idea to use extra. You can never be too wet."

Alice let out a nervous chuckle and shifted back down the bed a bit. She was kneeling between his open legs, eyes bouncing around as if she wasn't sure if she should be looking at him or not. And she should be, if she wanted to get any useful information out of this. Not that Tony minded if they were just doing this for fun.

"Does it hurt?" Alice asked. She had her head turned to the side but was watching as Tony easily slid his pointer finger inside himself.

It had been a while since he's done this, but he shook his head to the odd sensation. "Nah. It's just unusual for a little bit. It shouldn't hurt," he continued as he moved his finger in and out, purposefully avoiding anything too stimulating so he could last for Alice. "And if it does, whoever you're with is doing it wrong and I'll be sure to beat them up for you."

Alice chuckled. "You sound like Liam."

Tony's hand stilled. "Please don't make me think about your brother while I'm doing this."

"Oh! Sorry!" Alice placed a hand on his thigh, giving it a soft rub. And that certainly helped. "No more family talk."

"Thank you." Tony adjusted a bit, itching in his shirt. He wished he could take it off, but Alice had been very certain that the more clothes they were wearing the better. That wasn't, usually, how sex worked, but Tony was nothing if not agreeable when it came to Alice.

He got back into the swing of things, watching Alice watch him as he fingered himself. He tried to think of what to say, but he wasn't sure, exactly, what information Alice was looking for, and she seemed out of questions already.

Tony shrugged a bit and circled around with his middle finger. He teased and tested himself, opening a little bit more each time until it was a comfortable slide in. He let out a satisfied little sigh. He really needed to do this more often.

"Is it hard?" Alice asked.

Tony looked down at his dick, resting against his stomach. Unless she was blind, she couldn't be asking about that. "Is what hard?"

Alice shook her head, as if coming out of a dream. "Sorry. Is it hard to find the g-spot?"

Tony kept his work up and wondered what kind of thought process was going on in Alice's mind that that was the next logical question to ask. But he answered it all the same. "It's not really hard to find," he said. "It's more a matter of 'can I be bothered?'."

"Hm?" Alice shuffled a little closer and turned her attention to Tony's face, missing what he thought was one hell of a show.

Tony stretched his back against the pillows, pushing his own fingers a bit deeper. "G-spot really isn't that hard to miss," he explained. "It's just a matter of angles. All depends on if someone's willing to look for it." He laughed softly.

"Malcolm would look for it," Alice said with certainly.

"He sure would."

"And the, er, prostate, is, like that as well?" Alice was back to looking at her lap.

"Sure is." Tony let himself touch his own as a reward for somehow not exploding by now. He let out a moan and then bit his lip.

"I just want to make sure I'm doing it right," Alice said. "When I get in there."

Tony looked to Alice's lap as well. A few minutes ago, he had supervised as she strapped the device on. She had been rather good at it too, he noted with a pout, as he had hoped he'd be invited to help her put it on.

"You'll do fine," he said. "I'm sure of it."

Alice nodded and sat back on her feet as Tony readied himself with a third finger. He hadn't bought himself anything too big, but he did want something that would give him that good stretch he's been missing. He figured a few seconds with three and he'd be all set to go.

"Thank you for doing this, Anthony," Alice said. "I really do appreciate all your help with everything."

Tony smiled at her. "You're welcome. And really, I should be thanking you." He pulled his fingers out and cleaned them on the cloth waiting next to him. "This is gonna feel good." He planted his feet on the mattress and held his legs open for Alice to slip on in.

Alice gulped, and her face turned a bright red, only a small upgrade from the pink it's been all night. "How should I, uh," Alice gestured to his body and compacted her own.

"Well, we aren't exactly aiming for long term here," Tony said, his stomach growling in agreement. "So legs over the arms works for me."

Alice nodded and closed her eyes as she crawled forward. Tony took pity on her and lifted his legs to help, placing them on her arms as she settled in position. The pillows under his hips threatened to slip away without any extra pressure keeping him down. And he could not wait to have her pressure surrounding him.

"Sure you don't want to do the honors?" Tony asked, hoping for a change of heart.

"I'm certain," Alice said, eyes still closed. "I wouldn't want to hurt you."

"You wouldn't," Tony assured her. He reached between them dropped some lube on the strap-on, rubbing it around. "And if you did, I'd tell ya."

Alice opened her eyes and started to say something, which was really bad timing because Tony had started to guide her in. Their eyes met, and Tony's body was too caught up in the sensations below to understand his brain was having a meltdown from staring into Alice's eyes as she entered him.

"F*uuuu*ck," Tony said with a hiss as the strap-on filled him up. As Alice filled him up. She looked so beautiful, leaning over him, face flushed, lovely blond curls hanging down and framing her face so perfectly. She really did look like an angel. And Tony was feeling very blessed.

"I, er, is that good?" Alice asked. Her eyes darted away, and she stared intently between their bodies.

Tony followed her gaze, only able to see a bit of what was actually going on down there. He nodded. "Damn good. Better if you move."

"Oh! Oh yes. Of course." Alice gulped again and wrapped her arms around his legs properly, hands warm and soft over his thighs. He knew, then, that this was a bad idea. He'd barely last a minute. "Like this?"

Tony laid his head back and covered his mouth, stifling the moan that bubbled through his chest. He had to close his eyes to focus all attention on how *good* this felt. One in and out and Alice was already pushing up against his prostate. He had his speculations with the blowjob, and now he was certainly convinced she was lying, and this wasn't really her first time.

"Anthony?" Alice asked. She leaned over to try and look at him, which only deepened the angle, making him groan more. "Is everything alright?"

Firsthand Research

Tony took a steadying breath and forced himself to look at her. He had to be strong. And seeing Alice's face riddled with concern and confusion helped him pull his resolve back to the front lines.

"Yeah, sorry. You're just surprisingly good at that." He laughed, if only to avoid another moan.

"Really?" Alice smiled and started moving again. Tony bit back a whimper. "Could you, I mean, if you can, er, tell me about it?"

Tony nodded and lifted himself onto his elbows. His arms shook, but it didn't matter. This was somehow slightly better than laying down. "It's good," he said. "It's like, fuck, uh, it's like eating something that you've had a craving for for a long time." Alice nodded, paying rapt attention as she moved her hips.

Tony's gaze wandered over her body, still dressed, unfortunately. He thought about how it would look, moving like this. He thought about how her breasts would sway slightly, forward and back. He thought about her curves, shaking with each motion in a sinfully delicious way. And he thought about her ass, about how it would clench and move, about how he could grab it and mold it to his fingers' every whim…

"Is that all?" Alice asked.

Tony's attention snapped back up to her. He shook away his visions. "Uh, sorry. So, uhm, the g-spot, yeah? It's basically a part of the clitoris." Alice made a little noise of understanding. Tony could feel something hot and delicious pool in his stomach. "So, uh, basically you can play with it the same way. Pressing against it, purposefully ignoring it, circling i-!"

Tony let out a sharp yelp and fell back to the bed, covering his mouth with both hands as Alice did exactly as he had told her to. She paid too much attention, he decided, as her hips *rolled*, keeping a pressure on his prostate that pulsated with every pass.

"I'm sorry," Alice said, her movements stilling. And Tony would swear against it, but he whimpered.

And his body decided that his brain had had enough of being in charge. He kept a tight hold on his mouth, for a reason he wasn't really sure of, and his own hips pushed down against Alice, forcing movement.

Alice remained quiet but held him again and continued her expert movements.

"Anthony," Alice said. And he only sort of heard her. "May I... make something up to you?"

Tony's brain was too shot to think, so he just nodded. Alice's hand left his leg and reached between them, grabbing his dick. He jumped and sat up, hands supporting him with a worrisome shake as Alice spread his pre-cum around, creating a slick surface for her to work with.

A few seconds later and Tony was gone. A warm relief spread through him, tingling through his nerves as he came. He would have time to feel bad about the thick globs that fell onto Alice's hand later. For now, all he could think about was how *good* he felt.

His elbows buckled and Tony flopped back to the bed, spent. He closed his eyes and listened to only the hard beat of his heart as he breathed. Then he remembered he was not alone in this little escapade and his eyes snapped open.

"I'm so fucking sorry," he blurted out, watching Alice pull herself free. He felt empty in more ways than one.

"Sorry?" Alice asked. She unhooked the strap-on and cleaned herself off on the towel. "What are you sorry for?"

"That wasn't exactly filled with knowledge," Tony explained. He had his stupid body to thank for that. It should *not* have reacted that strong and that quick.

"What are you talking about?" Alice sat back, looking as if they didn't just have the best sex of Tony's life. "That was very informative."

Tony cocked an eyebrow. "It was?"

"Oh yes." Alice smiled, sweet and sincere. "See, you were right! I really was able to get inside Malcolm's head and... well I'm really not sure how but, watching you and listening to you, it... well, I think I know how to write it now!"

Tony smiled back, the adrenaline of his realization slowly fading away to exhaustion. His stomach growled and Alice's eyebrows rose.

"You rest," Alice instructed. "I'll make dinner."

Tony nodded, too weak to argue, and laid back down. He felt Alice get off the bed and then listened to her clanging away at something in the kitchen. He felt a little weird. He was supposed to be the one in control here, the one who knew all the answers. He was the one supposed to be taking care of Alice. Yet here he was, practically taking a nap while she cooked for him.

Tony hummed and thought about the past few weeks. Maybe he had been wrong all this time. Alice had, after all, always been cooking for him. And she had helped him with the job thing. And the falling into the pond thing. And the having no self-esteem thing. And the more Tony thought about it, the more he realized: Alice *had* been taking care of him all along. He just hadn't realized it because, well, no one had taken care of him like that before.

Tony creaked his eyes opened and stared at the door. On the other side of it was Alice. On the other side of it was the woman he loved. On the other side of it was the only person in the world Tony figured might possibly be capable of loving him back.

That was a lot to deal with. And he needed to do something about it.

Fast.

Chapter 29
Three Little Words

The end.

Two words that used to bring such joy and elation. Two words that would be followed by celebration, a time of rest and fun, before the real work of editing began. But now, as Alice stared at them on the page, they brought nothing but heartache.

"I guess that's that," she said to herself, pulling the page free. She should be bouncing up and down with joy, should be calling her family to proclaim another work done. Should be already too busy planning the next one. But all she could do was focus on what was going on just a few doors down the hall.

Alice sighed and opened the door. It was dark in most of the house, just the hall and study light on by her, and just the sliver of light peeking out through the bottom of Anthony's door. If she listened very closely, she could hear him shuffling around in there, opening drawers and packing bags. He didn't really have all that much to pack up, but he sure was dragging the process out. Alice couldn't blame him.

Alice grabbed the stacks of paper off her desk and glanced at the time. It was much too late for either of them to be awake, and it wasn't fair of her to ask Anthony to stay up any later, but she needed his expert opinion, one last time.

She knocked softly on the door, hoping a little bit that he wouldn't hear her. But he did. He always did. Anthony looked very soft, backlit by the lamp in his room. He had a frown on his face, and Alice wished she could just snap her fingers and fix this whole situation.

"Everything okay?" Anthony asked, always worrying about her before himself. Maybe that's what she liked about him. Maybe she was just too selfish. Maybe that's why all this was happening.

Alice nodded and looked down at her pages. "I hope I'm not interrupting." And then, because she wasn't selfish, "And you don't have too if you don't want, but…" She kept her gaze on the paper, knowing that Anthony would be able to fill in the blanks. It was like he could always read her mind, know exactly what she wanted to say even if she couldn't say it. Maybe that's why she liked him.

"I would be honored," Anthony said. He took the papers from her gingerly, their fingers brushing against one another, perhaps lingering just a little too long. "I'm very excited to see how Naomi and Malcolm are getting along."

"Very well," Alice said, looking up into Anthony's eyes, "I think." Even though Alice knew she would be seeing Anthony again, the very next morning, in fact, she couldn't help but feel like she would never see those wonderful, beautiful eyes again. And she tried to think of something, anything, that would keep the conversation going, keep those eyes in her line of sight always.

"Big day tomorrow," Anthony said, and Alice blinked away her fantasy, looking back down at her now empty hands. "You ought to get some sleep."

"You're the one who needs the rest," Alice argued. And she really was selfish, asking him to stay up and work for her when he had tomorrow to deal with. She winced and tried to grab for the papers, but Anthony held them out of reach.

"I want to," he told her, once more reading her mind. "And besides, I operate better on less sleep anyway."

"That can't be true," Alice said.

"Well, it is."

She huffed and put her hands on her hips. "Then it can't be healthy!"

Anthony chuckled and shrugged. "Healthy has never really been high on my list."

"Well, it should. You need to take better care of yourself."

"Yes, Ma'am."

They smiled at each other, and there was a small spark of hope in Alice's chest that she wished would go away. She had felt it every time in the past, and it had been wrong every time in the past. And every time she thought it would be different. But this time seemed to be playing out the exact same way.

"I'll see you tomorrow," Anthony said. "Get some sleep."

Alice nodded. "You too." She walked back to her room and laid down in her bed. But sleep never came.

*

Anthony and Alice sat next to each other at the kitchen island, neither of them touching the breakfast before them.

"You too, huh?" Anthony asked. Alice looked at the dark wrinkles under his eyes and the slouch of his posture. She nodded. "Yeah, figured. Good day for a nap." Anthony tried to chuckle, but he just ended up coughing a bit. "Are you sure you don't want me to stick around? Give you a ride back after or anything?"

"I'm sure," Alice said. She wanted to smile, but her face didn't seem to get the memo. "Liam is going to pick me up this afternoon."

"All packed?" Anthony asked.

"All packed."

"Good."

Alice picked up her fork and looked at her eggs. She poked them a few times, but her stomach was in knots, and she feared anything she ate wouldn't stay down very long.

"Hey, uh," Anthony started, then cleared his throat. "I know this is a hard thing for you to do." It couldn't be harder than what he had to do, Alice thought. "But I'm glad that you are, and I'm...I dunno. Proud? Is that weird?"

Alice's face finally woke up, mouth forming a small smile. "Not at all. We're friends. We can be proud of each other."

Anthony scoffed, a sound she was becoming familiar with as it was always followed by something like, "Well, one of us more than the other."

She was back to frowning again as she placed her fork back on the countertop. "Now you listen to me, I am very proud of you, Anthony. You have done some truly remarkable things since I've known you, and you should be proud of yourself, too."

"Yeah, and all of that's going away when I leave."

"That's not true." Alice reached out, grabbing Anthony's arm. It was much too cold. "You are an amazing friend, a wonderful brother, and much too good a son and grandson for your family." She rubbed his arm a bit, trying to warm him up. "That's not the kind of thing that can just go away."

Anthony smiled at her, but he didn't really mean it. "You're right," he lied.

Alice puffed up, ready to argue more to the point until he accepted it as truth, but the sound of a car pulling into the driveway cut her off.

"That'll be them," Anthony mumbled. He slumped off his chair and stretched a bit. "Sure you don't want a ride to town?"

Alice shook her head. "I'm okay. I think a nice bike ride will help wake me up anyway."

Anthony nodded and walked over to the door, where his two bags sat. He plucked the keys to his car off of the keychain rack and returned to her, holding them out.

"No!" Alice said, standing up and scurrying away from the keys as if they were contagious. "Absolutely not!"

"I can't," Anthony said.

"It was a gift!"

"Alice, please."

Alice looked into his pleading eyes, wide, earnest, hurt. She felt a similar way. She bit her lip and thought about the little package stuffed away in one of her bags.

"Fine," Alice said, snatching the keys up from him. "But you have to accept something else." She hurried to her room, hoping he wouldn't try to make a break for it as she rummaged. She had bought this little gift for Anthony one day when her heart was being hopeful. She had never intended to give it to him, but she had to do something.

Anthony was waiting by the door when she returned, one bag on his back, the other held in one hand. He took the small, wrapped gift from her with the other. "Better not be anything expensive," he said with a small smirk.

"It's not," Alice said. "Just a little something. A thank you. For all your help. You probably won't even have much use for it now but, well, I still want you to have it."

"Thank you."

"Thank *you*."

They stared at each other. Alice wrung her hands together. She tried to think of something to say, something to keep him there. But time was ticking by fast, too fast. She was losing him. She always knew she would, but that dreaded hope in the back of her mind had kept echoing to her that maybe this time would be different. But it wasn't. It never would be.

Anthony cleared his throat again and then laughed. "Don't know why this feels so dramatic," he said. "It's not like we won't see each other again."

"Right," Alice agreed. They would see each other again. But it would be so different, and not nearly as satisfying.

"By-" Anthony started. Then he smirked and opened the door. "See ya later."

"See you," Alice agreed. And she saw him. Saw him walk out the door and down to the car. Saw him get in with his family, come to collect. Saw him drive away, down into the town. She saw him more clear and precise than anyone else in the world, perhaps.

She had seen him. And now he was gone.

*

It was quiet in the car. And that was nothing new. Tony couldn't remember a single time when a family road trip held more than 10 minutes of conversation max. Not even the radio played, just the sound of tires over asphalt, and four bodies of repressed emotions bumping slightly into each other.

Tony sat hunched over in his seat, ignoring the protesting look from his father. He stared at the gift Alice had given him, hanging limp in his hands. He felt Sandra shift beside him, and then one of her hands was covering his own. "I'm sorry, Tony," she whispered.

"I love her," he whispered back. Because what was the point of hiding it anymore?

"I know," Sandra said. She gave his hand a little squeeze. Tony looked up at her with as much of a smile as he could muster. He didn't know many siblings that got along well, but when you had parents like theirs, you had to bond at least a little.

"I think I could have really loved her, you know, like loved her." He closed his eyes.

"Maybe you still can," Sandra offered. "It's not like you'll never see her again. What's stopping you?"

Tony shook his head. There were so many factors at play that even he couldn't fathom them. There was no solid reason why he couldn't go home, work for his Nana, meet up with Alice when she came in from time to time, date her properly, and end up having some weird fusion of his old life and his new life. He just knew it wouldn't work like that. He'd go back to his old place, and he'd go back to his old ways. And no one would ever come close to Alice. So why would he even try?

"At least you have something to remember her by," Sandra said.

Tony sighed and looked down at the little package. He felt around, but it was only a box, hiding the real gift inside. He could open the wrapping, anyway. One step closer as he stared at the white lid. He spent the next few moments trying to guess what could be in there. Maybe another set of keys. Alice would trick him like that. Or maybe a nice pen. She was trying to get him to be a writer too. (Or making a joke about holding pens, he thought, with a shudder at his past stupidity). Or maybe-

"Oh, would you just open it already?" Sandra said, nudging him in the side with her elbow.

Tony glared at her but agreed that was for the best. He pried the lid off, shaking fingers barely holding their grasp. There was yet another layer to remove, a soft, cottony-like bed protecting whatever was beneath. Great, she had gone and gotten him something expensive, hadn't she?

Tony picked the fluff away, eyebrows furrowing at what lay beneath. It was a keychain, not that he had any keys to add to it. A small link of chains hung off it, and a little silver heart reflected the light as he pulled it up to examine it.

Three words were engraved on one side.

For the book.

Tony's breath caught in the back of his throat, and he felt like he might be choking. He rolled the window down, despite the protests from his family as the cold air filtered in. He was suffocating and he needed fresh air.

Because those three little words meant three other little words.

"She loves me," he whispered, more to himself than anyone else. Then he chuckled with giddy glee and looked up, declaring, "She loves me!"

Sandra was smiling at him, but on the other side of the car his father and grandmother were looking rightfully confused.

"What are you going on about?" his father asked, because talking in a car was against the family code. But this wasn't his family anymore.

"She loves me!" Tony said again. He bounced in his seat, eager to do something with this newfound but always known information. He stilled, eyes landing on his Nana's face. "And I love her!"

He was sure he had to be thinking something as he clicked open his seatbelt and reached for the door. Clearly it wasn't about his safety, the street passing by below him too fast for that. He must have been thinking only of Alice, and how wonderful she was. And how wonderful his life would be with her. And how he had to get to her no matter what.

His family all yelled, "Stop!" at the same time, but only Sandra's was followed by, "the car!" The tires squealed as the car slowed down. Tony didn't even wait for it to finish properly. He jumped out, hit the ground running, and just kept going, following his heartbeat in the direction of Alice.

"What do you think you're doing?" his father asked. His head was stuck out the window, the car having turned around, following Tony in his trek back through the town.

"I'm going to stop this!" he told him. "I'm going to stop you!" He pointed in at Nana Jan with a shaking finger.

"Young man, get back in this car," Nana Jan responded, peering past her son to glare at Tony.

"You'll never take me alive!" Tony declared. Then he remembered he wasn't in the car. He didn't have to follow roads. He shouted a celebratory, "ha-ha!" and took off between two of the buildings, following alleyways and side paths towards his destination.

His legs burned as he ran, but he didn't have time to stop. He may have shortcuts being on foot, but he still had to outrun a car.

Please, don't let me be late, he thought, visions of Alice's smiling face propelling him across the ground. *Please, please.*

Snow started to fall, large, wet flakes sprinkling against his skin. And it was fitting. He already had a dramatic run to check off his list, add some bad weather, and he was really making for a classic forgive-me scene. Alice couldn't possibly turn him down when he was out of breath and covered in snow.

Tony turned down the street leading to Nate's office just as he caught the car doing the same on the other end. He pushed himself harder, feeling a deep burn in his chest with each breath. He just had to last a little while longer…

There was no time for elevators as Tony burst into the building, making a beeline for the stairs. The heat hit him all at once, and yet he shivered. So close. He was so close. He couldn't relent now.

"STOP!" he said, throwing open the doors to the meeting room.

Nana's lawyers sat on one end of the table, seemingly unfazed by this outburst. Nate and Alice sat on the other, staring at him with raised eyebrows. Nate held a pen in one hand, his other splayed over a piece of paper, half signed.

Tony strode forward and snatched it off the table, ripping the contract into little shreds.

"What are you doing?" Nate asked.

Tony opened his mouth to explain, but all that came out was a few raspy breaths. But the deed had been done. He could rest now.

"Water," he managed to croak out as he fell into the nearest chair and closed his eyes. Everything ached and he was sure he looked like a proper mess. But it was worth it.

"Here," Alice said. Tony peeled one eye open. She was hovering over him, holding a cup out, looking all kinds of scared and worried.

He tried to tell her that there really was nothing to worry about. That he was here now. And he would always be here. And she would never have to worry about anything ever again. But he really did need that water, so he took it from her and chugged it all in one breath.

There was a slow shuffle outside and then Nana Jan was walking in, Sandra quick on her heels. "What is going on in here?" she asked.

Tony hissed and forced himself to his feet. He couldn't be seen being weak now. But he had run quite hard for some time, and he was weak. So he swayed a bit until Alice reached out and grabbed his arm for stability. "What's going on is I'm stopping the train," he said.

Everyone else looked properly confused, but Alice's mouth fell open a bit in understanding.

"What on earth are you talking about?" Nana Jan asked.

"I'm not letting you just muscle your way in and take over Nate's company like this."

"Tony, it's fine," Nate said.

"No, it's not!" Tony huffed and leaned on Alice for a little extra support, his head starting to spin now. "It's not fine. It's never been fine. She thinks that just because she has a lot of money she can just, just push people around. Well, I'm done being pushed!"

"That's all nice and good," Nate said, "but the reasons we agreed to this don't just go away. I'm selling the company."

"No! I'm not going to let you! And you know why? Because you love this company! And you can't just let it go! You have to fight for it! And, yeah, it's gonna be hard. And sometimes uncomfortable. And you're gonna sit up some nights wondering if you made a mistake and threw everything away on another whim. But you know what?" He wagged his finger in Nate's general direction. "You didn't. You won't have. Because *nothing* you can gain from this deal will ever come close to a life spent with her."

"Her?"

"IT! The company! A life with it!"

Everyone stayed quiet for a moment, and Tony swallowed hard, hoping his blunder hadn't been noticed. But judging by the looks everyone was giving him, it had been. He felt Alice's grip on him weaken a bit. He couldn't bring himself to look at her, focusing all his intense energy on Nate.

"Tony-"

"We can do this," Tony interrupted. He tightened his own grip on Alice, hoping she knew he was talking to her as he looked at Nate. "We make a pretty good team. There's nothing we can't do together. We can...we *will* survive this."

"Anthony..." Alice whispered.

Nate stared at him, hard and unflinching. "And are you going to pay my bills when this whole thing goes belly-up?"

"I won't have to," Tony told him. "Because it won't."

Nana Jan hadn't spoken in a while and Tony glanced over to the door. She was gone, leaving only Sandra there, hands folded before her chest, big smile on her face. And the lawyers were gone too, Tony noticed, having slipped out during his grand speech, he assumed. He hadn't even heard them move.

"You better be right about this," Nate said as he stood up. "Because you just talked me out of a whole lot of money."

"Trust me," Tony said. He finally looked down at Alice. "This is worth so much more."

Nate groaned.

Chapter 30
Sex – Because I Love You

Nate had given them a very silent and awkward drive back to the cabin. He, thankfully, didn't say anything, but he did give Tony a very knowing look when he slipped out of the car. It was the kind of look that said, 'I'd better be seeing some Facebook relationship status updates soon'.

The awkward silence followed Tony and Alice into the house. They stood in the entrance, glancing at one another, neither making an effort to move.

"So," Alice finally said, saving Tony the mortification of having to speak first. "What changed your mind?"

Tony took a deep breath. All that courage and adrenaline was knocked out him with every step as he ran. Now he was weak and pathetic again. And he hated it.

"I, uh...I just realized you were right. Is all. You know? About, er, not letting her win and fighting for the company and all that." He shrugged and wished he could crawl inside himself. Alice was standing right there. And he still couldn't say it.

Alice smiled softly at him. "Well, I'm glad you came to your senses." She nodded stiffly and then turned to walk away.

And Tony's body reacted before his brain even had a chance to process what was happening. His hand shot out, grabbing Alice's and holding her back. "There's something else," he said.

"Oh?"

Tony gulped. Fuck him he just couldn't say it. And he didn't know why. But he could show it. He pulled Alice closer to him and kissed her. Kissed her like he always wanted, pouring every pent-up act of love he had in him into that one kiss. And what a kiss it was, with Alice's lips moist and soft, with her pushing closer, leaning into him as he held her tight. He knew he had to say *something* if he wanted to keep those kinds of kisses in his life.

He reluctantly pulled away, leaning his forehead against hers. "I want you to be my girlfriend," he said.

"You do?" Alice's voice was soft and gentle and quiet. And he wanted to hear it every day of his life.

Tony nodded against her. " I do. I... I love you, Alice." And it wasn't as hard to say as he thought. "And I can't lose you."

"Anthony…"

Tony closed his eyes, prepared for the worst. He had over thought the gift, just like he had over thought everything. And now he really was going to lose his best friend.

"I love you, too."

…

Tony opened his eyes again. He expected to be lying in his bed, having had another dream where Alice was his. But it didn't seem like a dream. He was still standing there by the door. Still holding Alice's hand. Still touching his head to hers.

He straightened up to make sure Alice wasn't an alien or robot that was just messing with him. It certainly seemed like she was human.

"Pinch me," he said.

Alice chuckled softly and reached her free hand over to pinch his arm. He winced at the pain, but he knew now it was real.

"You do?" he asked. Just to be safe. Alice nodded. "So, if you do. And I do. Then... we're dating?"

Alice's smile widened. "I do believe we are."

Tony laughed in relief. Giddy joy shook through his hands as he grabbed

Alice's face, kissing her again and again. He didn't think he could ever grow tired of it, kissing Alice. Her lips were perfectly plump and delicious. And when he thought about those lips on the rest of his body, his autopilot brain kicked in, and he pulled Alice closer, moving his hands to her back, holding her tight as if she would simply float away without him.

"Mph," Alice mumbled, a delicate vibration against Tony's mouth. She pulled her head to the side, but Tony's autopilot continued on, kissing against her jaw, getting any taste of her he could. "Liam!" Alice exclaimed.

And that certainly stalled his brain long enough for him to take back control. He leaned away and raised an eyebrow at her. "I thought we agreed we wouldn't be using your brother's name during this kind of stuff."

Alice laughed and bumped his shoulder lightly. "I need to call him," she explained, reaching to dig her phone out of her pocket.

"To talk about this?" Tony asked.

"Of course not," Alice said. She started dialing Liam's number and fixed Tony with a hard stare. "I would call Katie for that."

Tony chuckled, nervous because he knew that was true. "So, why are you calling him?"

"Because he's supposed to be by to pick me up in about an hour," she said.

"Oh, don't want that." Tony shook his head and pulled the two of them closer together. He rubbed his nose against her jaw line, wondering how lovely it would be to bite all over her neck. "Definitely don't want that."

"Hello, Liam," Alice said, shivering as Tony continued to press delicate kisses to her neck. Nothing too intense. He didn't want Liam to get wise. "You haven't left yet have you?... Oh, good. Because I've actually decided to stay another day or two. Just finish some things up... No, no I do not need you to come. I'm perfectly fine I assure you... It has nothing to do with that... Look, I promise I'll call you later and talk more, but I really must get some work done. Goodbye."

Alice hung up and placed the phone down on the table by the door. "Now, where were we?"

Tony smiled at her and kissed her. He couldn't believe his own luck. Alice was his. Truly. Not just in his imagination and wild dreams. This was real. She was real. They were real!

"About my earlier request," Alice said once they had parted, both a little out of breath. "Do you think you could reevaluate your answer?"

Tony furrowed his eyebrows at her, because there wasn't a single request he could think of that he had, or ever would, deny her. Alice bit her bottom lip and looked up at him through her eyelashes.

Tony smirked and kissed the tip of her nose. "Are you sure that's what you'd like?"

"Yes, please," she said. "Right now."

Tony laughed and kissed her again as he walked them back to the bedroom. He was overcome with joy. This morning he didn't even think he'd have a friend in Alice. Now, not only was she his girlfriend, but he was going to have sex with her! His autopilot kicked back in, hands roaming over Alice's clothes, looking for buttons and straps that needed removing.

Alice pushed him away gently, and he cursed himself for being too quick. "I just want to do one thing first."

"You know you don't have to do anything-" Tony started, cut off by a finger to his lips.

"I want to."

Tony nodded and watched as Alice slipped away into the closet. It was a good thing, he figured, as he sat at the foot of the bed with a sigh. He needed to cool off and compose himself. This was Alice's first time, after all. And it was up to him to make sure everything went well. He had to keep a lid on that autopilot of his.

"Okay," Alice said after a minute or two. "I-I'm ready."

"You sure sound it," Tony responded with a laugh.

But the laughter got stuck in the back of his throat when the closet door opened. Alice must have been reading his dreams. For there she was standing before him in that light blue and white lingerie set he had put together for her. He was pretty sure he blacked out. There was no way he could process the delicate skin and smooth curves he saw before him in the beautiful image that was Alice without passing out.

"Did... did I do it alright?" Alice looked herself over, checking for any misplacements. But everything was perfect.

"You're beautiful," Tony said. And his voice was foreign to him. Because anything that wasn't Alice simply didn't exist in that moment. He stood up and walked up to her, hands tracing over her body without touching, for surely he did not deserve such greatness.

Alice blushed and looked down at her feet. "I just figured... you did such a wonderful job helping me put it on... you deserve the chance to take it off."

Tony smiled at the beautiful angel he had been blessed with. He cupped a hand under her chin and raised her head to look at him. "Thank you," was all he could say. And it was all that needed saying.

Alice smiled and leaned into him for a kiss. And as much as Tony wanted to touch and explore and truly appreciate the gift he had been given, he couldn't ignore the slight shake in Alice's body, or the wary look that had been in her eyes. She was still nervous. And Tony could not have that.

"Gimme one minute," he said, slipping behind her into the closet.

"What?"

"One minute," he repeated. "Trust me. You'll like it."

*

Alice sat on the bed and counted the seconds. She knew that whatever Anthony was doing in there would be something she'd appreciate. But every second that they delayed the process just meant more time for her to lose her nerve.

Of course she wanted to have sex. And she certainly wanted to have sex with Anthony. But she knew she worked best off impulse. Like that first night, when she had just been prepared to do it and get it done. But now she had time to think. And when she thought about things, it always ended up getting muddled in her mind.

Anthony had said he loved her. Had kissed her with such passion. Had asked her to be his girlfriend. So why, oh why, did she still feel like it was all a lie? Or some kind of joke? Maybe she was rushing into things. Maybe she should stop this whole process and wait until she knew for certain how Anthony felt.

The door to the closet opened and every worry in her mind disappeared in her laughter. Anthony was leaning seductively against the door frame, one hand on his hip, the other raised above his head for support. He was wearing some of the lingerie that Alice had bought earlier, featuring a red corset that threatened to fall off with how loose it was, even at the tightest tie, and a black silk skirt that hung low on his hips. Alice broke into another fit of laughter when she noticed he was wearing a pair of her heels to match.

"What do you think?" Anthony asked. "Too much?"

Alice nodded, trying to hold back her giggles. "Just a little," she managed to say.

Anthony hummed and looked down at himself. "You're right. It's the shoes." He kicked them off and then raced over to the bed, bouncing on the edge next to her. "Hi."

Alice calmed herself and looked at him. "Hi," she said back. And there was something about those golden-brown eyes, illuminated by the red of his outfit, that just spoke truth to Alice. Anthony did love her. And, quite surprisingly, he found her beautiful. And that was all she had ever wanted from a boyfriend.

So what if it was too good to be true? It was good. And she intended to keep it, true or not.

Firsthand Research

Alice leaned closer to him, drawn in by his warmth. "I'm not really sure how this all works," she admitted. She had played out this scenario in her mind countless times, but how would it play in real life?

Anthony smiled at her and kissed her. He certainly had to feel some way about her with how often he was doing that now. "It's not that hard," he told her. Then he smirked. "You've already got quite a lot of practice."

Alice felt herself blush, and her gut reaction was to turn and hide in shame. But Anthony grabbed her chin, a gentle reminder that she didn't need to do that anymore. Not with him.

"So, how should we start?" Alice asked.

"How would you like?" Anthony leaned over, kissing along her jaw. And she quite liked that.

"I'm not sure." She tilted her head, inviting his kisses lower. And lower they went, just as Anthony's hand slid over her thigh, giving it a little squeeze. "This is nice."

"Then this it is."

Anthony kept his kisses up along Alice's neck. They were very light, and she was thankful, despite her wonderings on how it would feel to have him nip, just a bit. Better they start off slow, she figured. Besides, she was much more interested in Anthony's hand. It slid up and down her thigh, squeezing at random intervals. And every time his fingers would get close to where it truly mattered, he would pull back. And every time Alice's excitement only grew.

"Y-you can touch me," Alice said. "Uhm, just in case... in case you didn't know."

She felt Anthony smile against her skin, and she cursed herself. "Thank you," Anthony said. But he still didn't, and Alice felt a fresh wave of hot embarrassment wash over her.

"Sorry," she whispered, trying to scoot away. Anthony's hand shot across to grab her other leg, holding her in place.

And his kisses were gone, and he was looking at her with a deep concern. "Are you okay?"

Alice wasn't really sure how to answer that. "I'm just so…" she sighed and hung her head. Even with a dictionary or thesaurus she was sure she wouldn't be able to find the words she needed. Anthony just waited for her, patient as ever. "I'm not sure how everything works. And I just don't want to ruin it."

"You could never ruin it," Anthony told her. Not that she believed him.

Alice glanced at him and bothered her bottom lip between her teeth. "Could we maybe just...do it?" she asked. And she hated her own voice, saying those words. "It's just, there's all the anticipation and... while I'm sure that's good normally, I think it's just sort of making everything worse? Like, once I do it then I won't worry about doing it? Does that make sense?"

Anthony smiled at her. Warm and loving. He truly was the perfect person for her in this moment. In any moment. "It makes sense," he said, and Alice let herself relax a little. "We can do whatever you want and not do whatever you don't," Anthony continued.

Alice shrugged half-heartedly. "I don't know what I want or don't want."

Anthony reached up, running the back of his fingers across Alice's cheek before using them to push her hair behind her ear. His touches were always so soft and gentle, and Alice wanted them all over her body.

"I want you to touch me," she said, before Anthony could speak again.

"Where?" he asked.

"Everywhere."

Anthony breathed out a soft laugh. "I still can't believe I'm not dreaming."

"You've dreamt about *that*?"

Anthony's smile widened, that troublesome twinkle back in his eye. And Alice wasn't feeling as worried anymore. "Almost every night."

She blushed again, but couldn't stop the smile from forming on her face. "You're just saying that."

Anthony looked her in the eyes, with all the earnest honesty he could muster. "I'm really not."

And *something* snapped in Alice's body. It was like a lightbulb had gone off, only it wasn't in her brain. It must have been in her loins. For all at once she was pouncing on Anthony, sending them tumbling to the bed with a laugh as she kissed him and touched him. For she had had dreams of her own.

Every sensation became mixed up in her brain as they kissed. She could feel Anthony's hands running along her body, sometimes on her legs, sometimes her back, most times on her ass. And she felt his skin and clothing under her own fingers, smooth and delicate contrasting hard and rough. There were just too many textures; some of them had to go.

Alice pulled away, earning a protested grunt from Anthony. "You aren't married to that outfit, are you?" Anthony shook his head and Alice grabbed the corset around the back, ripping it open.

Well, she *tried* to rip it open, but it didn't seem to budge.

"Ah, sorry," Anthony said. He sat up on his elbows as Alice puzzled over the complexity of clothing. "Tied it extra tight to keep it on."

"Well, get it off," Alice ordered.

"Yes, Ma'am." Anthony winked at her and sat up fully, reaching around to undo his ties. Alice rolled to the side, watching him wiggle and jerk until he was free of all clothing confides.

Alice had never seen someone else that naked in her adult life. At least, not in person. And it was a bit of a strange sensation, because she still felt a little too exposed in her own outfit. Yet there Anthony was, all on display and casual. As he was about everything.

"You're very handsome," Alice told him. Because she would want the reassurance. And because it was true.

"Thank you," Anthony said. He leaned over to kiss her again. "You are oh so very beautiful."

Alice blushed at his words and kissed him back. The snap had cured her of her hesitations, but she was still uncertain how to properly proceed. "What now?"

Anthony hummed, his eyes scanning over Alice's body. She squirmed under his close examination, but she told herself he only saw good things. "I think we should start at the beginning," he declared.

Alice followed his eyes down to her lap. She saw him lick his lips. That she was more than comfortable with. "I think I agree."

Anthony smiled and kissed her again before getting up to his knees. Alice settled herself on her back, arranging the pillows to support her, so she could watch the master at work. Anthony nestled himself between her legs, laying between them on his stomach. He kissed at her thighs as his hands slid up to unhook her stockings. Alice shivered as he pulled her panties away, the thin fabric and straps leaving her easily, as if they, too, were excited to be getting on with things.

Anthony made that hum of appreciation he always did whenever he saw a part of her undressed. And she liked that noise. And she hoped it would never go away.

"Just don't do too good a job," she warned as Anthony slid closer.

"Why's that?"

"I don't want to finish before, well, before the grand finale." She chuckled at her own joke.

"I'm sorry." Anthony's head popped back up. "Were you under the impression that you were getting away with just one orgasm today?"

That question sent a shiver through Alice's body. "I-I well, it wouldn't be good to wear me out!" Although the concept of multiple times was alluring, Alice wanted to be fully conscious and aware when they did do it.

Anthony squinted at her, judging the situation. And she gave him her best pleading face. "Okay, you make a fair point." He lowered his head again. "We'll just do the big one for now." Then he lowered his voice to a whisper, "but there's still a lot of time left in the day…"

Alice sat up a bit and opened her mouth to argue but all that came out was a moan as Anthony wiggled his tongue between her labia, pressing to her clit. She fell back to the bed as sensations started to wash over her, warm waves of pleasure with every movement of Anthony between her legs. This was the third time he's done this with her, and it felt better each time. Maybe because she knew more of what to expect. For instance, she wasn't even the least bit surprised when Anthony's tongue ventured lower, prodding at her opening in a soft, gentle pulse. And it felt good, every time she stretched a little bit at his suggestion.

Oh, so very good.

Too good.

Alice realized she was already edging towards an orgasm. She was certain she would burst if she tried to talk so she just reached down to grab Anthony's hair, which only seemed to encourage him. He really was too damn good at this. But Alice was resolute in her decision to just have the one. For now, anyway.

Alice tugged on Anthony's hair, and he relented with a grunt. He let Alice pull his head back up and when she looked at him, he was scowling. Kind of adorably. She laughed softly at him.

"We'll have plenty of time for that later," she reminded him. They were dating, after all. They had quite a lot of time for that.

And Anthony realized the truth of her words, his frown morphing into a smile. He started to crawl up the bed towards her but stopped half-way. "Lemme go wash my mouth real quick."

He scrambled off the bed before Alice could even think to thank him for his consideration. She waited for him only semi-patiently. She bit her lip and let her hand wander down to where Anthony's head had recently been. She was quite wet, and not just from Anthony's mouth. Oh no, she had made quite a lot of that wet herself. And when she explored around her entrance, she found her finger didn't have that hard of a time easing its way in. But she pulled it back. She was nervous, and she trusted Anthony with that job much more than herself.

"Sorry about that," Anthony said, returning to the bed. He laid himself down next to her and pulled her in for a minty kiss. "I promise I'll be good from here on."

"Thank you." Alice kissed him this time, just for good measure, and he melted into it, rolling so his body was a comforting, warm pressure on her side.

Anthony's hand slid across her thigh again, and this time when it reached her vagina it didn't stop. "Just tell me if it hurts, okay?"

Alice nodded and closed her eyes. Anthony placed soft kisses over her cheek as his finger did what hers wasn't brave enough for.

It was odd. Just like last time. Not painful or uncomfortable, just odd. But odd with a hint of exhilarating. It was the stretch, Alice decided, as Anthony successfully wiggled one finger in there. The stretch felt odd but good. Something she was sure she would come to appreciate much more once she got used to it.

"Doing okay down there?" Anthony asked. A second finger was waiting eagerly as the first did little circles inside her.

"I think so," Alice said. She wasn't even aware how fast and hard she was breathing until she talked.

"Think?"

Alice opened her eyes just so she could roll them at him. "I'm good."

"Good." Anthony smiled at her as that second finger made its way in. Odd again, but not bad. And not nearly as hard as Alice had imagined.

"I really am close," she whispered. Because the good feeling of the stretch was amplifying her need, even if Anthony wasn't curling his fingers like that first time.

"I know," he whispered. "And I'm sorry, but I'm not doing it until I know you're ready."

"Don't apologize for that," Alice said. She was never more certain that he was perfect for her. "I appreciate it."

Anthony leaned down to kiss her as his fingers worked. And as time bled away into their kiss, so too did the oddity of Anthony's fingers in her. She never even felt the third one until it was already knuckle deep.

"Grand Finale time, eh?" Anthony asked. He pulled his fingers out, wiping on them on a small towel he had brought back with him. Alice had been right about that stretching sensation. She certainly missed it.

"I think so, yes."

"Bottom drawer, right?" Anthony rolled off the bed and went digging for the condoms. Alice had to grip the sheets to stop from touching herself. She was much, much too close. She wasn't sure she would actually last the finale.

Alice watched as Anthony masterfully applied the condom in a few quick seconds. She was very glad she had somebody so knowledgeable on her side.

"Beautiful," Anthony reminded her as he knelt before her on the bed.

"Thank you," Alice said, drawing her legs up and open. She was too lost in the sensations to even consider being self-conscious right now.

Anthony smiled, his eyes turning hungry as he took her in, rubbing a drop of lube on himself. Alice hadn't even seen him get out the bottle, but there it was, suddenly on the bed next to them like a ninja. Anthony grabbed one of Alice's legs, squeezing it as he inched closer. He was nearly there.

"Anthony, wait!" Alice said, her brain clicking back on for a brief moment. He stopped without any hesitation, alert eyes watching her. And she didn't want him to worry. This wasn't a that kind of stop. She grabbed his face between her hands and looked him in those gorgeous eyes. "Because I love you," she said, to make up for every lie up to that point.

Anthony's breath hitched, and he gulped a loud note. And his eyes went from dry to misty awfully fast. And a tear managed to escape before he could curse and pull away, rubbing the hand that had been holding Alice's leg over his eyes.

"Oh, goodness," Alice said, sitting up on her elbows a bit. "I'm sorry!"

Anthony shook his head, wiping at his face. He pulled his hand away, no longer crying, but still a little wet in the eyes. "I love you, too," he said, rather forcefully.

Alice nodded and figured she'd better shut-up and let them get to it lest the finale becomes a flop. She settled back down and waited for Anthony to recalibrate himself.

Alice had ruminated over Anthony's words from the other night, when the roles had been reversed. She had used them in her final scene, because they sounded right, but they didn't make a whole lot of sense to her until that moment when Anthony kissed her and started the slow slide of his hips, pushing himself into her.

She was full, of something she didn't even know she was hungry for. Anthony's dick was scratching the itch she didn't even know she had. And that thought made her chuckle a little.

"Everything okay?" Anthony asked, halting his progress.

"Oh yes," Alice said. She lifted her hips up, a giddy wave of joy spreading through her nerves as that pushed Anthony in further. "I just realized you were right."

Anthony smiled, taking matters back into his own hands. "It had to happen eventually."

Alice smiled back and pulled Anthony back down into another kiss as he finished his first, and by no means last, entrance. Alice hummed a happy and content note against his lips as she felt his hips against her legs.

"Just let me know when you're ready for me to move," Anthony mumbled into the kiss she would not let up on.

"I'm ready," she mumbled back.

"You sure?"

Alice pulled away with a huff and fixed him with a hard stare. "What part of really close did you not understand?"

Anthony laughed, a delightful rumble that spread across Alice's skin. "Fair. But I really don't want to rush anything."

"I promise, Anthony. I'm ready."

She pulled him back to their kiss before he could try arguing anymore. And since his energy wasn't spent on talking, he could put it towards more useful things. Like rocking his hips.

Anthony pulled out just a little bit before pushing back in. Just once. Then he adjusted himself, pushing his hips lower, raising Alice's legs a bit higher so that when he pulled and pushed again, he was hitting that spot that made Alice's heart skip a beat.

Breathing was difficult, as if all of her breath was stuck in her core, building up and waiting to get out but with nowhere to go. Alice let her head fall back, unable to continue kissing Anthony as she tried to steady her breath. But it was hard to do as each movement of Anthony's hips just seemed to add another block on her lungs.

Anthony, however, seemed to have no trouble kissing. He just moved his lips to Alice's neck and collarbone, keeping them light, with just the occasional brush of teeth that sent goosebumps down her arms. And the one hand that wasn't holding Alice's leg came into play too, fumbling between them until it got the tie on her top open before moving to massage one of her breasts.

Anthony kept his thrusts shallow, not really pulling out so much as gyrating around, just as he had told her to do. And she could understand the look on his face and the harshness of his breath from that night, for no feeling in the world compared.

Firsthand Research

Alice came with a flash of light behind her closed eyes, her legs shaking as warm, golden energy spread out from that block in her core to the rest of her body. She let out a deep, shuddering breath as her hips moved against Anthony's by their own accord. That wave of pleasure didn't just stop at that, for once the feeling had reached her toes and fingers it seemed to double back before returning to her center and repeating its course. She only heard the echoes of her moans of delight.

"That was fucking hot as hell," Anthony said.

Alice blinked her eyes open, surprised she could still have the energy to do so. She was very glad she had decided to stick true to just the one orgasm. For now, of course.

Anthony had stopped moving and was smiling at her. Alice wanted to tell him to keep going, that this wasn't just about her own pleasure. But the sensation inside her gave her the feeling she was not the only one who had just seen stars.

If Alice could feel anything outside the buzzing on her skin, she was sure feeling Anthony pull out of her would be weird. But she just felt a sort of emptiness. Not painful or uncomfortable, just odd.

"You alright?" Anthony asked, kissing her forehead.

Alice nodded, sure she looked a mess, hair thrown about, skin covered in sweat. But she didn't care how she looked. Because she *felt* amazing.

"I'm going to go clean up," Anthony told her. And she frowned. She knew he needed to (and she needed to), but she didn't want his warmth to go away, leaving her cold and shivering. "And I'll get us a snack." Alice's frown turned to a smile, and she nodded.

Anthony truly was perfect for her.

*

Tony had always hated the expression 'walking on clouds' because he was of a slightly scientific nature and clouds, as he learned in school, were not walk-onable. But it was the closest expression he could think of as he practically skipped down the hall to his bathroom, leaving Alice's free for her if she could get to it.

He wanted to be quick about things, so he could get back to his girlfriend. His *girlfriend*. Holy fuck! HE HAD A GIRLFRIEND! Nothing could stop him from dancing in the room as he cleaned himself off and slipped into the robe hanging on the back of the door. He wasn't just walking on clouds; he was having a full on rave on them!

He could hear water running in the bathroom in Alice's room. Wait! THEIR ROOM! BECAUSE THEY WERE *DATING*! So he made his pit stop in the kitchen to get a bowl of replenishing fruit and two glasses of water. He took a gulp from his glass and set it down on the nightstand with the fruit, waiting patiently by the door for Alice.

She emerged with a smile on her face and a fluffy robe wrapped around her body. Tony had to admit, he would have loved to see her in that outfit again. But, as she had rightfully pointed out earlier, they had plenty of time for that.

"Water?" he offered.

"Thank you." Alice's voice was hoarse, which was fair given all that moaning she had been doing. And Tony smiled. He was going to be hearing those noises in every dream he has from here on out.

"How you feeling?" Tony asked when Alice handed the empty glass back to him.

"A little tired," Alice said. She closed her eyes as her face melted into a relaxed smile. "Mmmm but good."

Tony did pride himself on a job well done. "Would you care for some post-coitus cuddling?"

Alice chuckled and opened her eyes. "Yes, please and thank you!"

Tony held Alice's arm and walked her to the bed, helping her rest comfortably against the headboard before he joined her. Alice smiled and pressed up against his side, sighing content as he wrapped his arm around her.

She turned to hug him, stopping when they heard something crumple under her arm.

"What is that?" she asked, reaching into his robe's pocket.

Tony shrugged. Alice pulled out a folded envelope that had his name written on one side. "Oh yeah!" He took the letter from her with a smile. "My eviction notice!"

Alice's eyes opened wide, and she snatched the letter back out of his hand.

"Hey."

"You don't want to read that." She chuckled at him, face returning to a lovely shade of red.

"Is it you telling me you hate me, think my sex is bad, and never want to see me again?"

"Of course not!"

"Then yes, I do."

Tony snagged the letter back with little resistance. Alice huffed at him but sat back against the headboard, arms crossed. And she was pouting again. And since they were dating, nothing was stopping Tony from leaning over and kissing that pout right off her lips.

"Just, don't think too much about it," Alice said when they parted.

"Me? Overthink something? Never."

Tony turned his attention to the envelope, opening it slowly, just to draw out the tension. Alice huffed again, kicking her legs a bit. He laughed and took mercy on her.

The letter read:

Dear Anthony,

Isn't it funny how we use the word dear at the start of letters and emails these days? Dear. Such a loaded word. Usually, when writing a letter, you would address someone by their title, unless that someone was close to you. So, before I waste another page rambling again, let me just say that you are close to me. Dear to me. Dear.

I know we haven't really had all that much time to get to know each other, not truly. And maybe we won't like each other once we do. But I'd like to know you, even if, in the end, we aren't really all that compatible. Because if we are, I think we could be good friends. Or maybe more. Or maybe not.

I guess what I'm trying to say is I like you as I know you. And I'd like to like you as I don't. And you've always been very kind to me, so I assume you like me as you know me. And I hope you can like me as you don't.

And really the only way to find out is to try, isn't it? So maybe, if you'd like, we could try.

But, of course, I'm perfectly fine if that is not something you want to do, and you certainly don't have to feel pressured to feel one way or another about me and, really, I do just enjoy your company, and I'll take it in whatever way you'd like me to have it.

I hope that makes sense, and I hope it isn't too forward of me. But I've spent a great deal of my life walking backwards recently. So, a jump here and there couldn't hurt.

Right?

Yours if you want,
Alice

Tony blinked at the words on the page. He rubbed his eyes. He even pinched himself for good measure because it had to be a dream. Or an illusion of some sort. Those couldn't be the actual words that Alice had written. Not to him. Not all that time ago.

He cleared his throat, ever aware of Alice staring at him. "So, if I had just read this when you gave it to me... we could have saved ourselves a whole lot of trouble?"

Alice smiled. "Yes. But, to tell you the truth… well, I'm sort of glad you didn't."

"Oh yeah no, I'm *so* glad we spent the last few months in turmoil, tip toeing around the issue when we could have been doing that all this time!"

Alice laughed and turned on her side, snuggling up to Tony, wrapping her arms around his waist. "I think it's a good thing we were friends first," she told him. "When you're dating, you're always trying to be your best. It takes a while to get to the point where you feel confident and comfortable being vulnerable, right? You want to be strong and attractive. But as a friend? You reach that point a lot faster. And I don't think we'd have gotten as close as we are if we did start dating that morning."

Tony hummed and thought about that. In a way, she was right. He never would have told her about subtraction. He probably would have gone out and gotten some kind of job on his own, just to prove he could, and then he wouldn't have met Nate or gotten a job he actually liked and was good at. And they wouldn't have had any sex lessons, oh no. They would have just had sex, which would have been good, but Alice would have been too shy and worried about being perfect all the time which would have been bad.

"I guess you're right," he said. He hugged her back and kissed the top of her head. "For once my inability to face a weird situation has actually improved it."

Alice chuckled. She leaned to the side and looked up at him. "Can I tell you something? As a friend?"

"Of course."

"I think I might be more afraid of being in a relationship than I was of having sex."

Tony smiled. "I'm fucking terrified."

"Neither of us have really done this before." Alice picked softly at the edge of Tony's robe. "What if we do it wrong?"

"I don't think there's really a right way to do it. Or if there is, it's different for each couple."

Alice nodded and licked her lips. She watched her fingers play with Tony's robe, and he could see the worries clear on her face.

"You know, that would make an interesting next book."

"Hm?"

"Two people who've never dated, dating. The drama, the mystery, the humor. Trying to figure out what works and what doesn't. Asking their friends and family and finding out that certain 'normal' dating things just aren't for them. And hey, we could always go on some classic date type things for research."

Alice sat up, a smile returning to her face as she looked at him. "Okay," she said. "But only if we go on some non-research dates for ourselves."

Tony nodded. They were done hiding behind books. They didn't need the façade of research to be together or do things together. They were in love. And that was the only reason they ever needed.

Happily,
The End.

Author's Bio
Anna Denisch

Anna Denisch was born and raised just outside of Baltimore City, but she has never called it home. When not traveling around the world or daydreaming about dragons, she spends her time looking at books she wants to read without actually touching them. She received her M.F.A in Creative and Professional Writing from Western Connecticut State University and considers daily if she is just insane enough to take her family's sometime suggestion of getting a PhD.